DO HER NO HARM

ALSO BY NAOMI JOY

The Liars
The Truth

DO HER NO HARM

Naomi Joy

An Aria Book

This edition first published in the United Kingdom in 2020 by Aria,
an imprint of Head of Zeus Ltd

A CIP catalogue record for this book is available from the
British Library.

ISBN 9781789543773

Typeset by Siliconchips Services Ltd UK

Cover design © Cherie Chapman

Aria
c/o Head of Zeus
First Floor East
5–8 Hardwick Street
London EC1R 4RG

www.ariafiction.com

For my wonderful friends

"All things are poisons and there is nothing that is harmless. The dose alone decides."

—Paracelsus (1493–1541).

PART 1

Prologue

Five Years Ago

20:00: She walks quickly, eyes wide, lips locked. *I can't go back now.* She's nervous. I can tell by the way she holds her handbag tight to her side, the quick-step of her gait, striding in time to the beat of her heart.

20:10: Her forehead is slick with summer, the thick air surrounding her thin body dense enough to feel. She passes a supermarket with her next step, the automatic doors opening for a moment, the air conditioning catching her peasant-top in the breeze, a glimpse of stomach beneath. She pauses to revel in the cold for a second longer, glittering specks of sweat evaporating from fake-tanned limbs. Her phone hugs the back pocket of her white jeans, printing a bulky rectangle into the material. He sends her a message – no time to waste – and the device vibrates obediently, sending shudders down the backs of her legs. She tells him she's excited to meet him.

He's excited too.

20:20: Her feet clip-clop to the bar, her toenails painted baby-pink, fingernails to match, plugging in a pair of headphones as she walks, pacing in time to a song about break-ups. *Apt.* She flicks her newly dyed hair behind bare shoulders and sings along in her head. She's happy, smiling, whole.

20:35: She arrives at the location he sent her – three miles from the nearest station – and orders a drink, casting her eyes over every shape in the room, double-checking he's not here. It's the kind of place she'd expect for a first date, so she's not immediately suspicious. It's upmarket, with velvet-cushioned chairs tucked beneath aged oak tables, bottles of spirits displayed artfully behind the bar.

She bites her lip, wonders where he is.

I watch her take a seat and reason with herself: *He's only five minutes late, I should calm down, relax. Maybe there's bad traffic.* Ten minutes later, though, when he hasn't messaged to explain the hold up, she swallows what's left of her strawberry daquiri and orders another. Sticky-sweet alcohol snail-trails her top lip and sweat flattens her hair to her neck, her perfect make-up beginning to melt. I watch her wipe her forehead with her serviette, the window across casting shadows on her face. It's getting late.

21:30: She's given it a good hour, sent five messages, called him a few too many times but she's lost patience now and, as she staggers from her seat – no dinner and five drinks down – the glass to her side thunks to the floor, explodes on impact, and turns heads, eyes spinning in her direction. She hates the attention. All she'd wanted were two eyes on her tonight.

His.

Sorry, she offers to the waiter coming over, drunk and

disappointed by the evening's turn of events. Promises had been made. Big ones. She is right to be angry.

21:32: She leaves the bar, handbag swinging loose, brow knitted in cross-stitches, furious with him. She types one last message, jabbing her fingers into the screen, wanting him to feel the hate she holds. *Where were you? I was counting on you. How could you?* She staggers from the high street onto the dark roads beyond, walking the backstreets because they make her feel dangerous, because she thinks by acting out she can get his attention. The station is still two miles away, and she's walking in the wrong direction.

22:00: From somewhere behind, she hears a car approach. She twists her face over her shoulder to look, her forehead creased in the glare of my full-beam. My vehicle rumbles closer, tyres crunching her way.

I watch through the windshield as she grows concerned that I'm slowing down, that my window is low. *Don't be scared. You want my help, you just don't know it yet.* Her lips are wet, she's been crying, and they shine in the bright. She looks away as I draw the car near. I shout to her from the window and, when she sees that it's me, her expression changes. Lifts.

Oh thank God, she tells me, chest heaving.

Newspaper Report

Five Years Ago

Disappearance of Tabitha Rice 'completely out
of character'

Report by Kay Robero for the London Times

On 21st of August, Tabitha Rice, a receptionist at the
Pure You aesthetic clinic, disappeared from the home she
shares with her husband, Rick Priestley.

As fears grow for her welfare, and the search enters
its fifth day without a breakthrough, public concern
has reached fever-pitch for the Battersea woman. Her
husband, a senior asset manager, spoke to us this
morning.

'When I woke up on the 22nd August, my wife was
missing. I thought she'd already left for work – she
often works early mornings – so, at first, I didn't think
much of it. By Saturday night I was growing extremely

concerned. It was then that I put in my first call to the police. I told them that Tabby had been acting erratically in the days before, but that it would be completely out of character for her to leave without talking to me.'

Rick continues, 'In response to allegations made in the press by Tabby's colleague and friend Annabella, that suggest I may have had something to do with Tabby's disappearance, I want to put it on record that I completely refute the accusation. I am cooperating fully with the authorities and any attempt to undermine my character is an attempt to undermine the search for my wife.

'Tabby, if you can see this, please get in touch. I want to talk, I want to help. Please don't hurt yourself. Remember that I'm here for you, at home. Please just come back.'

Annabella

Now

I wake up thinking about the last conversation Tabby and I ever had, about the twisted look on her face and the downward curve of her lips. She'd been trying to sell me the idea of quitting our jobs at the white-walled cosmetic clinic we worked at together and running away. At first, I'd thought she'd been joking, or smoking. It was only later that I realised how serious she was. I'd messaged her after work, trying to make amends.

> Sorry. But I can't do it, I can't just leave. I have a home, a job I love, a life here in London…

I curl my fingers round my waist, warm skin heated under the winter duvet, and breathe long. I've worked hard to become an aesthetic nurse and I adore what I do. My job is to meet people who feel trapped in the bodies they were born with, people who are desperate to break free but need my help to do so. Not many people know this, but I understand what it's like to feel that way. At work it's as though I have a superpower – the gift of transformation – and at the Pure You clinic I get to unleash it every day. Tabby, who worked front-of-house, didn't understand that. Her job was a job, she worked her hours and went home. But still, I don't like letting people down. Least of all Tabby.

'Look,' she'd said, getting serious, tucking blonde hair behind studded ears. 'Thousands of people travel to Turkey for cheap face lifts and boob jobs, but they're scared about botched procedures. If we set up our own surgery, we can charge a little more than the Turkish practices but still undercut the prices over here. We'll absolutely clean up. We'll be booked out, living on a beach, raking it in...'

I'd laughed gently, rolled my eyes wishfully, assuming this was a flight of fancy, a daydream Tabby was vocalising. I'd turned away, clicked through the day's appointments, heat rushing to my fingertips as I'd scrolled through the back-to-back schedule I was only halfway through. There'd be a few minutes for lunch, if I was lucky, if one of my patients was late. I'd started setting up for the next, my mind elsewhere, when Tabby had pressed it.

'What do you think?' She'd twitched, her eyes following me as I rushed to get the room ready. Her focus was in the wrong place and it had irritated me – it was a busy day and she should have been upstairs on reception, doing her job.

'We're young,' she'd said. 'Now is the time to travel, to explore, to find ourselves. Do you really want to stay in the same city for the rest of your life? Why don't we just try it, go on an adventure. Six months, even. Or a year.'

'Where has this idea come from?' I'd asked, straightening the towels on the patient chair, assuming she was going to tell me she'd just read an article about moving to Turkey, that this sudden spontaneity was being driven by something she'd have forgotten about by this time tomorrow.

'I've been thinking about it for a while,' she'd replied, able to read my mind, knowing exactly what I was thinking.

The phone rang, cutting our conversation short, and I'd picked up. Caroline, the owner of Pure You, was on the other end, slightly flustered, telling me my patient was on her way down, and to send Tabby back up to reception. *What is she doing down there? Why am I having to check patients in? What on earth do I pay her for?*

Looking back, I wish I'd taken a breath and been kinder, calmer. Tabby's invitation, tied with a metaphorical pink bow, hung by a thread. I'd sharpened my scissors.

'Tabby, what do we know about setting up a business, much less *running* a business? What do we know about the Turkish tax system? About working visas, about marketing our business in the UK, about the new qualifications we might need to get before heading out there, about buying or renting a house for us to live in, about leasing office space, about—'

She'd stopped me there. She'd called me cautious and pessimistic, too desperate to iron out every detail, to plan our relocation in its entirety before we'd even had an initial conversation about it.

'Please,' she'd pleaded, wounded by my realism. 'Just think about it. We can figure out marketing and running a business and everything else together. All I need to know is if you're at least open to the idea. That's all.'

'What about Rick?' I'd asked quickly, keen to nip this

in the bud, trying to make Tabby see sense, wanting this delusion to end. 'Would he come too?'

She'd tucked her lips defensively, just as I'd heard the smack of a footstep on the stairs. *Patient coming down.* 'No,' she'd replied. 'Just me and you.'

And, with that, the motivation behind Tabby's drastic plan stepped into the light. Rick and Tabby. The switch on their relationship set to off again.

'Rick and I, we've been through so much together.' She'd looked away. 'But we need some time apart.'

'Does he know that?'

'I think he's cheating on me,' she'd said, footsteps approaching the door. 'He keeps meeting this woman, he says she's a friend but—'

A knock at the door, conversation over. As I'd greeted my patient, Tabby had slunk out and retreated to the reception desk upstairs. She'd left work earlier than me, probably annoyed by my reaction and, when I'd messaged her later that night to tell her I was sorry and that I couldn't leave, she'd ignored me.

It was the last conversation we ever had.

On the other side of the shutters, it's not quite morning but the beginning of the thawing of the night, imperceptible brushstrokes painting the sky from black to indigo to blue. Thoughts of Tabby, and all the guilt and sadness that come with her memory, swirl.

It's been almost five years since she disappeared and, to this day, no one has any idea what happened to her. The police led the initial search, pointed a few fingers and shackled a few wrists, then, once the public interest died down, explained to her close friends and family that the hunt for Tabby would be more 'reactive' than 'proactive' from now on. What it meant was that they were downing tools completely, moving swiftly on to the next missing person, the latest woman lighting up the news agenda. Tabby's whereabouts were shelved, gathering dust. As soon as the police bowed out, her foster parents scuffed their shoes and shrugged their shoulders, desperate for the whole thing to be over and done with. It was clear to me then that if I didn't do something, no one would. I went to visit her foster mum, pulled up outside the semi-detached house Tabby had grown up in, hoping for *something*. Limp-eyed and drunk-she'd sniffled at me to leave it alone, '*Everything happens for a reason. We just weren't meant to find her.*'

That explanation might have been good enough for her, but it hadn't been good enough for me.

After the police had scaled back their investigation, a private investigator contacted me, offering to dig deeper into the case. At first I wasn't convinced – he was a sly-eyed, gel-haired American, promising the world in exchange for, basically, all of my savings – but though I was sceptical, it's fair to say that Chad has delivered some good intel since he picked things up from the police. Today he's called a meeting, and, as ever, I'm hoping for a breakthrough.

I swing my legs out from the covers and force myself into loose jeans and a jumper. I strip my covers and pillowcase, ready for the wash, and dust down the bedside tables, anxiety dissipating as I perform these rituals. By the time I pace into the kitchen, I'm ready to fire the coffee machine into action, but I take the time to clean the container with careful cloth-strokes first. As it spouts black water into my cup, I lean against the countertop, breathing in the earthy smell of beans. Today could be a big day.

The coffee machine bleats behind me and I pull the cup from its position, bringing it to my lips, steam rising. It occurs to me, as I drink, that my optimism shows I probably put too much faith in law and order, in the police, in people like Chad. I want to believe that the system is careful and ordered, that the people in it will do the right thing, act in good faith in any given situation. I swallow, not allowing the thought to go any further. All is not lost. Chad will prove my faith was not in vain. He has to.

Chad and I always meet in the same dark pub. He sits in the corner with a pint of real ale he doesn't drink – which, in my opinion, rather draws more attention than it deflects – and gives me the latest. I never ask him anything about his personal life, I don't care to know, but I'm polite and civil, and, if he ever makes a *real* breakthrough in the case, perhaps I'll throw him a bone and ask him if he irons the collars of his Ralph Lauren polos himself or if his long-suffering partner does it for him.

Feeling hopeful, I make for the bus stop on the corner. My new-build apartment sits just off a major road into the city, a thick artery of tarmac that pumps people into London all day and all night, and the familiar rumble of traffic rises as I walk. The numbers will begin in earnest at the turn of 5 p.m. but, for now, the road is relatively calm and the bus pulls in a few minutes later. I slap my card against the reader and watch my flat shrink into the distance as the bus heaves forward. I wonder if I'll ever be the kind of person who will own a car. I'm not sure I will – anything above fifty miles per hour and my mind wanders to how easy it would be to kill someone with a careless swerve of my steering wheel, schoolchildren squashed thanks to my split-second distraction at a zebra crossing. *Yes*, I think. *Better to stick to the bus.*

I haven't bothered to dress up for today's meeting and the perfectionist in me hates my failure to make a formal effort, but it is too late to worry now; my boyfriend jeans and slick-backed hair will have to do. I roll through south London and eventually close in on my destination. Heavy clouds hang overhead, covering the capital in a too-thick blanket, the city strangely humid for winter, and I step over smashed green glass to get inside. The pub itself – a pokey post-war affair – is a vision in wood: the furniture, the walls, even the pool table at the back, all of it is mahogany-inspired, the smell of beer stuck to every surface. It feels strange being here before lunch.

I spot Chad towards the back. He's wearing a pale-yellow polo tucked into dark jeans and a black mac hangs like a shadow on the back of his chair. His brown belt is pulled a notch too tight over his thicker-than-he-thinks waistline and a pair of clunky white trainers glow from his feet, his cell-phone holstered to his hip as if it's a pistol. I will myself to be positive: Chad Cummings is going to find out what happened to my friend and, even though he looks like he wouldn't be able to solve the mystery of a missing cat, it's not only my money motivating him to do the best job he can. If he can find out what happened to the *MISSING WOMAN WHO WANTED TO HAVE A BABY*, the *BATTERSEA BEAUTY WHO MARRIED HER UNIVERSITY SWEETHEART*, he'll be a hero. I raise my hand as I approach.

'Hi Chad,' I say, noting his leather briefcase-suitcase wheeled into position behind him, handle still high.

'Hi!' he booms. Then, 'Is everything all right?' His expression changes; he's not used to seeing me without make-up.

'Fine,' I reply, curtly, though I spot my deflated reflection in a teak-framed mirror opposite and wonder if it's the truth. From a distance, the healthy plump of my face belies me – the result of a few surgical enhancements that make me look better than I feel – but, look closer, and you'll see my hair is brittle from over-washing, my eyes underlined with grey buckets, my lips chapped and bitten. I pull my stare from the mirror, grab the seat opposite Chad, and fall in.

He looks down, realising his faux pas, clearly weighing up whether to backtrack and compliment me on something else instead. Thankfully, he decides not to.

'Wanna get to it?' he asks.

'Gladly.'

Chad whacks a photograph on the tabletop and spins it round. I look at a grainy CCTV image of a woman getting into a car and, though it doesn't show her face, you can see one of her hands on the door, one of her legs stretching into the interior. If I saw the next frame she'd be sitting pretty in the passenger seat. Though the inhabitants are blurred, the number plate of the vehicle shines luminous yellow, an EU flag at the side, *'PL'* underneath.

'Check the date stamp,' Chad says, leaning back.

'The night she went missing,' I mutter, frowning, but my forehead barely moves.

'Yup.'

'And you're sure it's her? Do you know who she's with?' I ask.

'Could be her.'

'Could be?'

'I spoke to a former officer on the case, managed to get this. This CCTV image was their first real lead, but the line of inquiry went cold. Darn shame. They gave up on it, in the end. Do you recognise the vehicle?'

The barman comes over – he wouldn't usually but the pub's empty and he's looking for something to do.

'What can I get you?' he asks from a slight distance, black apron tied to his waist, bushy eyebrows meeting in the middle. I wait for Chad to order first.

'Pint of real ale,' he replies, and I wonder if he's made a mistake by ordering alcohol this early – it makes him stand out – but the barman doesn't flinch.

'Sparkling water,' I add, forcing a smile, covering the photograph with my arms.

I pluck it from the table when the barman leaves, bringing it close.

Immediately after Tabby went missing, the police followed the theory that she disappeared of her own accord. There was no break-in, they said, no struggle, and the fact that she'd taken her phone and a few possessions meant she 'must have planned her escape.' At first, I agreed with the theory – she'd told me herself she wanted to move abroad – then days passed, weeks, and I still hadn't heard from her. If she'd run away, she would have found a way to get in touch with me to let me know she was safe. To me, at least, it didn't add up. When that story fell flat, the papers shifted their focus onto Rick. Why had he kept so quiet? Why wasn't he out searching for her? Why wasn't he acting like a *normal* husband? Eventually, after weeks of pressure, Rick went public. He reiterated that he didn't know any more than we did. When he woke up on the morning of 22nd August Tabby was gone. He never offered any more than that, never guessed or speculated about where his wife was, never ruminated on the possibilities, never showed any real emotion, or worry, or care.

If you ask me, I think he killed her, disposed of her body, did a decent enough job to make sure she was never found, then set about playing the victim. Why? I think he wanted her gone so he could start over. Tabby had told me she suspected there was another woman in Rick's life – not that he'd admitted it to the police – so I knew Rick was hiding *something* from them. I wanted Chad, among other things, to find out if my theory had weight.

'This supports the police version then… that she ran away of her own accord. That she planned it.' I pause. 'Where's the number plate from?'

'Poland.'

I push the photograph back towards him. 'Tabby didn't know anyone from Poland. I don't think it's her.'

'How do you know?'

I look up at him, hopes rising. 'Are you about to tell me different?'

Chad shakes his head and my body sags anew.

'What about Rick's other woman?' I ask.

'Nothing yet,' he replies. 'It's difficult to find someone without a name. I can only trail Rick and hope he leads me to her. But he hasn't…'

I can tell by the way Chad's eyes skirt off to the side that he doesn't believe Rick's other woman exists. He once asked, *'What if Tabby made her up so she didn't feel guilty about leaving Rick? There's no evidence of another woman besides what Tabby told you… don't you think that's a little odd?'*

I plait my fingers and jut out my chin.

'Where *has* he led you, then?'

Chad sighs as he reaches into his case, popping the catch open and reaching within. 'He goes to work, he catches the bus to and from, he goes to the gym, he comes home.' He fingers out a wedge of logs, all handwritten. Date and time in the left column, location in the middle, notes on the right. There are precious few observations: *blue shirt, black tie* – that kind of thing.

He'd produced a similar set of observations the previous time we met. I feel my fists clench and try to keep calm because I really want this to work out, but what Chad's been doing – following Rick in and out of the shadows – is pitiful. *I could do that myself.*

'Investigations take time,' he says, picking up on my dissatisfaction.

You don't understand, honey. This is the game, darling. Gotta be patient here, angel.

'It's been almost five years since she went missing,' I say, tense. 'Two years went to the police, and nearly three years to you… and still we're nowhere.'

I sigh as I say it – more false starts and empty promises.

It had been the same with the police investigation, I'd put my faith in their considerable resources and been let down. I'd turned to Chad when the leads dried up, but perhaps I should have taken matters into my own hands earlier, shouldn't have left it for so long in the incapable palms of too many incapable men.

Chad ruffles his lips and exhales like a shire horse.

'I get it. Three years. It's a long time. And, you know, maybe we should take a break for a few months. I don't want to keep taking your money when I know I'm not about to uncover anything new, it's not fair.'

Excuse me?

'I like you, Annabella, you're a good person, but you deserve to know that this case is dead. You're not going to find what you're looking for, no matter how hard you hope for it.'

My eyes crack as he lets me down. For the first time I see the game he's been playing for what it really is. This is what he does, pounces on the friends and families of missing people at their lowest ebb and drains what's left.

'Rick's clean. I've followed him for years and he hasn't so much as exceeded the speed limit.'

He reaches across and touches my skin with slimy fingers.

'It's time to move on, Annabella. It's time to put what happened to Tabitha Rice behind you.'

Tabby

Five Years Ago

I shift from foot to foot as I fumble with the key, my hands slippery.

'Not now,' I gasp as the lock jams. I press my weight against the frame and push hard, re-aligning the lock and freeing the door. Was it already open? It's just gone ten and the surgery *technically* opened an hour ago. My nose enters first, ears pricked for signs of life from within – I'm praying the lack of commotion on my phone means I haven't been rumbled – and step gently into the building.

'Hello?' I call quietly, waiting for a cavalcade of *where-were-yous* and *you-should-have been-here-an-hour-agos*, but hear nothing. The truth is, I was up late last night waiting for my husband to come home. Then I slept through my alarm. I've been doing that a lot recently.

I breathe out as I sink into my office chair, my armpits slick, and feel the wheels bounce over the dark grout between the white tiles of the reception floor as I pull myself into the desk. Luckily no patients have arrived yet but, as I fire my computer into action, my forehead crunches with confusion when the system fails to recognise my log-in details.

My desk phone rings and, reaching for the handset, I startle at a clipped knock at the surgery door. I'm jumpy this morning, anxious; I need to relax. Make a pot of mint tea or something. I buzz open the door, the sound of the mechanism echoing off the tiles, and watch the threshold intently, relieved to see Annabella on the other side. Her brown-blonde hair is poker-straight today, barely a strand out of place as she steps from the outside in. 'Morning,' she talk-whispers, noticing the phone in my hand, her voice light and fresh.

'Morning,' I mouth back, then put the receiver to my ear.

'Tabitha, it's Caroline.' My heart beats a little faster. Caroline's the owner of the surgery and I've been wearing her patience thin with my timekeeping recently. 'Can I have a word? I'm coming down.'

The colour drains from my cheeks as I check the number. Caroline's dialling from her office upstairs. I swear under my breath.

'Everything all right?' Annabella asks, pulling up her sleeves, swirling a Mr Whippy of foam from the anti-bac dispenser into her palms. She's clocked my sudden activity.

'I was late, I was really late,' I splutter. 'And Caroline, she…' I stop mid-sentence as I open the drawers beneath the desk, looking for my notepad, panicking, wanting something to hold, something to act as a barrier, but they're all empty. Even my personal things aren't there – the packet of chewing gum I keep on hand for breath-emergencies, the multi-coloured hairbands that litter every drawer, the half-peeled perfume samples I rip out of the surgery magazines – they're all gone.

'My things,' I mutter, glancing up at my friend. 'Bella, she's moved all of my stuff.'

This is a nightmare, this isn't really happening, I'll wake up in a moment, in bed, Rick breathing heavily by my side. I'll get up and dress and arrive here on time, just as I should have…

'Tabitha,' Caroline announces, her heels striking the tiles as she moves into the sterile space, her angular chin pointed slightly upwards, the smooth contours of her heavily edited face fixed firmly on the bumps of mine. Her weave sways behind her, shiny black hair stretching long to her waist. We're twenty years apart, but Caroline hasn't aged a day since she turned thirty.

'I'm very sorry, darling,' she begins, and it's then that the jigsaw pieces of this morning begin to tessellate. The reason why my computer wouldn't log me in, the obvious explanation behind my empty drawers. Caroline probably arrived early, reasoning she'd give me one final chance to prove her wrong and, when nine became nine-thirty, she made the decision to fire me on the spot. I shiver with humiliation; I can't bear to look at Bella. 'This morning was your last chance,' Caroline begins.

'She was with me,' Bella interrupts. 'I had a home-visit this morning and needed help getting my equipment back.'

Goose bumps bubble beneath the thick cotton of my uniform. Bella's lying to save me, and Caroline knows it.

Caroline's eyes narrow. 'Why wasn't it in the calendar?' she asks, her voice tight and distrusting.

'Last minute,' Bella replies. 'I got the call this morning.'

I nod at Caroline as she twists her dark gaze back towards me, my blue eyes shining with nervous tears. I didn't mean to start making a habit of late nights and missed alarms. I don't want to spend the small hours of each morning pondering my husband's every move. I want to lead a normal life, stable and settled, to have a partner I can trust. Perhaps my foster mum had been right that getting married young was a mistake. Why the rush? If it's meant to be, it will be.

Bella steps forward, gaining in confidence, and my heart twangs, my memory flitting to the first time we met, the smile behind her aqua eyes as I'd welcomed her to Pure You. It's not often you meet a best friend at work, but that's what we are. We have our little routines – Thursday night dinners, every other Saturday night out, coffee every weekday at the café across the road, quick gossips during break-time, instant-messaging between patients. She even fits in with Rick and me; she isn't jealous if I cancel our plans to spend time with my husband, she doesn't judge me like so many other young twenty-somethings in the city for having a husband. And, the more distant Rick grows, the closer we become, the more time we spend together.

'What's more,' Annabella continues, 'Tabby has had this great idea. You have to hear it. We were going to tell you about it today, actually.'

I swallow, my mouth dry, wondering what idea I've had.

'She was telling me,' Bella continues, 'that she's noticed how most of the aesthetic clinics round here just focus on the usual – Botox, fillers, IPL – but Tabby said she'd heard from a few customers that they'd love it if we also offered some beautician services.'

Caroline's gaze bores into my soul and I find myself waxing lyrical about a brain wave I never had. 'A pedicure with your fillers, lash extensions alongside IPL… that sort of thing. I was thinking, if we bundled up the procedures, we could give discounts, really make it attractive to our clients.' I smile, selling it with shiny teeth, jazz hands at the ready.

Caroline grips the skin at the top of her nose and closes her eyes. I dart a look at Bella and mouth a thank you. She shakes her head quickly and it's then that I realise this was her big idea. She'd spoken about something she was excited to run by Caroline the other day – this must have been it, and she's using it to save me. She should be using it to get a promotion! I feel terrible but, at the same time, I need this job. I'm not sure I could cope with interviews and job hunting, with telling Rick I've been fired, with failure in my professional life as well as my personal.

'Fine,' Caroline retorts. 'But this is the condition,' she snaps, pausing. 'Annabella, you've been asking for an assistant for a while.'

'But…' Annabella protests unsuccessfully, Caroline bulldozing her way through the conversation.

'Well, here she is. She's not very experienced but you seem to believe in her. Let's hope you're right to.' Caroline turns to me. 'Understood?'

With that, they both leave to start the working day. Caroline will be in the office for another hour or so, then leave early to 'work from home'. Bella's first patient will arrive imminently, and I'll have to get through the day without an electronic schedule because Caroline's frozen me out of the system. I put in a call to the external IT department, leave a message, then tug the cardboard box Caroline had packed for me out from beneath the reception desk, its bottom scraping across the floor, too heavy to lift. I begin putting my things back in their places, but end up throwing away most of it, a worrying amount of nothing but worthless junk from years of being sat in the same seat.

By midday, I'm hunting for things to do – still logged out of my computer – the day's patients slow and steady, a quiet weekday, the kind of day I long for when it's Saturday afternoon and there's barely time to breathe. I sort through the office post next, swiping my palm across my face, still reeling from what happened earlier, wondering how I'll ever face Caroline again. I'd have to start looking for a new job, what Bella had done for me had given me a lifeline, sure, but Caroline didn't want me here and that was the bottom line. I pick up the first envelope addressed to the surgery and edge my index finger into the top of the triangular fold.

Job application: Dr Alex Daniels.

We get a couple of these a week. Mostly they're sent in over email but the ones that are posted are usually of a higher quality. I'll find a smart covering letter and a sharp CV inside, then I'll pass it up to Caroline and let her deal with it. But something about this application gives me pause. The photo.

An olive-skinned, green-eyed man beams from the corner of the wedges of paper, his perfect proportions distorted by the paperclip pinned over his face. It's not a headshot, but a selfie, and I glow with the fact that I'd applied here with a selfie, too. I read through his CV, devouring the contents – a medical degree from the University of Toronto, a specialisation in plastic surgery from somewhere in Paris, a keen traveller whose life has brought him, right here, to London.

A mobile number glistens beneath his sign off and, before I know it, I've committed another fireable offence, his digits added to the contacts in my phone. If Caroline finds out about this, I'm dead.

Annabella

Chad had left me alone in the pub with a final bill and sorry eyes, though I'm sure if I'd squinted I'd have seen the dollar signs in his pupils – he'd taken me for a ride and I was supposed to be grateful.

First the police, now him. His parting shot was to ask me out for dinner – he told me he'd been wanting to do it for a while, that part of the reason for him terminating our contract was so we could start dating.

'*I can't ignore this spark between us any longer...*'

'*Well,*' I'd replied, angling a pointed look at his wedding ring. '*I certainly can.*'

The truth was, I'd given up on dating since Tabby went missing. Her disappearance had isolated me, sent me back into the cocoon I'd inhabited before she'd come along and pulled me out of it. I'd stopped connecting with people, their questions, their problems, their lives. I just didn't have the energy to care about anyone else the way I still cared about her.

Tabby had meant so much to me that when she vanished, I think part of me did too.

I push a soggy bag of broccoli into the microwave – the last thing left in the fridge – contemplating how I'll deal with the forever fact that I've failed my friend. Coming up to five years gone, and not a single step forward.

I must start over, begin a new life, forgive myself. I begin to close the dozens of webpages I'd kept open in relation to Tabby's case, the blue from my computer illuminating my face, the night sky twinkling through the dark kitchen windows, when an email catches my attention.

Subject: Tabitha Rice.

Dear Annabella,

I hope this finds you well. I am getting in touch with you about Tabitha Rice, your missing colleague/friend. I have followed her story over the years with interest. In fact, I was part of the team at the *London Times* who first reported on it. I have been putting together information on her case for the past year and I plan to launch a true-crime podcast about it. I hope it will lead to new evidence and that we might be able to help figure out what happened to her.

I've been digging through early media coverage and wanted to talk to you about the allegations you made against Rick Priestley in the early days.

Please contact me if you'd like to be involved. I'd be grateful for any input you're happy to make.

Do write back or call me on the number below.

Yours sincerely,

Kay Robero+447516177089

My eyes choke over the words. Another lifeline. But this one's different, this is public, this is the media. In the past I'd deemed it too risky, too uncertain. I search Kay's name in Google, my brain wired, long past bedtime, and retrieve a cavern of information about her illustrious career in journalism, articles pinging back with headlines such as *London's rising star … Journalist of the year…* I realise I've read her pieces before, all of them, dozens of times, in the weeks after Tabby went missing. Her website tells me she left traditional journalism a year ago, citing a desire to work on a new project, a true-crime podcast series that she hoped to release this year. I scan my eyes over the headshots accompanying Kay's biography: fierce and unsmiling, plain and untouched. Kay is the kind of person who demands to be taken seriously, who doesn't want anyone to make the mistake of complimenting her looks before her capabilities. I learn from her website that she's part Nigerian, part Spanish, educated in Scotland, and that she'd sent a serial rapist to jail last year after she dug up a raft of new evidence against him. I begin to get excited – Kay could really reinvigorate this case. I scrape my hair from my face into a ponytail as I think about it. Perhaps it makes sense to get involved, especially if someone revered is behind this investigation, someone who'd been there from the beginning, someone with an automatic fan base and considerable resources.

Without thinking, I call her back, the dial tone ringing fanfare-like as it connects.

'Kay speaking,' she says as she picks up, her voice lighter than I'd imagined from her headshots.

I take a second to compose myself.

'Hi, Kay, this is Annabella. I just got your email.'

'Annabella,' she says brightly. 'Thanks for getting back to me so quickly.'

I hear her take a sip from something and imagine a vat of coffee in her hand. She'd be the kind of person that drinks it right up to bedtime, caffeinated to the hilt from dusk till dawn.

'I'm so happy you want to help,' I tell her, heady on the thought I might not fail Tabby after all.

'No problem,' she replies, composed. 'Tabitha's case is absolutely fascinating.'

I cringe at her choice of words but, though I wouldn't choose to describe Tabby going missing as fascinating, I understand what she means.

'Why now?' I ask, wondering what's taken her so long.

'Tabitha's case, it's stayed with me. It had seemed so straightforward in the beginning, suspicious husband, shouldn't take long to convict him, and then the investigation just… flopped. I want to find out why.'

As she speaks, I type Rick Priestley's name into Google. My search brings up a raft of news articles relating to Tabby's disappearance – still top of the results after all these years – and I scan a few of them to refresh my memory of the time, the mood of the reporting, the cut and thrust of the blame.

'Do you remember Rick's statement?' I ask, rolling my eyes across it on the screen in front of me as though no time had passed between then and now. I read it down the phone.

'*When I woke up on the 22nd of August my wife was missing. We'd gone to bed, as normal, the night before... I am extremely concerned for her safety. Tabby, if you can see this, hear this, please get in touch. I want to talk, I want to help you. Please don't hurt yourself. Remember that I'm here for you, at home, if you need me. Please just come back.'*

'To me,' Kay says, 'it sounded desperate at the time, contrived.'

'Just reading those words again made my skin itch,' I tell her. 'Tabby and Rick hadn't spent a normal night in together for weeks; he was cheating, she was unhappy. They were barely living together, let alone sleeping in the same bed.' I pause. 'I must admit, though, that the "crazy" card was a clever red herring, it delayed the investigation, set it off in the wrong direction, positioned Rick as a long-suffering, but caring, partner who was guilty of nothing besides supporting his damaged wife.'

I hear Kay taking notes down the line.

'He knew what he was doing,' I continue. 'The way he orchestrated that statement wasn't an accident. It was premeditated.'

I think back. During those first few days, the early-early days, people hadn't paid any attention to Tabby's story, a crazy woman running from her loving husband wasn't a narrative they cared about. Then, when the focus shifted to Rick and it was rumoured he'd kidnapped and murdered her, reported by a blogger that he'd *cut her body into quarters and sunk her in the deepest part of the Thames,* then by a gossip site in the US that he'd *strangled and defiled her, buried her corpse in the woods somewhere near his family home in Norwich,* people began to get excited. Stories started to stir. He'd been seen leaving the property *in his pyjamas* by a neighbour in the early hours a few weeks prior. An ex-colleague said he'd once taken a very angry telephone call and had slammed the device onto the ground afterwards. His school-days girlfriend came out to say he was into bondage, the paper she'd sold her story to somehow able to convince her to dress in lingerie and handcuffs for the accompanying image. I could just imagine the paper's gruff editor barking that the picture would *'really bring the piece to life,'* rubbing his greedy fingers together as he thought about the copies he would sell if she agreed.

'Million-dollar question, then,' Kay says. 'What do *you* think happened on the night of the 21st of August?'

I take a breath. 'Honestly, I don't know.'

'Speculate, please, be my guest.'

I want to reply straight away, to tell her that Rick is guilty as sin, that he has so much to answer for that he's never *once* had to justify… but I'm aware of coming on too strong. I don't want to put her off, I don't want her to think I'm as biased as I am.

'Like I said, Tabby wanted to leave Rick. She was desperate, she was even talking about moving abroad to get away from him. He was having an affair and… I don't believe in coincidences as big as that. I have no doubt that he was involved.'

'Do you think he killed her?'

'That's what I've always wondered.'

'Do you know anything about Rick's other woman?' she asks.

'No.' I curse Chad Cummings for his failure to deliver on that front.

'Rick's living with someone else now. Her name is Mandy,' Kay says, dropping the bombshell I'd spent so long trying to find. 'But, we're five years down the line, so I'm not suggesting Mandy's the same woman. And I don't know how long they've been together.'

My hand trembles as it reaches my mouth. 'Mandy,' I repeat quietly, trying to remember if I'd heard that name before.

'Do you know when this alleged affair started?'

I gather my thoughts, try to keep the nerves from my voice. 'It had been going on for a while before Tabby vanished, but I don't have an exact date.'

'I can't believe the police didn't dig it up. Why do you think that was?' she asks. 'I mean, I certainly didn't find any evidence of it when I was reporting the story for the *London Times*.'

I settle into her questioning, my guard down. 'Laziness, incompetence, bribery… take your pick.'

'Do you have anything to support your theory?'

'No,' I reply, a bit defensive. 'I hired an investigator, but he was a waste, trailed Rick for years and found precious nothing. I've heard nothing about this Mandy woman until now.'

She pauses. 'That's interesting.'

'Is it?'

'Do you know what kind of an investigator finds nothing?'

A shit one?

'The kind that's gone to the other side and asked for more money to keep their secrets hidden.'

Blood rushes to my ears.

'Did he tell you anything at all? He might have told you some information that Rick wanted you to hear.'

'Err,' I stutter, my mind reeling, the thought of how much money I've wasted on Chad piercing me. Had there been signs Chad was playing both sides? What had I missed at our last meeting? Had he even been following Rick at all? I shake my head, thinking back. 'He showed me logs of Rick's activity, examples of how accommodating Rick had been in helping the police investigation. And there was a photo... it was of a woman getting into a Polish car.'

'The CCTV shot?'

'Yes,' I breathe.

'I've seen it. Do you think it's Tabby?'

'Impossible to tell,' I reply. Then, 'What do *you* think happened?'

There's a slight hesitation before she speaks.

'The police have left a lot unsaid,' Kay sighs. 'And I pride myself on fighting for the people that others have forgotten about. In this case, I tend to agree with you: Rick's story just doesn't add up. His statement was so cold, his lack of caring... You know they only searched his place once? Just *once*.'

Her words play in my ears like nostalgic music, but

DO HER NO HARM

the melody is melancholic and I don't know if I want to keep listening. I am so used, too used, to being the only one who cares about Tabby that now there's someone else, someone with the resources to make a difference, it makes me double-take. *Do I really want to dive back into this?* Tabby's case has dominated every decision I've made for the better part of five years, do I really want to do it for another five? Could I cope if another attempt to find her ends in failure?

'If you're interested,' Kay says, 'I'd love you to work with me. I always find these things go easier if the people who truly knew the victim are close to the investigation... they tend to see the connections I miss.' She pauses, picking up on my reluctance. 'You could really make all the difference, Annabella.'

I keep quiet, weighing it up as she continues to talk.

'If there was a way of getting into his home,' Kay pressed, 'we'd find something. I know we would. Killers, or kidnappers, always leave mementos, little trophies reminding them of what they've done and of how clever they've been. Mark my words, if he did it, there'll be something in that house. We just need to figure out a way of getting in there. What do you say?' she finishes up. 'Are you in? Do you want to help?'

And with that, I know I have to agree. Not for me, but for my friend whom I've spent too long letting down. At least I have a life. Giving up five years of it is the least Tabby deserves.

'I'm in.'

'Brilliant,' Kay says. 'Pleasure to have you on board.'

At that moment, the line drops, and I realise Kay's hung

up on me, as though our conversation has come to its natural conclusion and she doesn't have enough time to finish it with a run of pleasantries. I put Kay's quirk to the back of my mind and replay our conversation. Though part of me is sceptical about starting again, I want to believe that this is it, that this is my chance to redeem myself, to honour Tabitha's memory and bring Rick Priestley to justice.

Tabby

Five Years Ago

'I'm sorry,' I say through a yawn, pulling up a seat at Annabella's clutter-free desk. It's gone eight and I've been at work for twelve hours now, bleary from my lack of sleep the night before, exhausted by the new responsibilities Caroline's assigned to me as Bella's lackey. It's not Bella's fault, of course, and I do want to take advantage of this opportunity, to learn from her. It was never my intention to be a receptionist forever.

'So,' she begins, clicking away at the white mouse under her grip. 'These are the latest rounds of before-and-after photos. I take them at each patient's initial consultation and again after treatment, then put them up on the website.'

She clicks through the process, showing me how it's done. It all seems straightforward enough.

I nod, agreeing. 'No problem.'

Bella smiles and gets up from her seat, a cloud of sharp citrus and cotton-fresh washing-powder in her wake. She picks up the camera she uses for these pictures, about to give me a tutorial in point-and-click no less, and clocks me looking up at the time.

'What does Rick make of your longer hours?' she asks.

I roll my eyes. 'He hasn't noticed, to be honest. That man is so wrapped up in himself that I honestly think it would take him a week to realise if I died in my sleep.'

Bella laughs, her water-blue eyes shining. We're closer than ever at the moment, which is why I feel terrible when my phone shudders on the desk and my first instinct is to hide it from her. *It's him.* Bella switches off the lights, then hands me the camera.

'For the sake of continuity—' Bella is nothing if not a perfectionist '—you want to stand five steps back from the patient, and to make sure their face fits perfectly into the guidelines on the screen.' She positions herself in front of the white surgery door, ready to be my model. 'And check that the flash is on.'

I set up the shot.

'Say cheese!' I joke, made funnier when Bella's expression remains completely unchanged. The flash shoots up from the camera, the click loud in my ear, freezing Bella on the tiny screen in my hands.

'Well, you don't look exactly... *ecstatic* about your upcoming procedure,' I observe, laughing, passing her the shot, reaching behind her to switch the lights back on.

Bella shrieks from behind me, covering her mouth with her hand, howling with disbelief. 'Take another one, right now, and *delete* that.'

I can barely hear her through my own laughter, stronger now that Bella's so horrified by the image. I look again at the picture and deduce it's something about the ferocity of her straight-face, the slight flare of her usually slender nostrils, the blur of her right eyelid, the camera capturing the very beginning of a blink, that's floored us both and I can barely keep the camera straight to take another shot.

'Tabby!' she pleads, and I gather myself together, taking a series of natural pictures that capture a more realistic image of my friend. Her high cheekbones and piercing eyes shine through, her naturally thick lashes and glossy ombre hair.

'Much better,' I say as I click through the pictures I've just taken, depressing the right-arrow button with the cracked tip of my fingernail, trying not to be envious.

I chastise myself even as the thought floats into my head; our relationship isn't like that, I should know better.

I pass her the camera and she hums a sound of approval. 'I was worried for a moment, but you're a quick learner,' she quips, glancing up from the camera. 'Just as well.'

'I'll finish up here,' I tell her. 'You should go home.'

She looks up at me. 'Are you sure?' she asks.

'Of course,' I insist, and watch her pack her things, observing her methodical approach to leaving the office. Everything in its place, everything tidied and put away. I expect my mere presence in her room is giving her a bit of anxiety, but she doesn't let on. She's been better recently, especially since we started doing CBT together. I don't need it, but I knew Bella wouldn't go alone.

I start uploading the rest of the patient pictures and guess the process will take me an hour or so, if I'm quick. Bella stands to hug me goodbye, wraps a slender arm round my shoulder, then pauses at the door before she disappears for the night. 'Bye, then, and thank you, you really are a better assistant than anyone Caroline would have found… despite what she may think.'

For a moment, I feel a pang of loneliness. I don't like being stuck here without Bella, but then my phone buzzes again, his name lighting up the screen, and I can't wait for her to disappear.

'See you tomorrow,' I call, and she flits into the hallway with a wave, a gust of warm air hitting my cheeks when she opens the door. We're on the cusp of summer, but the weather has been stormy and unpredictable all week, casting a gloom over the capital. The pale sun, occasionally visible through the cloud cover, bides its time, the turbulence not over yet. I wait until Bella has left the building and then, finally, I pick up my phone.

My skin vibrates. This isn't something I'm used to. A run of flirty messages, none of them from my husband.

My heart thuds, it's like he's knocking on a door inside me, asking to be let in. I pick it up, unlocking it, and the world falls silent as I read.

How was your day?

You know, it's not fair that you have that photo of me and I have none of you. I want to know who I'm talking to.

After Dr Alex Daniels mailed in his CV, I sent him a message. I told him I'd passed his application on to our owner and that I'd let him know if I heard anything. He got back to me a few days later to thank me but explained that he'd accepted another job, something closer to where he was living. It was mundane, boring, and uneventful, and yet I felt electric every time I heard from him. It was unthinkable to me to just… stop. So I didn't. I told him I'd spent some time in Paris on my gap year (a lie), that I loved Toronto (I've never been), so I was sad that he wouldn't be joining us (the truth). He replied, asked me about myself, and the conversation went from there…

Now we're on to pictures.

Crikey.

I glance at my reflection in the mirror to my side, my tired eyes and frazzled hair not exactly up to the task of taking the picture of a lifetime. Which is when the thought occurs to me that there is *something* I can send him that would pique his interest. I glance at the camera on the desk, my stomach churning. I can't do this, I tell myself, I can't send him a picture of Bella. Can I?

Annabella

Now

My teeth chatter together, holding their own frosty conversation at the bus stop on Lavender Road. My limbs are frigid, the tip of my nose iced over, the scene around me near-frozen in a bleak cloud of grey. I rub my gloves against each other and remind myself why I am here. It's January and my New Year's resolution is simple: the truth.

My senses heighten, my head spinning to the right as I spot the red double-decker I've been waiting for, to lumber into view. It should be tied with a bow like a late Christmas present because, given what's inside, that's exactly what it is. I stay seated on the half-bench in the bus shelter, toes numb despite wearing two pairs of socks, unable to keep my eyes from forensically examining each passenger until – *there he is*.

Rick Priestley.

My next breath shudders from my chest and I clench my legs together. *This is it*. He sits on the top deck, second row back on the right, a workman in a paint-splattered hoody just in front.

I notice things about him from this distance I hadn't before: the way he stares out of the window, the turn of his neck, the veins that protrude, a ligament under stress as he cranes to follow something that's caught his attention.

The indicator fires and the driver spins the wheel into the kerb. Rubber squeaks against concrete. Fleshy, almost, as the hard surface refuses to relent. I push my mouth and nose beneath my coat to avoid the effervescent fumes as they fill the air with toxic perfume. It backfires when it comes to a stop and breathes a noisy sigh of relief. They always sound so tired, buses.

I flit my focus to the top deck just as he's pushing himself to standing and let my pale eyes dance all over him. Part of me is almost tempted to wave, as though he might be aware that I've been following him. I smile to myself. I am always, somewhat perversely, excited to see him.

I follow his sharp haircut as it disappears below deck and my heart presses hard, knocking against my chest, as I wait for the doors to open. A few passengers are spat out before him, plastic bags and fold-up bikes negotiated through the gap and out into the wintery evening. He carries a briefcase, gripped to his side, and he steps from the bus to the road in the thick of the crowd. In the hubbub, a flustered woman grazes Rick's arm as they pass. Her hit was light, inconsequential, but he shoots her a stern look in response. The woman gasps, apologises, blushes, lingers, explains that she's clumsy and that she's terribly, terribly sorry. He flashes her a picture-perfect smile. '*No problem*', he says, lying through his too-white front teeth.

I hold my breath as he pulls away and, in the seconds that we're uncomfortably close, I can't help but notice how little he has changed. The same dark hair, smoothed to a side-parting, the same heavy brow and wide-set jaw, the same steely expression, taut and unforgiving. I cut the thought as it crescendos and tune into the sound of Rick's shoes striking concrete, fifty yards or so ahead. My focus needs to be here. I shake my head once, quickly, and hone in.

He walks steady, sturdy, not particularly heavy or light. Average, I'd say. I wonder if that's what he wants people to think. *But you're not average, are you Rick? It's a cover. A guise. A façade to hide just how remarkable you can be when you put your mind to it.* But people like Rick can't hide in mundanity forever, no matter how much they practise. A leopard always shows its spots. He hides his with his disarming smile and dull-blue eyes, with a suit so banal you'd forget anyone in it, no matter how notorious. He's styled this image of himself to hide what lies beneath. If he looked like a serial killer, I probably wouldn't be so worried about him, but this man, this everyman, is so normal that he *has* to be hiding something. My imagination fires, invented images flashing as I follow him. Tabby. Make-up running down her face, pleading with Rick to let her go, clawing towards the front door with her one remaining arm, the other loose and broken by her side. She's nearly there, she's nearly free; then Rick rises in the background, bruised from their fight, and clatters her with blood-thirsty fists. Later, a woman sobs to the media, adding her voice to the many that didn't see it coming. 'I thought he was a nice man, he's just, he's so *normal*.'

The streetlights glow as I follow him in and out of the

dark, past Neighbourhood Watch stickers and home security systems, discarded Christmas trees littering the pavements, the smell of pine needles hanging in the air. I slow slightly, fifteen or so paces behind, hands in my pockets, hood low. My breath quickens, the light hair on my arms bristling with anticipation. Which way? The same as last night, the night before? Part of me enjoys following him, but I am growing impatient.

I watch the way his feet move, note that the left overpronates a little, examine the way his free hand sticks rigidly to his side. I wonder if he senses me, feels me drawing closer, warmer. I let my gaze travel up his legs and catch a glimpse of red sock beneath suit trouser. *Loud.* Interesting. A glimpse of the *real* him. That tells me a lot. You want people to comment on that, don't you? If only you were wearing red gloves, Rick. *Red-handed*, I think. *Caught. Guilty. Twenty-five to life.*

He swings back his garden gate and I hover in the dark beneath two orange orbs, watching. I am used to this ritual. First, he closes the gate behind him. *Tidy.* Then, he walks to the front door, whistling. *An act.* He pulls a set of keys from his pocket. *Careless.* He fits them into the top lock, then leaves it on the latch. *Double careless.* I take a few steps forward and scan the front of the black-bricked house; there are no cameras, no alarm, the windows are single-glazed downstairs and up. *He thinks he's untouchable.* I hear the door bang as it closes behind him. I imagine the latch clicking into place. *Home sweet home.*

I visualise the way he'll slide off his shoes, red socks on show, then head upstairs to change into sweatpants and a loose jumper. He'll throw his work clothes near the washing basket but not in. He'll sigh long and loud as he thumps down the stairs. He'll ask what's for dinner with hungry eyes.

I approach the front of the house with another set of cautious, careful steps and watch, pupils wide, as a woman comes into view. Mandy. She moves round the space in red lipstick, a black top hugging her shoulders, dark curls pulled into a wild ponytail.

I observe her surroundings. From a distance, she stands in a light-grey kitchen with sharp edges and sparse personality but, look closer, and you'll see the cast iron shelves are decorated with well-thumbed recipe books, a marble island topped with post, fishbowl lamps hanging from the ceiling like spiders dropping from silver-spun webs. Rick drifts into the kitchen moments later, paces over to Mandy and wraps his strong arms round her middle. She half-smiles when he touches her, her shoulders shrugging to her ears as if she's uncomfortable. *Trouble?* She rests the back of her head on his shoulder, waiting for him to kiss her and, though it sounds affectionate, something about it looks perfunctory, well-rehearsed. Brief. He pecks her forehead, lets her go, then glides to the set of matching sofas in the living area beyond. He sinks into the seat and out of view. She sighs as he leaves and her smile disappears, replaced with pursed lips and frigid eyebrows. She chops at something I can't see, blade piercing flesh.

Cold air curls round the back of my neck.

I wonder if she loves him.

I wonder what she knows, what she doesn't.

I wonder if she feels the danger that lurks outside her house, that scratches at her door, that presses its face up against her windows at night.

Tabby

Five Years Ago

The Pure You office is stifling, swimming-pool humid, the dank air clinging to the skin beneath my uniform, the walls dripping with sweat. I don't mind the heat, not when I can be out in it, a linen dress whipping blushed skin rather than thick cotton. But, behind reception, the air sits heavy and I find myself counting down the hours to lunch.

I look down, the back of my hand still stained jelly-red, and four letters – XOXO – blurred across my skin. I cast my mind back to this time yesterday when the owner of XOXO had stripped to her underwear and flattened herself onto the surgery table, ready for a few rounds of laser therapy. Quite quickly, I'd noticed a fault line appear in the white plastic and I'd had to move fast to coax the woman down from it.

'Caroline's corner-cutting strikes again,' I'd whispered to Bella as we lay the patient seat as flat as we could make it. 'Let's hope she spent more than fifty pence on the seats.'

'Don't worry, I'm used to breaking things,' the woman

had said, her yellow-brown eyes sparkling beneath well-crafted brows. 'My mother fed me fast food when I was a kid because I was prettier than her and she hated me for it. Wanted to do everything she could to stop me from picking up the compliments she used to get.' Annabella and I had shared a look as she'd continued. 'I often wonder if I could sue her for child cruelty. It should be her paying the price for my ill health, not me. Don't you think?'

Child cruelty isn't the best subject to bring up with Annabella and me – both of us have survived difficult upbringings – and, at the time, I could tell the idea of this woman suing her own mother was affecting Bella. I'm sure she'd told me that her father had done something similar. Sued her mother after their divorce, stopped her from selling the tiny house she'd been exiled to, that all of her mother's money ended up tied up in the property, so much so that she couldn't afford the heating bills, or even food, and, rather than counter-sue, she'd let him win. Suicide, I think Bella had told me, in the end.

'Ah, I don't know,' Bella had replied. 'I think most parents are just trying their best. Besides, you're beautiful, *being thin* is not the be all and end all we were once led to believe.'

Bella's compliment had worked and, at the end of the appointment, two tickets to XOXO's Wednesday night Perspextacular were pressed into our palms.

Bella hadn't wanted to go – too loud, too dirty, too crowded – but I'd begged her, and dragged her back to my house after work to get ready. Perspex had made a fashion comeback a few years ago and, though it was often levelled at me as an insult, this time my trend-following obsession had paid off. I'd squeezed Bella into clear-heeled sandals, the top of her foot clad in a jelly-shoe-like band, an ice cube-inspired plastic clutch swinging from her arm. She looked amazing and, finally, she relented.

Honestly, if she'd said no, I would have gone without her. I was desperate to escape, seeking oblivion to punish myself for caring too much about Alex, who'd been broadcasting radio silence since Sunday night. I'd been trying my best not to dwell on it, alcohol and nights out the best way to forget and, before I knew it, I was doing the same again. Bella and I downed watermelon shots at the bar, danced to too-loud-to-hear music, mouths agape at the amazing podium dancers wrapped in clear-plastic dresses, our arms in the air as we'd enjoyed it all together.

We were having fun, then, motivated by self-destruction, I went on to have a little too much. Not much later, Bella had my tresses in a hand-held ponytail to stop me from turning my blonde hair watermelon-pink. She'd stood behind me trying not to touch the surfaces, dabbing a stack of toilet roll against my clammy forehead, pushing a bottle of water into my hand, forcing me to drink, then held me as I'd heaved into the toilet once more – 'You're OK, you're OK' – she'd cooed as she patted the space between my shoulder blades. Over my shoulder, though, I could tell she was panicking. Bella didn't like public toilets at the best of times, let alone vomit-stained ones. Bella, patient and perfect, waited for me to finish, then got me home, safe and sound, despite the fact she was on the verge of an anxiety attack herself.

'Do you always make a habit of ignoring your patients?' My neck whips towards the voice across from me and my heart flutters as I realise my mistake. The woman ruffling her feathers is one of our textbook patients, an entitled lady in her early fifties, a neat top wrapped tight to her torso, her silver-blonde hair cut sharp to her chin.

'Sorry,' I say, grabbing a bunch of forms. 'I'll take you down now, you can fill these out later.'

I guide her down the stairs and mouth an apology to Bella as we enter, shuffling towards her as the woman hangs up her things behind the door.

'She hasn't had time to do the forms,' I explain under my breath. 'But I'll make sure they're done before she leaves.'

My hair stinks of cigarette smoke and my eyes are tired and crusty. There's a faint ringing in my left ear – the lasting effect of last night's loud music – and a stale taste on my tongue. Bella doesn't look much better.

I head back upstairs and nap with my head on my desk until Bella's patient leaves. I shift her next one over to Anya's schedule. Anya won't mind, she has a quiet day today.

I give Bella five minutes to clear up, then trudge to her room to debrief on last night's events. Her head rests heavy on her forearms and she groans when I come in.

'Why?' she asks. 'I didn't even drink that much. It's not fair. It's as though my brain has been scooped out and replaced with avocado.'

I imagine a head full of mushy, green flesh and my stomach burbles.

'Have you managed to get this off?' I ask, showing her the back of my hand.

'No,' she groans again.

I fill the surgery sink with hot water and scrub at the red stamp with renewed determination.

'You'd think they'd make them easier to remove,' I say. 'Does no one else have to go to work the next day?'

'They want people to wear them as badges of honour,' Bella replies.

'Hmm.'

'Seriously, though, I'm too old for three hours' sleep and work the next day.'

I sound an agreement, though I'm not sure I really mean it.

'And clubs are just... filthy,' she says.

Bella gets up from her desk, her complexion pale, and joins me at the sink. She grabs the scouring pad on the side and scrubs at the back of her hand. I don't think much of it until the water in the sink begins to redden, the back of her hand cut to shreds, the look in her eyes distant and fogged, unmoved by the pain she should be feeling.

'Bella,' I say, breathless, breaking the scourer from her grip. 'Stop!'

Her eyes roll towards me and she visibly crumples. I reach my arms around her, pulling her close, then feel her head nestle into the nook of my neck.

'Sorry,' she whispers. 'I'm tired and I'm—'

'It's OK,' I say, sitting her down, cleaning the wound with antiseptic and bandaging it up. I feel terrible. Bella's symptoms are always worse when she's tired, or stressed, or hungover. 'We all need help sometimes. It was me last night, it's you this morning.'

Before I have the chance to ask her more about how she's feeling, her hand freshly bound, we're interrupted by a knock at the door.

'Hello?' a voice calls on the other side.

Bella gets up, bandaged hand by her side. Behind the door is her next patient – the one I'd moved to Anya's schedule. I roll my eyes with frustration at Anya's laziness, acknowledging the irony in the way I feel mid-roll.

'Can you stay?' Bella asks, turning to me, then to the patient. 'Tabitha's shadowing me, do you mind if she sits in?'

The woman bristles. 'Not if it won't cause any more delays. You're already running quite late enough.'

This surgery has a habit of attracting impatient patients – *we should call them impatients* – and I can tell Bella's trying her best not to rise to the bait.

'Of course,' she replies calmly, guiding the woman to the patient seat. 'How can we help you this morning?'

'I've always been like this,' the woman explains, peeling back her sleeves to reveal a coat of thick, dark hair. 'And I need it all gone. Permanently.'

Bella runs through what will happen next, hiding how awful she's feeling behind a mask of professionalism. She tells the woman she'll need to shave her arms first then, once they're smooth, she'll fire a laser deep into her hair follicles, destroying them. She tells her to expect a bit of discomfort. 'But please don't worry, you're a fantastic candidate for this procedure. I'm confident we'll achieve a really good result.'

She says that to all the impatients.

'Will there be any scars?' the lady asks.

'No, but the area will be very sensitive to sunlight afterwards. You'll have to wear a high factor SPF outside but, ideally, you need to keep your arms covered.'

Bella looks over at me and I offer the woman a razor. The patient hurries out to the customer toilet, and returns to the chair moments later, ready for the main event.

'Here we go,' Bella says on autopilot as she administers

the first hit. I watch as the patient's hands turn yellow as she squeezes the armrest. 'The first one's always the worst,' Bella assures her, then aims her conversation towards me. 'It's really important the area is clean and smooth before you start IPL, it also helps if the room is cool – although on a day like today we can't always control that.'

I nod, taking it all in, learning from the best. It's my dream to follow in Bella's footsteps and become an aesthetic nurse one day. I must admit, since I've been speaking to the doctor, that my desire to be more like her – not just professionally – has intensified. I find myself staring at our respective reflections in the mirror opposite. Wisps of peroxide hair cling to my forehead, my pink lipstick long melted, electric-blue eyeliner smudged across my eyelids. I am the kind of person who longs to look groomed and polished but always comes off a little scruffy, even when I'm not cripplingly hungover. *Rushed*, that's how Rick described my Valentine's Day outfit last year. Bella, in contrast, though she's paler than usual, shines in a way that I never do. Her jaw is fine and chiselled, created by a top cosmetic surgeon, her pouty lips subtly plumped with filler, her eyes a deep, mysterious aqua-blue. She is the very picture of perfect. No wonder Alex Daniels has fallen for her.

I look deep into the reflection of my friend, feeling guilty. I still haven't told her my secret. Mainly because I know what she'd say: that I'm being stupid, that I need to walk away, that I need to *stop*.

But I can't.

I turn away and check my phone, swiping my keycode over my love-heart screensaver.

No new messages.

My heart sinks and my brain wanders. *Where is he?*

I blink quickly to hide my disappointment, my mind looping to thoughts of alcohol and escapism, to another night trying to forget the person who's already forgotten all about me.

Annabella

Now

A branch snaps in two beneath my right foot, invisible in the dark that engulfs the back garden.

I'd accessed it through the garden gate to the right of the property. I'd noticed during my weeks of surveillance that it's often left open overnight on a Tuesday after the gardener has been to tend to the weeds. It's the kind of detail that meticulous people like me pick up on. I'd smiled as the circular handle had given way freely, the swing of the hinge silent, the click shut barely perceptible.

I slip into a gap in the hedge, my breath coming quicker at the sound of the branch breaking beneath my weight. To me it had sounded like a gunshot, a fork of lightning kissing the earth, but to the world it had gone unnoticed. As much often does. I look up once I am sure I have not been caught: the windows of the house remain dark, glass-like, reflecting the sway of the trees in the park beyond. I pull the black balaclava down over my face, my eyes my only visible feature, my breath panting into the material. I do not have props, or tools, just a bag with a change of clothes and a simple plan, a clear purpose.

The man inside this house needs to face justice.

Rick Priestley: arrested in connection with the disappearance of Tabitha Rice. Rick Priestley: accused but not charged. Rick Priestley: the cheater. The liar. The narcissist. The partner you wouldn't wish on your worst enemy let alone your best friend.

There is something hypnotic about being this close to him, about being in the confines of his garden *finally* taking action after years of none. But I must be careful. He's dangerous. I check my watch, wondering what it is that I am waiting for. It has to be now. Mandy's routine is erratic and she spends most of her time at home. I'd wanted to break in during the day when the house would be empty but I couldn't take the chance of Mandy coming back and raising the alarm. My teeth chatter, goose bumps rising along my forearms, dotting their way down my legs. The cold of the grass seeps into my skin and chills me further. I look up once more into the dark windows, checking for the slightest of movements. I imagine them lying in bed, side by side, sleepy limbs stretched across the mattress. I think about their routine, a perfunctory kiss before bed, then a synchronised roll to their respective sides. Mandy's hair will be tied back, her face washed and scrubbed clean, her eyes covered with a fluffy mask, chest rising and falling. He'll be snoring. noisy, grunty. My heartrate quickens as I imagine being near them. *What if I am caught?*

I close my eyes and pull on the gloves – gardening ones I'd found in their shed – clammy palms fitting the space. My mouth is dry, parched, every sense heightened, every sinew tense. I know already what I have to do, I just don't want to do it. *It will be worth it*, I tell myself. He'll have been careless, there will be *something* in that house which proves his guilt. It will be hidden, probably, something he can't risk throwing away. I just need to build up the courage to go in there and find it, whatever it is.

I rise gently from the undergrowth and take a few silent steps towards the back door, leaving my bag by the exit. I move the plant pot up, drag the spare key from its hiding place and fit it into the lock.

I take my first tentative step inside, towards a man who should be seeing bars for the rest of his life, and wonder if he's proud of himself.

Not many people get away with murder.

I wait until silence has engulfed the house once more, until the hands of the hallway clock are the loudest noise, tick-tick-tick, mirroring the beat of my heart. Only then, when I am calm, do I press on. *I must hurry.*

I pad through the hallway, hearing my own muted footsteps, and crack open the door to my right which leads to the living area. It's a plush open space, the chrome and marble of the kitchen sweeping to the creams of the lounge, a Jacquard print rug on the floor. I scan the room, my eyes landing on a white-gloss cabinet, photo frames, and a small stack of mother-of-pearl boxes on top, pushed up against the far wall. I fumble with the handle-less drawers, realising eventually that you have to press them to open them, the latch mechanism inside the drawer rather than out. I depress, then open, all three.

But there's nothing inside.

I open the boxes on top, spending too long fiddling with the clasps. All empty. I turn, spot a bookcase pressed up against the opposite wall, and hurry over to it, levering out multi-coloured spines one by one. But I don't find anything I can use. Dust whips the air and I stifle a sneeze into the sleeve of my black windbreaker. A muffled squeak, as though I've just stepped on a mouse, carries through the house and I freeze once more, waiting to be caught, my heart beating so loud I'm afraid it will give me away.

When I'm sure that the coast is clear, I move faster, to the kitchen, into the silver edges I've been observing for so long, the surfaces near-vibrating as I run my excited fingers across them. I duck down and scatter the kitchen with bills and manuals and scrap pieces of paper shoved into drawers and forgotten about. But still nothing grabs my attention.

I'll have to go upstairs.

I sneak from the kitchen to the hallway, the glass window of the back door reflecting my macabre image back at me, all black, my pupils sparkling as they pick up the glow of the moon from beyond. I hardly recognise myself. Which is a good thing. I do not want to be recognised.

I take a deep breath, fill my body with oxygen, the peachy, floral scent of their home thick in my lungs, and tell myself I'm ready for what's next. I grip the wood of the handrail and place my foot on the first step. I take each more quietly than the next, attempting to glide over the carpet rather than step on it.

Three doors greet me when I reach the landing, standing one after the other in a line, the corridor reaching long to the back of the house. I tiptoe towards the first and press my ear to the frame. Nothing. I twist the handle: porcelain features sparkle back. A bathroom. White subway tiles, a matte-black basin, a house plant with green tendrils curling round the windowsill. I must keep going. I leave the door ajar and move on to the next. The sound of slumber rolls from within – it must be their bedroom – so I slip past it, but a loose plank betrays me and squeals beneath my weight. Sweat trickles from the nape of my neck.

'Rick?' Mandy's voice seeps through the door just ahead.

I stop. Confused.

I hear her ask again.

'What?' Rick grunts from the door behind me, annoyed. *Separate bedrooms. Mandy's room is in front of me, Rick's behind, me in the middle.*

'Was that you?'

'What are you talking about?' he sleep-shouts back. I listen to him half-turn, the springs of his bed stirring with him. I pick up the irritated trill in his voice. *Stupid woman*, he wants to say. 'Go to sleep. It's nothing. You're always hearing things.'

She is.

His mistake is not believing her.

She settles down. I don't know why. Why does his patronisation make her feel better? It's perverse.

I am not here to hurt her. I wish I could tell her that. *Just go back to sleep, listen to Rick, let me get what I'm looking for and I'll leave you in peace.*

The final door is about ten steps away and it's ajar, inviting me in. I could wait here, quietly, until I'm sure they're both asleep again, or go for it. As I'm weighing it up, long before I have the chance to make up my mind, Mandy's bedroom door handle twists and the mechanism turns slowly from inside. The movement is cautious, which is lucky, because it gives me a chance to dart to the room at the end of the corridor – my hips stretching the full range of their sockets as I leap out of sight. I flatten myself into the wall as she pauses at the threshold, my breath heavy, hers light. I imagine her sticking her neck, giraffe-long, into the hallway, checking right then left before tottering out. Her footsteps pad across the landing, then fade as she walks towards the bathroom. Mandy will be wearing grey jersey pyjamas with love hearts for buttons, her mess of dark hair wild and untamed – as though drawn by an angry child looping furious circles with black crayon on white paper. I close my eyes and try to steady my breath. Cold sweat sticks to my body. That was close.

While she's in the bathroom, I take the opportunity to examine the shelves to my left. I don't have long. I must hurry. I look around, deducing quickly that I'm in Rick's study, a desktop PC resplendent in the centre, an office chair tucked neatly behind a sturdy desk. A framed certificate of his Oxford University degree sits behind it and I make a snap judgement: clearly nothing in his adult life has eclipsed this achievement, still pride of place after all these years. But then I suppose they don't give out certificates for well-executed executions, do they?

My gloved fingers flick through papers and notepads and, just as I am losing hope, I find something: a cardboard box marked 'OLD'. I pull off the top and, buried beneath a few books about espionage and cyber-warfare, are a collection of old passports, the tops snipped away at the corner. I open a few – they're all of Rick – and then, right at the bottom of the box, I find something else. Bank statements. I shuffle through the top few and notice a pattern. On the first of the month, Rick transfers £1,000 to somebody. There's no name, just a collection of letters as the reference.

I shudder, my mind looping to secrets and pay-offs and, though there must be more to find in here, I know it's time to leave when I hear the toilet flush and, moments later, the bathroom door whoosh open. The draft glides into the study, I feel it on my eyelids, the only part of me exposed. I clutch the statements in my hands, then make the decision to leave them where I found them: they're more powerful here, hidden in Rick's study, waiting to be unearthed, followed up with a series of uncomfortable questions about why he's paying someone off. Silencing someone, silencing his secrets.

Kay and I are going to get him, I think. *Finally.*

I stand tall, press my body against the wall once more, and wait for Mandy to leave the bathroom. I feel the drumbeat of her footsteps as they cross the landing and, just as I'm expecting her to turn and go back into her bedroom, she hesitates. She knows something's wrong. Her intuition is telling her to investigate.

Her footsteps crescendo as she draws near, coming right for me. My mouth is chalk, my head wool, as I weigh up my options – *fight or flight* – in the milliseconds that follow. My first instinct is to hide behind the door, but I won't have time to get there. My second is to hide beneath the desk, but it sits on four exposed legs and wouldn't cover me. My third is to jump out of the window but I'm not sure it's big enough. My fourth is to grab the paperweight on the desk, the glass mass heavy in my gloved palm, and rush towards the door. I can't give her the opportunity to scream. I have to reach her first.

We meet at the threshold, her eyes wild and wired as I ambush her, not giving her a second to react, or for me to change my mind. I watch the paperweight in the reflection of her eyes as I lift it high, then dive it towards her skull. The sound is dull, her head absorbing the worst of the impact, her heart-shaped face broken by the hit, the paperweight still whole as it clatters to the floor. *Glass beats bone.*

My heart flutters as I stand over her, the horror of what I've done to protect my mission, to find out the truth, creeping up on me. I stare at her brick-red cheeks, her right eye caved inwards, her lips covered in cherry-coloured blood, her throat making a horrible choking sound. *I didn't want to hurt you*, I want to say, but my voice is trapped in my mouth, something glue-like keeping my tongue from moving. No, I tell myself, *I can't speak to her, I can't risk being caught.* I go to move, to run from here, but find that I can't, something in me paralysed.

Rick's voice trickles from his bedroom – *'Mandy?'* – and it's this that breaks me from the spell. I snap my neck upwards, thudding back to the present. 'Is everything OK?' he asks from the warmth of his duvet.

The annoyance in his tone rises to worry as she doesn't respond, and I know I must get out or everything will be lost. I take a series of skip-like steps across the landing, fly down the stairs, yank open the door, grab my rucksack, and escape into the dead of the night.

I have what I want – *proof for the world that I am right, that Rick has been buying his innocence* – but it came at a cost. I run away from what I have done, from the horror of it, but the fear in Mandy's eyes as I attacked her, plays on a loop I know I am not going to be able to forget.

PART 2

Rick

Fifteen Years Ago – 2005

Perhaps it was hard to believe, coming from someone like me, but Oxford University was never a dream of mine. Not because I hadn't wanted to go, but because I never thought it would be an option. My family weren't particularly privileged or wealthy, they weren't able to buy my place with a large donation to the university's treasury or butter up the admissions secretary via influential friends. Instead, I went to a state school and, though I was a prize-winner in maths and physics, top of the year in biology, and taking an extra A level because I wanted to, I didn't also play eight different instruments and professional-standard rugby. I dropped my T's, found it hard to make eye contact, and answered their questions with 'Yeah' rather than 'Yaaaarrrhhss'.

So, it was a surprise, you see, when I was accepted. It meant a lot at the time. I got in – so I thought – for me. Off my own bat. My stellar grades, genuine interest in my chosen subject – Economics – and admissions interview enough. My ego was at an all-time high that summer, I waved goodbye to the lesser mortals from my hometown – most of them choosing to stay and study in the county they grew up in – and set off in late September, wind blowing through the slightly longer hairstyle I'd crafted during the break, a moody side-fringe batting up against my left eyelashes. I was Rick Priestley and I was going to Oxford. These were going to be the best years of my life.

My first lesson came sooner than expected. In fact, it kicked off the moment I arrived, stepping confidently into the wood-panelled corridors, poking my head curiously into the grand dining hall, breathing in the smell of old books, running my eyes across trophies and honours and the gold-plated names of previous alumni. I remember it well; it was a brutal out-of-hours seminar entitled How The World Works. A quick-smart reality check in Who Do You Think You Are?

I was stopped by a student on my way to registration. 'Sorry,' she said. 'The college is closed for visitors today. We have our freshers arriving! Here, let me show you to the visitor entrance.'

I corrected the student, turning her cheeks grape-purple, but the way she looked at me said it all: Oh. You're one of 'those' freshers.

A political storm had been brewing for a while, Oxford had been lambasted for not accepting high-flying state-school students citing their 'lack of potential', and the public were biting back, forcing its rusty gears into a new and reluctant action.

It quickly became clear that I wasn't here for me. I wasn't here because I was good enough – far from it – the only reason I got into Oxford was because I wasn't. The place needed a rebrand, a reputation overhaul, a new kind of student to wheel out to the press when the headlines made for uncomfortable reading. I was in the right place at the right time, one of the chosen few from a splattering of comprehensive schools across the country intended to 'prove' that not everyone was a quiff-haired, cravat-necked, double-barrelled somebody. The university resented taking people like me – felt we sullied Oxford's reputation as a world class institution – but needed us for the right interviews and press releases and for the pages of the matte-finish brochures, as opposed to the glossy ones heading for Eton, our dreary clothes a subliminal message that anyone could make it to Oxford if they tried hard enough. And why wouldn't you want to go to Oxford? The question was so rhetorical no one ever thought about the answer. And this, unfortunately for me, meant I blended into these hallowed halls like a counterfeit bank note crafted by a plucky eight-year-old.

It took fifteen minutes to cycle from college to the McDonald's on the outskirts of town, and every time I made the journey, I hated myself more. I could almost feel it: my ego flattening under the front wheel of my bike as I set off. Unlike my privileged peers, I had to work to keep myself afloat. I don't think I would have minded if I wasn't the only one, but I was, which meant that before the end of the first week I was already behind. I was certain that if I didn't have to work, I'd have been able to keep up here. As it was, while I looped the ends of my apron to my waist, mopped sodden chips from the restaurant's dusty corners and swirled sky-high McFlurrys into disposable cups, they learned about Nietzsche and Marx, and debated the great economists of all time. They swapped theories and revision notes while I rummaged through the stock cupboard for the last of the ketchup the franchise owner – Darren – never ordered enough of.

At first, I lied about where I went when I was at work; I told the boys on my landing there was someone I rode off to see, a gap-year girl, toothpick thin with red hair, pale skin and a couple of trips to Malawi on overseas-aid projects under her belt. Refined. The type of girl I was supposed to be interested in.

It was a slow Friday midway through an unusual October heatwave and my shift was dragging, just the occasional sticky customer inside, sweat stains on the back of recently occupied chairs because the air conditioning wasn't working. I pushed a strawberry sweet into my mouth, bagged up the afternoon's rubbish and thought about what my gap-yah girl would be called, what her favourite colour was, her favourite food. I settled on Poppy, red, steak. A theme emerging. Any discerning listener would see right through the lie.

Later, working the tills, I played games to pass the time, guessing people's orders before they made them. A skinny girl approached, legs poking out from the frayed hem of her denim skirt, a gingham blouse on her top-half tied with a bow. I guessed her order just as she asked.

'Diet Coke,' she said, avoiding eye contact with me, shoving a twenty-pound note on the counter as though it were Monopoly money. I took it, slid the note into the till, plucked out her change, then prepared her drink.

'Your Diet Coke and…' I reached beneath the counter, feeling for the paper wrappers. 'A straw,' I said, handing them both to her.

'Thanks,' she said, then scooped up the change I'd left on the counter, leaving behind a cluster of brown and silver coins.

'Keep the rest,' she told me. 'Your tip,' she smiled nastily, and I ground down on my back teeth as she left the restaurant with her friends, laughing. Though I wanted to stand there, offended and angry, I stole a glance behind me and scooped the coins into my greedy palm, shoving them deep into my shallow pocket. Nowhere made me hate myself more than inside this garish red-and-yellow McNightmare.

Once my shift was over, I cycled the route back to halls – couldn't risk a job that was nearby – and, just as I arrived, the heavens opened. The heatwave vanished with the rain and, rather than T-shirts and jeans, the boys were getting ready with jumpers and blazers and expensive leather jackets for tonight's night-out. I joined in as best I could, wore a dark-grey coat I'd found in a second-hand shop back home, and headed with the rest of the boys to their preferred nightclub, forced to spend all the money I'd just made on expensive rounds for my moneyed mates. I thought about the 80p in the pocket of my uniform when I handed over thirty pounds for a round of Jäegarbombs and shook my head at my stupidity. When I handed the drinks out, none of my friends blinked an eye, only a few of them even said thank you. That wasn't because they were all horrible people… they just didn't understand. The people here weren't like me, the previous rounds had been Veuve Cliquot and Krug. I'd watched as one of the boys had bought an extra bottle and chugged it straight from the neck, champagne drooling down his face as he'd tried to finish it in one, half of it tipping to the floor, jeers from the other boys. Down it, Down it, Down it! He'd puked it up almost immediately –inside, right on the dancefloor, he didn't care, someone would come to clean it up. He'd laughed about it afterwards. Bought another round. It would be my turn again soon. And you know what was bad? I wanted, more than anything, to be like them, to buy champagne like it was tap water, to make the people who couldn't feel inferior.

Later, drunk, gone midnight, I laid eyes on a girl with chunky highlighted hair and pink pearly lips. She was walking towards me, her round face illuminated by a shaft of white light from the strobe overhead, and I watched a smile break across it when our eyes met. The light clicked off, the club dark, and when it fired again, strobe-effect, her smile was gone and her position had changed. She was in front of me, now, saying something about the university. I morphed into one of the boys – she didn't know any better – and it felt good. I let her know I was the heir to a confectionery company, coy with the details.

'Really?' she asked.

'How old are you?' I fired back, changing the subject, and she replied, eyes to the sky, that she was twenty-one. I knew she was lying – there was no way she was older than me – and we debated, jokingly, on the dancefloor. Eventually she handed me her driver's license, a naughty smile on her pearlescent lips. She was eighteen, and only just, finishing her last year at school. Her white lie resonated with me. She wanted to be someone else, too. I looked at her, a little sad, and leaned in.

'Never lie about who you are again,' I slurred into her ear, a gold stud in the middle of the lobe. 'Who you are is enough.' And, even though I was drunk, distracted by the way her halter-neck gaped at the front, her shiny hair twisted round her finger, I really meant it.

She told me about herself, about her foster parents and normal high school, about the fact she was going to drop out because she hated being there. She reminded me of the girls at home. The summer-soaked sixth-formers I'd meet on the beach in Great Yarmouth with loud-mouths and short-skirts. She made me realise what it meant to be homesick. I fancied her and, not only that, her humour was the exact same as mine, her references, her interests.

Though we'd only just met, it was as though I'd known her for years. I think she even said it, her blue eyes blinking up at me. I was so happy to have found her, a piece of me in a haystack of others.

'This might sound weird but… I feel as though I know you already.'

Annabella

Now

I duck into the moss-green shed of number 50, the frantic scene before me illuminating the night. Red and blue kaleidoscope sirens, high-vis yellow uniforms, blue and white tape, a stretcher loading a woman into the back of an ambulance. *I hope she's OK.* A tumble of Mandy's blood-black hair identifies her as she's wheeled past and I watch as neighbours' curtains flicker, snatches of yellow-light breaking into the dark. A few of the more curious among them are already outside, slippers in huddles, arms crossed over waists, excitement dressed as concern dancing across their faces. A man with a haphazardly tied dressing gown walks, head bowed, towards the activity. *A few of us, you know, are just a bit concerned. Could you tell us what's going on, please?*

The policewoman he approaches shakes her head.

I retreat into the shadows of the shed, remove my balaclava, the gloves I'm wearing, pull off my black windbreaker and change into a smart coat and scarf from my rucksack. Then I wait. The couple from number 50 are either out, or heavy sleepers, and the windows behind me remain black. I sigh deep with relief and wait for the commotion to begin. What have I done?

I sink to the floor of the shed and let my mind travel back to my teenage years, connecting the dots from then to now, showing me who I've always been, revealing that tonight wasn't a one-off, freak event, but entirely and utterly in character. I bottle up my emotions, I always have, allow them to fester. For some reason I'm always surprised when the glass explodes.

I spent my formative years growing up in a mews house just off Holland Park with my eccentric parents. Whenever I think of that house, I remember the tiny ground-floor toilet first, the plush pink hand towels and the rose-scented candle that sat on the windowsill for years and never burned. I think of that room first, then remember my mother teaching me how to bake, watching endless repeats of *Murder, She Wrote* together. I adored that show and that tenacious old woman who'd get to the bottom of every crime thrown her way, thirsty for justice, satiated only by unravelling the truth from a pack of lies. When our family cat went missing that summer, I'd used her as inspiration and broken into the garden of the big house at the end of the road. I was caught looking for cat-poo among the bushes and, though I was told off, I was found again the following week when I thought the family were out, picking through the gravel of their front drive with my father's antique magnifying glass. *Don't tell me your mysteries: I will only try and solve them.*

I have to face it: what I did to Mandy tonight, though horrifically violent, was all me.

At the turn of 5 a.m., just as my eyelids begin to droop, I recognise a presenter from the *Breakfast News* arriving at the scene, a clutch of cables and men in anoraks following behind. Adrenaline flares. Her face is usually squashed into unflattering 2D on the screen, but today she's right in front of me, fully formed. I feel as though I've nabbed a backstage pass, exclusive access to the inner workings of her off-air world. The early mornings, the late-nights, the last-minute concealer drawn in beige paint-strokes under her tired eyes. *The news never sleeps, so neither does she.* My finger twitches for the volume on my imaginary remote control. I want to hear what she's saying but, of course, I can't. I draw closer to read her lips.

'*Rick Priestley – ex-husband of the still-missing Tabitha Rice – was the victim of a break-in overnight. His partner, Mandy, has been taken to hospital with a head injury described as 'severe' by a close neighbour. According to the same neighbour, there were raised voices in the property earlier in the evening.*'

I take a breath as a police car revs, lights flashing down the twist of the cul-de-sac. They've probably just had a tip. Or they're *pretending* to have just had a tip, they want the news to think they know what they're doing. That they're 'exploring all avenues of inquiry'. But they're thinking it too: Rick Priestley's guilty as sin. One girlfriend missing, presumed dead, the other in hospital. *We cannot comment on ongoing investigations*; the line they will deliver. Then Mandy will wake up and exonerate him. '*He's telling the truth, there was someone in our house, someone wearing a balaclava and gardening gloves holding a paperweight.*' But everyone will think he's manipulating her, that she's scared to tell the truth. *What kind of intruder attacks someone with a paperweight?*

No, it was him, in the heat of the moment. It's obvious. It's sad. I pity her.

I know it already. Though I deserve it, no one will come looking for me.

Streetlights line the way back to my flat. I don't live far from Rick and Mandy in Battersea, and I'm sure one of the reasons I haven't moved from the area is because of Tabby: I've never really been able to let her go. The fact that Rick hasn't moved tells me he hasn't either.

I push open my front door, number 413, desperate for bed, aware as I take my first step inside that the air smells different somehow, greasy with leftovers and takeaway food, but perhaps it's just my imagination. *Has someone been inside while I've been out?* My palm pushes the door shut, closing it behind me with a cautious click of the latch.

'Hello?' I call.

Silence.

I steady myself. 'No one is here', I say out loud. No one has found their way into my space. The smell I thought I could detect disappears. *I'm projecting.*

I breathe. I let the remaining fissures of adrenaline leave my body, then pull, tug and peel winter layers from my limbs, my dyed, dry hair filling with static electricity as I unfurl my scarf from my neck. I hang it over the iron coat holders in the entranceway and move towards the wooden console table in the corner. I place my keys on the far left, stroking them in line, then straighten the stack of letters beside them, which I need to post tomorrow. I unhook my feet from the depths of my winter boots and tuck them neatly beneath the table. Three other pairs are out on display: old trainers, work plimsolls, and a pair of sheepskin slippers. I steal a quick glance at myself in the oval mirror that sits above the table, my skeletal features and bruised cheeks from a recent tear-trough procedure appearing ghoulish, somehow. I do not like to look at myself for too long: I always find something I need to improve. I shake the thought away, push my feet into the slippers, and walk into the living area, squeezing anti-bacterial gel into my hands and up my lithe arms as I go, enjoying the sterility. Performing my rituals calms my breathing and helps me to rationalise the situation: *There's no point in panicking until you know how Mandy is. She could be fine. You're not a killer, you're not like Rick.*

I let the thought percolate and watch, in the flat opposite mine, a yellow-lit young family in the throes of breakfast. I can't make out the details, but I know that they are happy, unified, and it makes me smile. I'm glad there are families like this in the world, that they aren't just the cynical invention of advertising companies trying to sell washing powder and package holidays with a smiling group of similar faces. I wish I'd grown up in a house like that, so full of warmth. I bet there'll be apple crumble for dessert tonight, thick custard on the side.

I watch for a moment as they make breakfast, morning TV playing behind them. Then I spot Rick's face and my smile disappears. His piercing eyes are etched with electric worry and I can just about make out what he's saying.

Vigilante groups are out of hand. This vilification of my character by the media has to stop.

I close my blinds. I do not want to see him. I do not want to hear what lies he is going to deliver to the masses watching him.

I move to the kitchen, parched, pushing him from my mind and pour myself a drink, letting the water run through my body, quenching my thirst. I reflect on the packed family home across the street. The surfaces had been so full of things, the room packed with stuff, brimming with life. In contrast, the shiny surfaces of my own kitchen are clean and empty, the hob sparkling, the fridge white and orderly. It's a little sad, in a way, but the cleanliness is an oft-overlooked upside of living alone. When I return to this place, I'm greeted by the same sanctuary I left, no one messes anything up while I'm gone, leaving stains across the surfaces, specks of mud trodden from the outside in. Other people are so unhygienic. I learned that first at university, forced to live with nursing students who clearly hadn't read the course notes on the spread of E.coli and the importance of washing one's hands. Filthy, that lot. I'm not sure how I'd come through it.

I run my glass beneath the tap, clean it, then stack it on the draining board next to the sink. Perhaps I'm not the kind of person who would be able to cope with a family, anyway.

Too messy.

I wipe away the tears that paint my cheeks.

Tabby

Five Years Ago

The humidity of earlier in the week has given way to monsoon-like downpours and my jacket is sodden as I wave goodbye to Bella at the end of the road.

'Feel better soon,' she urges as my arms slip from our rushed embrace. *I feel terrible for lying to her. For pushing her away in favour of my secret crush.*

'I will!' I reply, over-enthusiastically. 'I just need an early night.'

I'm not planning to get an early night, of course, but I had to cancel our plans. I can tell she's disappointed – it's the third time in as many weeks I've cancelled our ritual Thursday night dinner – but, listen, the new Mexican in Soho isn't going anywhere. It can wait another week.

I feel my phone vibrate in my pocket, shuddering against my hip, dancing up to the flutter in my chest.

He's waiting. *Dr Daniels*. He wants to talk.

I've missed you, Tabby cat.

He calls me by my real name but talks to a different face. Bella hasn't noticed – no one has – but I switched our names on the company website, just in case he looks at it. I can just about bear him thinking about her face but calling me by her name would have been a step too far. What's in a face, anyway? Shouldn't love be based on connection rather than physical attraction? Another text message arrives.

I have an hour tonight, between shifts, if you're free?

My heart skips beats. It's not unusual for him to only have an hour here, a couple of hours there, and I've learned to make the most of every available moment he gives me. When we do find a moment to talk, our connection burns fast and bright, swirls pink and red and hopeful, exploding like fireworks, my eyes saucer-round and wondrous, the blaze always fizzling out too soon.

'Send my love to Rick,' Bella calls as she turns away from me, her eyebrows raised. She can probably tell I'm up to no good but has decided not to force the truth from me. She's a good friend.

Rick gets home late, gone ten, and I try to remove the disappointment from my face when his frame fills the doorway. I hurriedly end my chat with Alex.

I hate to feel upset that my husband is home, I really do, but as the door slams and an angry grunt follows, I remind myself that the bad feeling between us is entirely mutual. What happened to us? I wonder, as I pad through to the kitchen in pink slipper socks, thinking back to the way I used to feel about Rick.

It had been cold the night we met, late October, the Indian summer we'd been enjoying blasted out by high winds, whipping in winter. My friendship trio had decided to brave the elements and head out regardless. We weren't about to let our first year of adulthood be marred by a bit of wet weather. Lisa, head of the group with a sensible haircut and a future in project management, had talked us into it and suggested wearing raincoats over our clubwear. She went for tight jeans, wedges, and a burgundy anorak. Fern slipped into a ski jacket, complete with snow guard, atop her little black dress, and I settled on a short skirt and low-cut halterneck, heels that I'd borrowed from Lisa's wardrobe, and a voluminous yellow top-layer: a splash-proof shell that began with a tented hood and ended in a wide-angled skirt. We'd staggered up to the queue in our sensible attire, trying to keep our made-up baby faces out of the rain, cuddling into each other to conserve body heat, our waterproof outers merging into one. We were glad of them but, to our dismay, the older girls that joined the queue later had decided to brave the elements: slick skin and wet dresses on show, looking down on us through lashings of waterproof mascara. *Did you get lost?* one of them had asked, blowing cigarette smoke into my eyes. *Or is this a stop on the hop-on hop-off bus tour now?* She flicked my yellow poncho and her group burst into laughter.

When we got to the front, the three of us had been asked for ID, while the older girls were waved through without a second look – hardly a surprise. If it hadn't been a quiet

Friday night on account of the rain, a persistent drip of water splashing from the bouncer's nose in a steady rhythm on the photo page of my passport, I doubt we'd have been let in. But we had! I burped vodka and Diet Coke up from my stomach with excitement when the rope across the entrance was reluctantly raised.

Heavy drumbeats shook through our feet as we stepped into the club, the music claustrophobic, the smell of alcohol and the rush of body-heat ambushing me. I took a moment while Lisa and Fern staggered for the bar, promises of sambuca on their lips. That was when I saw him, standing in a cluster of fellow students, puffed bodies in white shirts, athletic legs in dark-wash jeans, a clutch of blazers draped over the backs of nearby chairs. I spotted the occasional flash of signet ring as they knocked back glasses of lethal-looking liquids.

Half an hour of furtive glances and nonchalant but seriously-please-notice-me dancing later, Lisa made the first entry into the group of student boys. Her forthrightness paid off and she splintered off to the bar with a boy in shiny brogues, shooting us a thumbs up moments later. But I couldn't do that – I simply didn't have Lisa's confidence – so I decided to bide my time, dancing with an inebriated Fern instead – scared to approach – and then, later, when the university girls these boys had been waiting for arrived, the group scattered and my boy, the one with the blue eyes, was suddenly by himself.

I made my move quickly, while Fern was chatting the ear off a girl she'd just met, and shuffled fast across the dance floor, ducking under the arms of his preppy friends to close in on him, electric beats and flashing neon pinwheeling around me. He looked down-to-earth, comfortable, safe, and, most of all, he looked normal. Like me. I knew already, as I went to speak to him, that we were going to be together.

'Hi,' I said. 'I'm Tabby. This might sound weird but… I feel like I know you already.'

I run my hand along the grey surfaces as I set about making a hot chocolate, the silver edges sharp and metallic beneath my grip – and freeze when he comes in. He's catatonic. Rigid. His gaze is focused on the middle-distance. He looks wrong, strange, uncomfortable and my gut churns with worry. *Does he know what I've done?*

My mind unravels, guilt and anger and self-loathing bubbling beneath the surface. Though I know things are over between us I can't help but feel guilty for my part in our most recent downfall.

I take a few silent steps towards my husband and wrap my arms like runs of ivy round his neck.

'Are you OK?' I ask gently.

He grunts in reply, his shoulders meeting his ears. I feel detached, distant, the man in front of me shutting down just as I try to coax him into opening up.

'How was your day?'

His breath is warm and wet on my neck as I pull close, his muscled body heavy. His hand traces the sides of my body and, involuntarily, I shiver.

'Fine,' he tells me, breaking away. 'Stressful.'

I study his face. I've seen him grow from boy to man over the years, and, somewhere in there, behind the muscles he's grown and the tight jaw, lies the sensitive boy I met all those years ago. There's something I want to ask that boy, the one who used to love me.

'Hey,' I begin. 'You know those cosmetic qualifications I was telling you about?'

He tilts his head. *Not this again.*

'A really great one starts next month. It's just a few days, a few hundred pounds.' I wrap clammy fingers round his palms. 'Would you be able to pay for me to do it? It would make me so happy. You know how I've been shadowing Bella at work? Well, she thinks I'm ready.'

Though it doesn't sound like much, I've just stepped on a conversational landmine. I watch the skin over his knuckles tighten as he grips the kitchen table and brace myself for the inevitable conclusion. Why I keep bringing it up, foolishly expecting a different outcome, I don't know.

'Are we really having this conversation again? Tabby, if you want these qualifications you have to pay for them yourself.'

I don't have the money. He knows that. What little I earn never seems to hang around for very long, probably because I'm always the one who buys things for the house, the one who'll remember to pick up dinner on my way home from work. I need to earn more than I make at the surgery – I am desperate to become financially independent – and these qualifications would really help with that. Rick earns more than enough to help me achieve my dream, to pay for these courses he just… doesn't want to.

So much for our wedding vows.

What's mine is miniscule, and what's his he doesn't want to share.

In my darker moments, I wonder if he wants to keep me in my position on purpose. I can tell he thinks my aspirations are delusional. He's used to being the clever and successful one in our relationship and I don't think he's ever going to be ready for that to change.

'I'd pay you back, Rick.'

He rubs his face and it reddens beneath his hands.

'No, you won't. You're in debt as it is, Tabby, don't lie to me.'

'Don't pretend you can't afford it,' I hit back. 'You'd just prefer to spend your money on other things.'

I stop short of accusing him of spending his cash on flash hotels and designer lingerie for his other woman. Rick's never been very good at confrontation.

He looks at me, picking up on my coded meaning. 'I take out my salary so I can invest it in shares, Tabby. In insurance policies. In businesses. In things that will help our future but take a little while to build up. You forget that I spent my entire time at university working, earning, trying to put us in a better situation so that we'd have more than either of us did growing up.'

I roll my eyes. Now that he's made his money, he doesn't want to let go of it. 'Where are these investments then? Show me.'

'They're funds, Tabbs, it's complicated.'

'If you wanted to invest in our future, you'd pay for me to get these qualifications. I'm a far better investment than stocks and shares you can't tell me anything about.'

At that moment, my phone presses against the curve of my thigh, hidden in the pocket of my pyjama bottoms and buzzes.

It's like he's here with me and knowing that makes me stronger.

Rick sighs, bored of the conversation, then heads upstairs. 'Are you coming up?'

'No,' I reply. 'I'm not.'

I'm lit by the glow of the phone, my face bathed blue, sinking into the sofa with *him*, rather than the mattress upstairs with my husband. I write, my fingers quick over the keypad, heart in my mouth.

Are you there?

Right where you left me, beautiful.

My heart flutters. Though I know this is ridiculous, childish, irresponsible, the feeling of having someone who wants me again is addictive. I couldn't leave our conversations if my life depended on it. Knowing Rick, it probably does. I write another message. Coy, flirty.

I just wanted to say goodnight…

I watch as three dots appear on my screen. He's typing. I wonder what he's going to say. A floorboard cracks overhead, startling me, but no footsteps follow – it's just the house settling down for the night, cooling. The three dots disappear, and a message lands:

I thought you were with your husband tonight. I'm glad

you're not. I like having you to myself.

My senses tingle. I like his protectiveness of me. His infatuation is safe, comfortable. It isn't real. I keep telling myself that: this isn't real. Until I take this offline, it's just a fantasy.

You sound jealous.

My stomach curls, embarrassed. Then releases its grip as he replies in kind.

Maybe I am.

I stifle my naughty smile with the sleeve of my pyjama top as another message lands in my inbox.

I want to meet you.

What? The words jump from the screen, shocking me. *Meet?* They blur into one another as I stare, disbelieving. Adrenaline surges.

How about it?

I type quickly.

Really?

You don't even know what I look like, I want to add, but of course I don't.

We might not get another chance.

I shift in my seat, paying attention.

What do you mean?

I'm moving to Turkey. The surgery I'm working for needs help in their office over there, I leave in a few weeks. I didn't want to tell you until it was definite.

For how long?

As long as they need me.

What about us? I write, then delete the message. Instead, I type:

You only just got here.

Why don't you come with me?

I laugh out loud.

I can't do that...

Really? You can't bear to leave the job your idiot boss almost fired you from? Can't walk away from your cheating husband?

You make some good points.

But as I send that last message, my mind flips to Bella. I'd have to leave her, too.

Later, I go through the ritual of deleting all traces of him from my phone, then slide the screen to turn it off, my heart pumping. *He wants to meet.*

I curl into bed beside my husband, taking care not to disturb him from his sleep and, at some point we drift off, our dreams full of other people.

Annabella

Now

I pace to my front door, Kay Robero's anxious face on the other side when I swing it open to let her in. Her tie-dye skirt ruffles as the gust catches it, a curiously contrasting black blazer strapped to her top half, fastened with four shiny buttons.

'I've seen the news, obviously. I barely slept last night,' she says, undoing the buttons as she steps inside, not stopping for the answer. 'Oh, God, are you OK? Is Mandy OK? What happened? Was there a fight?'

We'd discussed the plan together. What had started as weekend research comparing notes between Chad's intel and Kay's, had quickly progressed into this 'information-gathering mission'. At first, we'd planned to wait until Mandy and Rick were on holiday but – frankly – we were impatient. We'd waited long enough to catch him already.

'Come in,' I say, leading her through to the living area, not keen to have our discussion in earshot of my neighbours.

'So…' Kay prompts as we shuffle through.

'I found something,' I say, taking a seat next to Kay on the sofa.

Her eyes widen and she clasps the black onyx hanging round her neck.

'There were a load of bank statements in his house,' I tell her, then pause. 'He pays £1,000 to the same account on the first of every month. Without fail.'

'Really,' she gasps. 'You think it's a bribe?'

'Exactly,' I tell her, enjoying riding on the same wavelength.

'How long's he been doing it?'

'I got back to ten months ago but there may have been more statements, it could have been going on for years. Five, maybe. As a guess.'

'This is brilliant,' Kay says gleefully. 'It gives us something to work with, somewhere to start.' Our eyes meet and my core swells with pride as I do my mentor proud.

'Do you have them?'

'I don't,' I reply. 'I decided to leave them. I didn't want him to realise they'd been found.'

'Good,' Kay agrees. 'Yes, far better ammunition in his red hands than ours. I'd rather avoid jailtime on account of the break-in plot so, yes, good idea… let him think he hasn't been rumbled.'

'There's something else,' I tell her. 'They sleep in separate rooms.'

'Really?' Kay replies. 'Trouble in paradise, you think?'

'I don't know,' I admit. 'I can't figure it out.'

'Seems a little strange,' she says, rubbing her nails into the beige corduroy of the couch, deep in thought.

'Do you want a tea?' I ask.

'Please,' she replies, pulling her notepad from her bag.

I walk to the kitchen and fill the kettle with water, the filler in my lips exaggerated in its shiny surface, bringing me back to thoughts of Tabby. She used to fill them for me occasionally when we worked together. Though Tabby worked on reception, she often sat in on my procedures, helped out where she could, and when she showed an interest in learning the ropes of aesthetic nursing, I was happy to be her guinea pig. She'd touch my lips with gentle gloved fingers, following my instructions, and take her time to select just the right places to plump. My stomach throbs with how much I miss her.

'What happened to Mandy?' Kay presses, remembering the real reason she'd shuffled over here at the crack of dawn to question me.

The kettle clicks in the background.

'She heard me.'

'Did she *see* you?' Kay asks, rising from her seat.

'No, well, not really,' I stutter, unsure how to tell Kay I'd hit Mandy, feeling terrible about what I'd done, about what I was capable of when I was pushed into a corner.

I look down at the floor, guilt tying my tongue, muting me.

'It's OK,' Kay tells me, reading between the lines, putting two and two together. 'Mandy's going to be fine.'

'I hope so.'

'God,' Kay sighs, rubbing her forehead. 'What a night. Have you checked what people are saying online?'

She comes into the kitchen and pulls my laptop, sitting on the kitchen table, open.

'Not yet…' I reply, logging into Twitter.

Surprise, surprise, Rick Priestley's partner packed-up in the back of an ambulance… anyone wanna bet she kicks it like his last one?

How many times can this creep get away with the same crime?

He makes me sick.

I thump our cups of tea on the side as we scan through the public's take on Mandy's visit to hospital. My bias confronts me as I scroll: I'd agree whole-heartedly with these people if it weren't for the fact I'd been the one standing over Mandy, blood on my gloves, and not Rick.

'Is he on any social media?' asks Kay, noting that none of the posts tag him.

I type Rick's full name into Facebook, Kay observing, sipping noisily on her brew. I click through various profiles and, when I stumble across his, I'm disappointed to find it still set to private, just his profile pictures publicly available. Kay asks to take a look so I click through and, before long, I find myself staring into the young face of a girl I used to know. I've seen these pictures before, of course – looking through Rick's social accounts were oft-performed rituals of mine a few years ago – but I am arrested by seeing Tabby today, breathless, for a moment. I forgot how rosy-cheeked she was back then, how colourful, how hopeful. In the picture I'm looking at, Tabby's yellow hair frames her young face in windswept waves. Her lips are painted pink, nails to match, wedding band gleaming, the rest of her make-up deceptively natural: her eyelids dusted light gold, her brows coloured warm brunette, her cheeks subtly blushed. She's wearing a ruffle-collar blouse, so all of your attention falls on her face. You barely even notice Rick beside her, his blue eyes and close shave his most stand-out features.

'Don't they look young?' Kay muses, leaning in.

I click forward, scanning through holiday snaps and selfies, and then, after a while, Tabby is replaced with Mandy. Mandy is beautiful, definitely, with pillow lips and messy dark hair, wild eyebrows and a tiny, pinched nose. I look closer, analysing them: where Tabby was soft, Mandy is strong, and where Tabby was a little scruffy, Mandy is poised and precise.

'Don't you think it's weird that they're polar opposites?'

'Not really,' I reply. 'Would you want to move on with someone who reminded you of the woman you killed? If anything, moving on with a woman so far from his type proves his guilt.'

I look at Mandy a while longer, deducing she's not quite the woman I've observed through their windows. Here, in these pictures, she looks carefree and in control. In person, I'd say she looks the opposite.

Kay pulls out her own laptop then, mumbling about patterns in the future-relationships of convicted wife-killers. *Do these men choose pen pals who look like their victims? What about the ones who go free, do they act like Rick and choose someone completely different?*

I dip in and out of Rick's profile pictures as Kay investigates and find myself entranced by images of his family, especially his younger brother: a rounder, lumpier, more logo-ed version of himself. Rick stands tall, clean-cut, and good looking, clad in muted well-fitting clothes in a picture taken on New Year's Day, his brother his embarrassing sidekick, pictured to his left, head to toe in highlighter-yellow sportswear, crooked teeth bared for the camera. It's clear from this picture alone that Rick sees himself as superior to the world he comes from, it's all there, in the details: the way his body doesn't quite touch his brother's, the uncertainty of his smile, the way he leans off to one side almost as though he wants to escape from shot. Unhappy families.

But perhaps you have to come from one to know one.

Rick

Fifteen Years Ago – 2005

I was very late getting out of bed, the weak winter sun peeking through my closed curtains. Debate club had kept me up last night and I'd been talked into buying pizza on the way home. It had only cost eight pounds, but I'd had to borrow money from my savings to pay the bill. Eight pounds was nothing to the people around me, but it was everything to me, and I tried to savour each slice as I stumbled along the pavement.

I'd checked my balance at the ATM on my way back to halls and, as the pitiful amount illuminated in front of me, I swore I would stop getting myself into these situations. I couldn't afford to get into my overdraft before the end of my first term here. It was supposed to last three years. I needed to be sensible with my money. One day I would earn enough not to worry about these things but, until then, I had to count the pennies and try not to spend the pounds.

I thought about Tabby, thought about calling her. Since the night we met, we'd been seeing each other casually, taking it slow. The last time we went out she'd come to McDonald's. It wasn't the most romantic of settings but when you're short on cash, and time, you have to make do.

'No one's seen me in my uniform before,' I told her, wanting her to realise what a big deal it was to me that I'd brought her here.

She looked at me with electric-blue eyeliner and smiled. 'You know, the moment you told me you were the heir to a confectionery company I knew you were lying.'

I gripped my forehead with my hand and cringed. *I'd forgotten about that.* 'How?'

'No one with real money ever brags about it,' she told me. 'They might be wearing an expensive watch, but they won't show it off, they'll simply wait for you to notice. This look though,' she said, standing up, parting my arms with her hands, admiring my uniform, 'is better than any fancy watch.'

She wrinkled her nose and I did the same back, frissons of electric energy running between us, the start of something special.

I could hear some of the boys playing FIFA next door – Freddie had more tech in his dorm than the Oxford GAME store – and I hurled myself out of bed, rushing my face under cold running water and combing my scruffy hair with my fingers, smoothing my fringe into place.

'Rick!' called Freddie, two bangs on the partition wall following shortly after. 'Get up, boy.'

I trudged next door, the smell of aftershave and sour-cream Pringles guiding me there, and sunk my backside into the floor as the boys greeted me. Bleary-eyed, I thought it was just the usual crowd – Freddie and his mates from school in baby blue and white striped polo-shirts – but, when the controller was flung my way, it skimmed the nose of a very pretty girl, sitting cross-legged in the thick of the boys. Her hair was dark, and a shiny fringe swept gracefully across her left eye. Just like mine. Our right eyes met. Blinked.

I smiled at her, and she smiled back.

'Saskia,' she said, introducing herself with a delicate handshake, a European accent leaving red-stained lips.

Saskia Silvetti, a Classics student with Italian aristocrat parents and feline features, beat me at FIFA, then came back the next day to win something else. Me.

Annabella

Now

'We've all heard the stories, haven't we?' Kay's voice trills through the airwaves, her podcast *The Cold Case of Tabitha Rice* going live to an audience of thousands. I think about the listeners, like me, at the other end of Kay's broadcast. Are they all regulars – Kay's fanbase – or are there new ears tuning in today… potential witnesses, internet investigators fascinated by the case, a few suspects, even? I wonder if there'd be a way to find out whether Rick's listening… not that it would prove anything.

'We've heard them a hundred times – the high-school sweetheart horror stories – but Rick and Tabby's relationship was… different. It wasn't a sweetheart romance, not even at the very beginning. While researching for this podcast, I got in touch with a number of old boys from Rick's college at Oxford University. Now, none of them would refer to Rick as a "friend", which is our first red flag, but, more than that, none of them were aware he'd even dated a girl called Tabby at university.'

What?

'I decided to dig deeper into the social archives to find out. And that was where I found her: Saskia Silvetti. Rick had a girlfriend at university all right, but it wasn't Tabby. *Tabby* was his bit on the side, the one he'd spend most of his time with but never introduce to his friends.'

Did Tabby know that?

'Saskia is yet to respond to my requests for interview so, more on that story as I get it.'

I dig out my laptop and start searching for Saskia.

'Allow me to fast forward. Somehow, somewhere along the line, Rick and Tabby got back together and the pair moved to London. A reliable source – a close friend of Tabitha's' – I blush, knowing she's speaking about me – 'told me that Rick had someone to hide at the time of Tabby's disappearance, too. Another woman.' Kay pauses. 'Again. Did Rick's history repeat itself?'

My heart speeds as she plants the seed for her listeners.

'We don't know who she was yet, but we're working to find out.' I press my headphones into my ears, taking it all in. *Was it Mandy? How long has she been in Rick's picture?*

'But it doesn't take a genius to see the patterns emerging: disloyalty, secrecy, silenced women.'

Kay pauses.

'Today, Rick's with Mandy Evans. An actress who's currently in hospital with a severe head injury after an alleged break-in. And, you guessed it, she can't talk either. Another hidden woman. Another suspicious event. And what have we heard from Rick?'

She stops to let the question hang. 'Let's go through his short statement to the media, shall we?'

She ruffles a few papers and affects an accent, mimicking him. *'My partner, Mandy Evans, was attacked in our home this evening in the latest of a number of events that have threatened our safety. I was asleep at the time of the break-in and, to those corners of the press who wish to blame me for this vile act, I implore you: this vilification of my character has to stop.'*

Kay clears her throat. 'So, let me get this straight,' she begins. 'Rick's girlfriend has just suffered a head injury and yet... his concern is with how *he's being portrayed?*' She guffaws down the microphone. 'The two sentences he's decided to give on the matter, the first a replay of the facts, the second a thinly-veiled excuse to make it all about him. What about *her?* Where's his concern for *Mandy?* Why do we always hear from Mr Priestley after-the-fact? He leaves his female victims silenced in his wake and uses their suffering to talk about himself. As the mother of a teenage daughter, I find it completely terrifying.'

She breathes heavily, sucking me in, riling me up. 'So, listen up, Rick Priestley, I'm onto you and this podcast has one aim: to give these women the voice you took away.'

Tabby

Five Years Ago

Bella and I were already similar before I started talking to Alex, but now I find myself studying her movements so I can copy them. When I watch her work, I take in every micro-adjustment that she makes: twirling her hair behind her ear, rubbing her lips together as she concentrates, creasing her forehead as she worries about a speck of dirt on her uniform. I've even started colouring my hair to look like her, changing the clothes I wear to align us closer still.

I feel terrible for cancelling our dinner the other night in favour of Alex. I feel terrible for treating her like Rick. So, I have done the right thing: I've re-arranged our reservation at the Mexican place in Soho.

We sit at a table overlooking the bustling street below. I look down at the people milling under the florescent lights – men wearing dog collars rubbing shoulders with corporate office workers, scantily clad women asking passers-by if they want to spend the night, giggling eighteen-year-olds swirling between the crowds, buzzed off pink-coloured cocktails.

Bella nibbles at our plate of tortilla chips and we joke about how we've turned up tonight in the same top – a black off-the-shoulder we'd both seen on offer. I watch Bella hold her water glass up to the light, checking for lip marks – the first sign of a poorly performing dishwasher. Though I like clean, Bella is pedantic about it.

'How's Rick doing?' she asks, putting the glass down, picking up mine to do the same.

I sigh. 'Worse and worse,' I reply.

Now that I analyse my relationship with Rick, it's clear we've been sleepwalking into a crisis. Sat smugly under different jars for the past few years, shouting what we want from the other into the glass that surrounds us, only hearing our own dissatisfactions echo back, never hearing the other person's.

'Don't judge when I say this. Promise me.' I look up at Bella.

'Go on,' she encourages. 'What have you done?'

'Promise me.'

She looks at me askew. 'That bad?'

I nod, then plunge my pink-manicured hand into my bag.

'I promise,' she says.

'I took Rick's phone.'

'Really?'

'Read this,' I say, downcast, though my heart is racing because I know that this is the excuse I need to leave him.

She takes the phone in her hands and reads.

I want to start a life with you, Rick.

I want that too, my love. Soon. Be patient.

'Oh, God,' Bella begins. 'What are you going to do?'

'I just want to run,' I tell her and then an idea bobs into my head. *She could come.* 'Do you ever feel like that?' I ask.

'I guess I know what you mean,' she replies. 'But you know me, creature of habit, woman of routine,' she laughs, looking at her watch. 'Talking of which, we should order.'

After dinner, Annabella and I go our separate ways. I hadn't plucked up the courage to ask her about Turkey, and it was a dream, anyway, it wasn't real. I watch as she paces back to her sanctuary, then I turn to walk with renewed irritation towards the unhappy home I share with my unhappy husband.

'Rick?' I ask, calling his name as I brush off the drizzle from my coat and close the front door.

No answer.

I breathe deeply with relief.

Knowing he's not here gives me time. I stalk upstairs, change into my pyjamas and slip into bed. I write him a message.

Can you talk? x

Twenty minutes later and the room is dark, the day extinguished, all light turned dark except for the glow of my phone. Rick still isn't here – he's probably with *her* – and I stare at the screen, waiting.

What if he's changed his mind about me? What if the way I'd brushed off his suggestion at first, slightly spooked at the thought of meeting him, had made him think I wasn't serious? My teeth draw blood from my bottom lip, a metallic taste pooling on my tongue as I curl it inwards. I re-trace some of our older messages.

Who was your first crush? he'd asked a few months ago.

A doctor, I'd said – a white lie. Sad as it sounds, my first *proper* crush had been Rick. When we'd first met, I'd been sure I'd found the love of my life, he was everything I'd ever wanted: funny and down-to-earth, dark and attractive. I'd spent weeks pinching myself, shocked that I'd met him so quickly, so easily, that the other half of me had simply walked into my life just after my eighteenth birthday. I remember smiling a big-girl grin the morning after the night we'd met, pushing pink arms into the university hoodie that he'd given me to keep warm as we'd said goodbye. The main colour had been navy-blue, white motifs down the side, royal letters spelling out OUDS on the front. I probably still had it somewhere. I recall the smell of it that morning, fresh aftershave stuck tight to its fibres, the faint whiff of something manly behind it, and I shrug my shoulders to my ears replaying wearing it for the first time, of feeling, like I do now, that I was falling in love.

The clock ticks eleven-fifteen and I worry Alex is going to stand me up, so I put down my phone and relax into my pillows. In the quiet of the house, I find myself thinking about Rick, about whether he's done the same to me: looked through my phone to find evidence that justifies his affair. I've been much more careful than him, though, so I deduce he can't know, and it saddens me – even though I'm not really in love with him anymore – that he'd made his affair real long before mine.

Tabby cat, you there?

All thoughts of Rick vanish and I sit upright, back like a ruler, my heart racing. At last.

I'm here.

I feel like a schoolgirl, embarrassed at how excited I am that he's back.

I thought you might have fallen asleep already, thanks for waiting up.

That's OK.

Have you thought about my offer?

I bite my lip a little harder, thinking about Rick, about the messages on his phone, and decide.

Yes, I want to meet.

There's a slight delay and I imagine his face breaking with a broad smile, thick fingers clenching to a fist, pumping the air with happiness. I type out another message.

When?

Next week. But I'm working dayshifts at the clinic so it will have to be at night. Is that all right?

My skin bristles.

Yes, of course.

For a few seconds there is silence, then:

I'm so excited to meet you. It's been too long.

Me too. I'd better get some sleep. Sweet dreams, doctor.

Sweet dreams, Tabby cat.

I sign off with a flurry of love hearts and flop back into bed, the mattress springing with my weight. I'm going to meet him! This is actually going to happen! But, even as I smile, wider than I have for weeks, a bubble of doubt floats: What if he's disappointed when he finds out who I really am? What if I am not enough?

Annabella

Now

I often think about Tabby when I'm at work but, as I walk there this morning, her image loops my brain and memories of us nipping and tucking together replay more vividly than usual. I recall one evening – stuck in the surgery till 8 p.m. on the after-work shift – where we'd shared secrets. Hers was a confession: she'd once swapped her foster mother's shampoo for hair remover, forcing her into wearing a wig for the better part of a year. *Trust me, she deserved it*, Tabby had said with a smile. I try to shake her away as the snow-white exterior of the surgery comes into view. Pure You in black signage on the window. *Why not get a manicure with your fillers; a back massage after your IPL? Double up for double discounts!* I smile to myself at how Tabby's legacy has lived on.

I push open the front door and wave to the silicon-chested woman on reception. She's nice but she's no Tabby.

'Caroline wants to see you this morning,' the receptionist announces before the door has time to shut behind me.

Caroline's our big boss and, though her visits are infrequent, she usually does us the courtesy of getting in touch to let us know if she's popping in. An unannounced visit can only be cause for alarm.

'Should I go up?' I ask.

'She said to wait down here.'

I nod and take a seat in the waiting area, my right foot bouncing in nervous anticipation. Caroline's been spending most of her time in LA recently and she loves to let everyone know how difficult that arduous task is for her. *'You know, as soon as I'm in London I'm like "trash, sidewalk, elevator", then I go to LA and turn into Mary Poppins like "war-ter, coriander, aubergine"... they all look at me like I'm insane! Like, clinically insane! Isn't that just so, so funny?!'*

I always have to remember to set my smile to manual when I'm with Caroline; her anecdotes leave a lot to be desired but demand appreciation.

I hear her before I see her, first the strike of her stilettos, then her reedy voice.

'Annabella,' she says. 'How are you doing, darling? I just need a moment, if you don't mind.'

I rise to greet her, and she kisses the air either side of my cheeks with glossy lips, then motions for me to follow. I walk behind, watching her navigate the staircase up to her office in stilettos and flared suit trousers. I notice she's changed her hair since I last saw her, her poker-straight tresses replaced with a tumble of thick curls.

She pulls wide the door to her office and lets me in. I'm hit immediately by the smell of Chanel No.5, then the little details of the room itself: plants hanging from baskets, a

DO HER NO HARM

sculpture of a couple intertwined in the centre, certificates behind her desk, a cafetière steaming atop the polished black surface. I feel as though I've stepped into a 3D Instagram picture and a few appropriate hashtags spring to mind. *Office goals*, mainly. She keeps this place locked when she's not in town. I wonder how she keeps the plants alive? Perhaps they're fake; we do specialise in that.

'You're in luck,' her excitable voice tells me as she closes the door. 'Pure You London is expanding faster than I can keep up with and you, lovely Annabella—' she smiles at me then, her cheeks bunching at the sides to make way for her grin '—are our most accomplished team member. I want to offer you a promotion: clinic manager. I need to transfer full-time to LA this year – the market is so much more competitive out there – so, over here, where things are pretty easy, I need someone to fill my shoes.' She glances quickly at the sensible plimsolls on my feet. '... So to speak.'

Caroline revels in being the most glamorous woman wherever she goes and, though she looks down on others for not meeting her standard, she'd be furious if anyone ever did. I've learned over the years, through the misfortune of others, that not competing with Caroline in the glamour stakes is a great strategy for survival: *don't try to be like her, it only makes her angry.*

'What do you say?' she asks.

I roll her offer on my tongue, savouring this brief moment of power, then relent. 'OK,' I tell her. 'I'd love to.'

'It will be more responsibility as I'll need you to be on the business side of things as well as the practical, but you're smart; I trust you can make it work.'

I look down at my hands – I don't want this to interrupt

my mission with Kay – but I force my gaze up and will myself to accept. Exposing what happened to Tabby is my priority, but this promotion is important. I should take it.

'You can count on me.'

Caroline runs her tongue over her front teeth, happy with her morning's work. 'Great. Congratulations, then!'

She sticks out an eager hand for me to shake. 'I'll pop your new contract through later and, if you could come up after work, we'll start the handover right away.'

I admire my room as I sit down to my day of patients and check it for signs of sloppy cleaning. The walls are sterile-white, stunning marble underfoot, a large silver mirror to my left and potted succulents across the surfaces. I snap on a pair of latex gloves and give my office seat a second wipe down, just in case. It's very important to me that everything is perfectly clean before I begin. If I spot a stray hair, or a greasy smear on the mirror, I simply cannot concentrate on the task in hand. That's when mistakes happen, and I don't like to make mistakes. Once I'm done with my preparations, the room looks brighter, somehow, perhaps because it's framed in the context of my recent good news.

I click through my day's appointments. First up, Botox injections for a young patient's underarms to stop her unstoppable sweating, a few mani-pedis and IPLs in between. Then, this afternoon, I'll assess an older woman for purple leg-vein removal, then pump a few late-teenagers' lips like party balloons. *All in a day's work*, I sigh, as the first knock sounds at the door, the radio in the corner telling me that Kay's podcast has attracted a record number of downloads.

'The cold case that's red-hot,' says the presenter. 'I defy you to find anyone who isn't listening.'

'What's your theory, then?' asks his co-presenter. 'Runaway? Kidnap? Murder?'

'I think she's still alive,' he replies. 'The fact that Tabitha Rice was thinking about moving abroad in the days before she went missing is too much of a coincidence.'

'Well, if anyone can bring someone back from the dead to answer for their crimes it's Kay Robero.'

Rick

Fifteen Years Ago – 2005

Saskia Silvetti was gorgeous, no doubt about it. When we were together, I basked in her glow, lit by her mocha skin, my eyes lost somewhere in the crease of her cleavage. What's more, our relationship brought me reputation points, opened doors I hadn't known were there, drew me into circles I had no business standing in.

She was kind, too, and forgiving of my upbringing. She told me she liked how I had to work my way through university. My poverty was, somehow, a plus, and because she knew I didn't come from much, she paid my way. Whenever I went out with Saskia, the Bollinger was on her. And, just like that, my problems began to disappear.

Except one.

I found Tabby after class rustling through my drawers a few weeks later – my stuff strewn across the floor. The first, silent question I had popped into my head: *How had she known which room to find me in?* Quickly followed by the second: *Had she been following me?*

My eyes widened as I took in the devastation. Too late to take the crash-course in How Not To Break Up With People. We never locked our dorm-room doors – we all trusted each other, plus, most of these people had too much money to care if something was stolen, and some of us didn't have anything worth stealing anyway. It was this weakness that had allowed Tabby to get in.

A cat among the pigeons.

Saskia was by my side and clutched my arm a little tighter when she saw the dread etched across my face.

'Who is she?' Saskia asked, and I shouldn't have lied. I really shouldn't.

'Nobody,' I replied, feeling guilty even as the word left my lips, the same insult levelled at me not long ago.

As the commotion grew, some of the boys came out onto the landing to listen. Freddie's frosted-blonde highlights caught the light.

'Trust me to have ghosted a psychopath,' I bemoaned as I passed him, reddening as soon as I was out of eyeshot.

They slapped each other's backs, laughing, and, as I went inside, I could feel them close in behind me to eavesdrop on what happened next.

'Do you at least use a condom when you're screwing other girls behind my back?' Tabby spat, spinning my way. 'Thought you might want this back, seeing as you're done with me now.' Her face was pink and splotchy, her fingers hooked under one of my OUDS university hoodies, a mess of my belongings on the floor behind her.

I puffed my chest and thought about Saskia and the boys

listening on the other side of the door, about the glasses they'll have pressed up to the partition wall in Freddie's room, the omnipresent sound of his Xbox suspiciously silent.

'Let me get this straight,' I began, trying to hide the tremor in my voice. 'You're here because… I told you I didn't want to see you anymore?'

She blinked back her surprise, not used to seeing this side of me. I was hurting her.

'Who is she?' Tabby asked, her voice cracking, embarrassed.

I tried to do it, I really did, but I couldn't bring myself to twist the knife in. I should have called her crazy, or pathetic, or desperate, instead I showed her I was weak. 'Why don't we talk about this somewhere else?'

Her blue eyes appeared almost green, watery emeralds of envy staring back at me. She didn't move a muscle.

'You hate these people,' she hissed. 'It's all you talk about. And now you're leaving me for one? It doesn't make sense. I think you're using her.'

'I've never said that,' I lied. 'And Saskia's got nothing to do with why I ended things with you. You're young, you're still at school, what we had wasn't serious. I'm sorry if I gave you a different impression but… I thought we were on the same page.'

Tabby looked at me, boiling from the inside out. 'Liar.'

She breathed heavily through kinked nostrils and I imagined her as a racehorse, pawing a hoof at the ground, ready for the gun to go off so she could gallop towards me and knock me out. I heard someone guffaw on the landing beyond.

'I think you should leave,' I said.

In response, Tabby took my laptop, ripped it from the plug and threw it, hard, to the floor. She smacked my face with a twitchy palm, her eyes watering, daring me to retaliate. I watched her tears build and felt every ounce of sorrow and hate and anger seeping from her pores into mine. She got in my face then, her lips wired, her breathing ragged.

'Do it then, break up with me. To my face,' Tabby snarled. 'Just say it out loud. Just once, that's all I want, then I'll go.'

Behind me, the door opened.

Tabby's face, previously plum-purple, settled.

'Rick,' Saskia mouthed, creeping in behind, the long dress she was wearing grazing the carpet. 'Do you want to tell me what's going on?'

'Do it,' glared Tabby.

'Is this… an ex?' Saskia's soft Italian accent glided over my shoulder and snaked towards Tabby.

'Bitch,' Tabby frothed.

I heard someone laugh outside. *He's absolutely fucked it.*

'Are you going to let her talk to me like that, Rick?' Saskia breathed, looking at me with doe-eyes, waiting for me to defend her, disappointed when I said nothing: my silence damning.

'Who the fuck do you think you are?' Tabby countered suddenly, making for Saskia with sharpened nails before I had a chance to think my way out of the situation.

'Stop it,' I said, stepping between them, trying to turn down the heat.

'I'm not getting involved in this,' Saskia said, taking the high road, and, just as I turned to stop her, the door slammed shut and she left, the smell of her expensive perfume lingering, jarring with Tabby's cheaper scent.

Tabby stood opposite me for a few furious seconds, breathing nosily, then followed Saskia out.

'Wait,' I tried, reaching my hand out towards her, my fingers catching air as she shifted to avoid my grip.

'Fuck!' I cried, crashing my palm into the plasterboard of my dorm and, with that, voices hushed, doors clicked shut, and I was alone.

Things changed after that day.

Though I worked to repair my relationship with Saskia, things were never quite the same between us and our committed partnership turned on-again off-again. The boys, though not outwardly nasty, stopped inviting me to things, the fact that I was already so different to them was the main driver, but now they were weary of mine and Saskia's turbulent ups and downs, and, after we got back from Christmas break, I felt the shift more than ever. They'd all met up, a few times in fact, and stories about a raucous New Year's Eve party did the rounds. *Sorry you couldn't make it*, they'd said, knowing full well I hadn't made the guest list.

I spent a night in January crying over it. I was still two years and two terms away from graduation. A lifetime. And I wasn't the kind of person who could cope without friends for that long, I needed the company, I craved it. I used to have friends at home. Happy friends, normal friends. Friends who I went to the cinema with on a Friday night, bowling on a Saturday. Friends who'd invite me to the beach and to their semi-detached house parties. I made a mistake, when I got into Oxford, of cutting them out. I left so many texts unanswered when I was riding high with Saskia, an immature part of me revelling in the power. I don't know why exactly, perhaps I was too desperate to suppress everything about where I came from, but I didn't care about them anymore, I made it clear that I was busy with my Oxford friends and Oxford girlfriend. So when Christmas rolled around and my Oxford friends and Oxford girlfriend were nowhere to be seen, it was my turn to feel the cold shoulder from my former set of schoolfriends. My question, *Cinema tonight?*, still sitting unanswered in my phone.

I wonder what they'd have made of Tabby, if I'd never met Saskia and kept in touch with them all. I'd have brought her back home with me for a weekend over Christmas, had her tag along to a bowling night with some of the girls my mates had met too. My mind immediately jumped to an insult. '*You can take the boy out of Norwich but you can't take the Norwich-taste-in-women out of the boy.*' But I knew deep down they wouldn't have said that. They'd have welcomed her, they'd have liked her, they'd have joked with her and she'd have joked back, witty remarks lobbed back and forth, all of us drinking a little too much, cheap rounds, going home to cold sheets, Tabby saying, *You have such great friends, Rick, they remind me of mine.*

So you can understand, perhaps, why I was surprised to see her one night in February. Tabitha Rice, back in the glow of my bedroom door, blonde hair shining, skin silky, her voice smooth. Tabby didn't blow hot and cold like Saskia, her fire for me raged year-round, and here she was, burning bright. She said she was sorry about what happened between us. I was too. She asked if she could come in. I stood to one side. She held up a bag of doughnuts, a boxset swinging in her other hand.

'Truce?' she asked, pearly gloss on her lips, shimmer on her eyelids. I'd never been happier to see anyone in my life.

She pulled herself close as the opening credits played, leaned in, and, though I knew I should have asked if she was sure, I was lonely and aching for the company. Tabby made me feel good and, what's more, it had been a while.

As the story played out in front of us, so did the next chapter of ours. She smelt sweet. Snowflakes of sugar I couldn't stop thinking about licking off her doughnut lips. I twitched with the thought, crossed my legs, tried to hide how I felt, but she knew. Was she doing it on purpose?

I noticed then that beneath the black skirt she was wearing were the fasten-tops of suspenders and, as she sucked the jam from her fingertips, I fell back under her spell. She laughed at something on the screen, but I wasn't looking at the screen anymore, I could only see her. Her body was hot as I curled my arm behind her shoulders and drew her close. Soft hair grazed my neck and I breathed in the smell of strawberry shampoo, her pulse throbbing against my chest. Then I whispered in her ear, my breath wet, moving down her neck, back up to her lips. I kissed her without asking. She said something like, *Only if you're sure.*

I was sure. I pinned her down, her smile wicked, hands rigid by her sides, lips sticky as I pressed harder.

'I'm sorry,' I moaned, forgetting everything, our motion together like second nature.

'Me too,' she breathed.

Annabella

Now

I find myself pounding the wet pavements to Rick's house after work. Kay texted earlier to say Mandy was being discharged from hospital and it was all I could do not to bolt there immediately. Mandy had released a short statement from her hospital bed, designed to quell the attacks being rallied at her husband. *The intruder was about 5'8, average build, male* – I chalked up that last observation to everyday bias. No woman expects to be knocked unconscious by another woman. It ends: *We are working with the police to bring the intruder to justice.*

I want to know how she is, to see if I've scarred her lovely face, if the pair of them are going to be able to get through this latest test together. I want to know if things are tense between them – Rick hadn't believed Mandy when she'd said she'd heard something outside their bedroom – and I wonder if he's apologised for that. I wonder if she'll hold it against him if he doesn't. I wonder how close they'll sit together tonight, if they'll polish off a bottle of wine with dinner against doctor's orders or stick to water.

But when I arrive, rain beating down, I find, to my horror, that the lights are off. There's a paparazzi in a car just ahead, on his phone, about to give up on getting a glimpse of them too.

I walk briskly across the street, flick my wet hair from my face, treading dangerously close to their front door as I cross the road to get a better look, just to check, and, when I don't see them, deduce they must still be at the hospital, that perhaps Mandy is being kept in for another night as a precaution. I wait for ten minutes, text Kay to ask if she's heard anything else, then, when no one appears and Kay doesn't respond, I jump on the bus to take me there.

My damp trainers squeak against the lino corridors of St. Thomas' hospital and I squeeze a mound of anti-bacterial gel into my palm before continuing up the stairs. I'd stalked the ground floor to no avail, not wanting to draw any attention to myself by asking the staff where I could find Mandy – they'd probably take me for a journalist and escort me out. I use the sleeve of my jumper to open door handles and try to breathe lightly so I don't inhale too many germs. This place will be riddled with them.

On the first floor, I walk into a massive waiting room of people, a faint whiff of something stale in the air as I pass through. A woman rolling in and out of consciousness wheels past me on a sad trolley-bed, her arm flopping hopelessly through the railings. I up my pace and flit past signs for *dermatology*, *pathology* and *radiology*. Then, a sliver of hope: the Acute Admissions Ward.

I curl my head round the door of the first room. Eight frail bodies are propped up in beds, clutches of visitors round a few, the majority empty, the smell of mince and potatoes heavy in the air.

Another ward is further down the corridor and through a set of double doors. I turn sideways and slide through, careful not to touch the surfaces.

A nurse smiles at me as I enter, something green stuck between her canine and first molar, waiting for me to ask where I can find my sick relative. I smile back, then duck my head as I pass, pretending to know exactly where I'm going. This ward smells stronger than the last. It's how I imagine a medical war-tent might smell – wounds fresh with blood, corpses waiting to be taken away. I realise why it smells so bad when I step inside; there are far more beds in here and the windows are closed. Though it's winter, this room is in dire need of circulating air, but I imagine the frail lady in the bed nearest the window has complained about the cold. I make my way out, still no sign of Mandy.

Down the following corridor are the private rooms, each with a name next to the door, scribbled frantically with marker pen. I wonder how much you have to pay for these. I find a young girl in the first, her hair in pretty pigtails, a tube running from her nose, the door ajar. There's a boy in the second with a broken leg, a man in the third with a bandage over his eye, an old lady behind the fourth door who grins at me as I come in, then starts shouting when I turn to leave. *Where do you think you're going, love? You need to give me my medicines!* I stalk down the corridor away from her shouts, passing a number of closed doors, busy nurses, porters rubbing mops across floors, doctors whizzing from room to room, chasing one emergency after the next.

I pause when I see her name come into focus. *Mandy Evans*. My fingers tremble as I step closer, her door cracked open slightly. I breathe in, and the scent of their home – freesia, peach – comes back to me in waves as I draw closer. I hesitate when I see the outline of Rick's back, his broad shoulders stretching a long-sleeve sweatshirt, his sharp haircut protruding from the top.

Mandy's awake, and they're talking. I take another step closer.

'I'm just not sure how much longer I can do this,' I hear her say.

'I'm sorry,' he replies.

'I can't stop replaying the moment.'

My body clenches. *Neither can I.*

'And what was it all for?' he asks, shakily. 'I don't understand it. Nothing was taken.'

His comment is met with silence.

'Has anything come out yet?' Mandy asks, voice breaking.

'No,' he replies.

'What if they come back?' she asks. 'They obviously didn't get what they wanted first time.'

Rick rubs his forehead.

'I think you need to start talking,' Mandy says. 'Let the world know who Tabitha Rice really was.'

I move closer.

'If you did… they'd leave us alone. All of this would stop.'

I double-take. *What does she mean?*

'Can I help you?'

A loud female voice sounds from behind me and I jump, spotting the twist of Rick's neck as her question carries into their room.

'I'm looking for the toilets,' I respond quickly. 'Could you point me in the right direction?'

'Back that way,' the woman replies, hooded eyes looking me up and down.

I hurry away, quick pace, then send Kay a text, fingers shaking.

I'm coming over.

Kay and I have met up many times since our first phone call, but I rarely go to her house. On the way, the streets are littered with crisp packets and debris and I'm guarded as I travel deeper into Camberwell, a gritty part of South London just poking its nose into the possibilities of gentrification. The street where Kay lives is drab and dirty, but Kay's home is an end-of-terrace with a vibrant mother-and-child mural covering the side that meets the pavement and, though it's not exactly Banksy, it brings some colour to the place.

Where Kay craves individuality, a home that will make her stand out as different, I crave the opposite. I bet she thinks my new-build in Battersea is mundane and obvious, too clean, too sanitised, too devoid of real life. I could just imagine her saying it and I smile as I thumb the lid of my anti-bacterial gel and slip it into my pocket. We really are chalk and cheese.

Kay's house, when I am welcomed inside, is unashamedly

messy. A kind of home-meets-hostel with trinkets and treasures strewn across the walls and windowsills. In a word it's... busy. Everything's covered in fabric, carpet chosen over wooden floors in most of the rooms – even the bathrooms – and my wide eyes flit over the dozen scatter cushions in the lounge, scattered everywhere except the sofa. I can imagine Kay's teenage daughter rolling her eyes with embarrassment whenever she invites friends over and, just as I'm finding a place to perch, Kay bustles in with a stack of paper.

Her haircut is bobbed to her chin, dark strands that intertwine with grey, a pair of reading glasses pushing it all back from her make-up-free face. She hasn't had any surgery whatsoever – *she's probably never even had a facial* – and I guess she's in her late forties, but her eyes look younger and dart, puppy-like, as she begs me to sit, patting a beaded cushion into a wooden chair, removing the stack of DVDs previously atop it.

'Sorry about the time,' I rush to say. 'I didn't mean to intrude on your evening...'

'Tell me everything,' she says, falling into a Scottish-flag beanbag opposite me, her crystal necklace clattering against an exposed bit of wooden floor as she shuffles herself forward. She thumps a wedge of papers in front of her, rendering the room floor-less now, completely hidden by cushions, rugs, papers, mugs, books, leads, shoes, clothes... I itch for the anti-bac in my pocket but resist the temptation. I don't want to be rude. I run my thumb nails under each other, just glad she hasn't asked me if I want a drink. I bet she'd offer a murky pond-water tea if I did, hand over a mug with a chipped rim, *Borneo '90* wrapped round the outside. I find it remarkable that someone with a home as cluttered as this can have such a sharp and brilliant mind. I'd be admitted after five hours of living here.

'What did you overhear?'

'It was odd,' I begin. 'Mandy suggested that she and Rick have a treasure trove of dirt on Tabby but have chosen to keep it to themselves.'

I watch as Kay's face pales and she jots a few frantic notes across the back of a bank statement.

'I don't know what exactly,' I continue. 'But we need to find out in case they decide to take it public.'

Kay pulls her computer to her lap to search for something. It's almost as though she knows what I'm going to say.

'We need to get out ahead of whatever bile he's been saving up for the right—'

Kay's eyes narrow as she hits upon something and spins her laptop round so I can see what's on the screen.

'I found this a while ago,' she explains. 'While I was researching – I didn't know if you knew. I think this might be what they were talking about...'

Student cleared of rape after underage-accuser says she 'made a mistake'.

First-year Oxford university student Rick Priestley was cleared today after all charges against him were dropped by his accuser. The woman branded him a 'rapist' who 'sexually assaulted' her after a drunken night in college, but now admits to lying about the non-consensual nature of their relations. Due to legal reasons, she cannot be named.

I stare at the picture of Rick on campus at university, his fresh-faced youth haunted by the obvious stress of his situation. The face of his accuser, the one that he should be pictured alongside, is missing, though I'm pretty sure I can fill in the gap.

I look up at Kay, baffled, then flick down to one of the comments.

> There's a special place in hell reserved for women who lie about being raped. Not only did this woman ruin this man's reputation, but she casts doubt on every woman who has actually gone through it. Shame on her.

'I've been wondering why he hasn't used this to his advantage, yet,' Kay cuts in as I skim the lines. 'It would have been enough to stop the public sympathy for Tabby in its tracks.'

I push my fingernails through my hair, grasping for a reason. 'He won't have said anything because there must be something in the lost details that make him look bad.'

'Stop being biased. If you want to find out what happened to Tabby you have to consider everything.'

A stone bobs in my throat.

'How did they seem when they were talking about it?' Kay asks.

'Cold,' I reply. I read the article again then turn the laptop back towards Kay. 'How do you know if this girl was Tabby? She's not named, she's not pictured. What if he *forced* her to drop the accusation?'

'That doesn't bother me,' Kay replies. 'Because if Rick comes out with it, she's not here to tell her side.'

She stops writing and leans back in the bean bag, eyes to the ceiling.

'So we have to tell it for her,' I insist.

'How?' Kay asks.

As we're sitting in thought, a heavy-set man appears, a friendly smile on his face.

'All right?' he says, his voice worn but warm and I assume he's Kay's husband.

'Can I get either of you anything?'

'No, Tom, thank you,' Kay says hurriedly, shooing him away. I sit back, enjoying the role reversal of a husband tending to his working wife, but Kay doesn't bat an eyelid, her mind full of thought and theory.

'I'm starting to have my doubts about Tabby.'

I tilt my head. Part of me knew this was coming.

'You need to meet him, AB.' I half-smile at Kay's new nickname for me. 'That's the next step. You need to find out what Rick has to say about this rape allegation. You need to find out what he wants to get off his chest. If he speaks before we can get in front of the story the podcast will suffer.' She fiddles with the frayed edge of the beanbag as she convinces me to get closer to a murderer.

'But... but...' I stammer. 'He knows who I am. He knows what I think about him.'

'So?' Kay replies. 'Convince him otherwise.' And, with that, her mind is made up.

Tabby

It's stuffy in the surgery today, which isn't helping, but the way Bella laughs at my suggestion of moving to Turkey, tearing it down before I've even finished my sentence, has fired me up.

'*What about Rick?*' she'd asked patronisingly.

Well, guess what, Bella: I don't need you anymore. I've learned so much here already, all I'll need when I get to Turkey is some money for a couple of pieces of paper to say I'm qualified and then I'll be able to go it alone. Not completely alone, of course. With Alex.

When I think about my husband, about the lengths we went to in order to make it down the aisle, I often conclude we'd have been better off meeting each other later in life. The problem is, if you meet someone when you're young, you have to experience your growing pains together, break into taller bodies side-by-side, bodies neither of you are quite ready to inhabit yet.

At university, Rick was deeply insecure, caught up pretending to be someone he wasn't, convinced he needed to impress a bunch of people he thought he wanted to be like. There was a night I don't like to revisit in which his deep-seated anger got the better of him and we slept together even though I hadn't said yes.

We'd called things off a few months prior, after I found out he'd been seeing a girl named Saskia but, rather than tell me the truth – that he'd met someone better and didn't want anything to do with me anymore – he batted me away with a text.

Sorry Tabby, I don't want to be writing this. We had a great time together, but can we cool things for a while?

I'd been in McDonald's the day he texted me, waiting for him, reminiscing about the last time we'd been there, eating fries like Lady and the Tramp spaghetti.

The night in question was about two months later and I knew for a fact that Saskia and Rick had called things quits. I'd plucked up the courage to go to his room to make amends, taking my chance because I wanted to get back together. I'd knocked on his dorm room door a little tipsy, gone eleven, in pink jeans and a band T-shirt. When we talk about it, he remembers it differently. He told the police I'd been dressed in lingerie and a short skirt – I guess he wanted them to think I was *asking for it* – and, maybe if he'd been the right kind of person, that would have worked.

I'm not sure exactly what I'd hoped for, I'd just felt our business was unfinished and eighteen-year-old me couldn't let that go. It had all happened so fast, that sudden rush of desire, the link of our bodies and the rhythm of his breath, but when I'd told him I didn't want to take things any further, that I wasn't sure, he hadn't listened. It was as though he'd been in his own world, his eyes staring right through me, shark-like.

'Sorry,' he said when it was over, lying in bed side-by-side.

'Me too,' I agreed. 'So, what's next for us?' I asked hopefully.

He coughed awkwardly. Retrieved his arm from behind my neck.

'Are we back together?' I mused, misreading him.

His jaw set into a locked position and the reality of what had just happened clicked into place.

'Do you want me to go?' I asked instead, my heart breaking.

'It's just…' he said. 'Yeah. If you could leave before the boys wake up that would be great.'

'I thought you were sure?' I whispered, but he didn't hear. 'What?'

'Nothing,' I told him, gathering my clothes from the floor, pink cheeked and embarrassed. Used.

I ground my heels into the floor as I walked the quick way home, furious. My breath was high in my lungs, shaky as I tried to keep myself together, my heart leaping from my chest then thudding back into position, rattling my rib cage with its ferocity. How dare he use me like that? After *everything* I still wasn't good enough for him.

My foster mum opened the door when I got home and,

for the first time, I let her in, desperate for comfort. I pushed my wet face into the hair that puddled at her shoulders and told her about it – that we'd slept together even though I wasn't sure I wanted to. Even though I hadn't said yes. Before I knew it, she was marching me to the police station to report him and, like any good mother, wouldn't take no for an answer. Over the course of the next few hours I did a number of interviews, a rape kit, and had filed charges against the love of my young life, convinced by the adults around me that I was doing the right thing. *I am doing the right thing, aren't I?*

'Don't be scared, sweetie, he won't be able to touch you again once we're finished with him.'

Have you ever set something in motion on a hot-head and come to regret it? This was one of those times and, looking back, I wish I'd done things differently. I wish I hadn't told anyone until I was ready to explain it rationally. It was a complicated situation and I was so angry at Rick, the entire episode clouded by what had happened afterwards. It wasn't as black and white as the people on the news, or the people around me that day at the police station, made it all sound. Of course, I understand there are black and white situations, but mine was lost in the grey and, as the anger dissipated, I didn't quite know how to tell them that.

I'd told Rick I wasn't sure if I'd wanted to sleep with him, I'd never explicitly said yes, and, when he'd rejected me afterwards, that crucial part of our conversation hit me like a sledgehammer. With a few nudges in the right places from the police, it was enough to kickstart an investigation against him. If he'd wrapped me up afterwards and told me he'd loved me and wanted to get back together I would have forgotten all about it, I wouldn't have minded giving myself to him if it hadn't been for nothing.

But most people can't understand that, it's either 'she's guilty' or 'he's guilty'. There's nothing in between.

People have no time for nuance anymore.

Rick certainly didn't. His surety that he'd done nothing wrong convinced me further that I was wrong to ruin his life, wrong to have brought it up, wrong to have said anything at all. I told myself that I'd taught Rick a lesson, and that was enough. He wouldn't do it again, he'd think twice before sleeping with someone without getting clear consent, and maybe that was enough.

I dropped the charges a couple of weeks later, I couldn't stand the scrutiny, couldn't deal with the pressure, the doubt. My foster mother was deeply disappointed in me for that. She'd been talking to a reporter, negotiating a fee in exchange for dropping my anonymity – and the university came out swinging. Suddenly I was a liar. I was the enemy. I was the bad guy. Death threats abounded.

Like I said, lucky for those couples who meet once their growing pains have subsided so that when you meet them, they're the best they've ever been. Rick and I never had a chance to turn into better people, our love an immature combination of spontaneity and fire, doused quickly when we argued. Extinguished now. Perhaps for good.

Annabella

Now

I stand in the shed peering across the road, the dark dawn matching the near-black bricks of Rick's house, staring up at the bright bedroom window that contrasts vividly with the sky. I take a long breath out, waiting patiently for him to pull the curtains open, and glance at my phone – 06:45 – wondering how late he will rise this morning, hoping he won't change his routine at the last minute because Mandy isn't here. What if he goes to hospital to see her first thing rather than head to the gym like I expect him to? These would be a waste, for starters. I look down at the tight Lycra stuck to my legs.

In preparation for our first meeting, I'd bought a whole new outfit based on the fact that he usually works out at the Spin studio on Wednesday mornings. I'd gone to an overpriced fitness boutique and chosen cobalt leggings, then black, then settled on navy-blue, pulling the tight material over my legs, at first sceptical of the ridiculously high waist, then converted. I'd kind of liked the way I looked in them. At first glance you wouldn't have guessed my lithe figure had been honed from nervous stress, overactive cleaning, and unavoidable undereating rather than a finely crafted gym routine. I'd chosen a silver racer-back vest and matching jacket, then a padded overcoat from the clearance rail in white. I'd wanted to put him at ease, to make him remember the common ground we shared despite the difference of opinion about how his wife disappeared. I feel like an undercover operative on a honeytrap mission. Today is the beginning of a new me.

Back in the shed, I notice the family at number 33 are already awake, can hear their baby screaming in the distance and watch as their ceiling spotlights turn on, first upstairs, then down, the mother moving like a blur between rooms. *Come on, Rick, wakey-wakey.* I tie the hood-toggle tight to stop the winter air from getting in, then push my chilly hands deeper inside my new puff jacket. I bounce up and down on the balls of my feet, working my calves. Then – whoosh! – his curtains draw back and he slides into view. Icicle eyes chill me.

Next, he flies downstairs – he's running late – and into the kitchen. I have a crystal-clear view of him as he makes breakfast, the blinds gloriously wide. Rick has nothing to hide, your honour! Look in, go on, observe his innocent home! I watch him pour cereal into a bowl, shovelling spoonsful into his mouth. He looks up and out of the window as he eats and, just for a moment, I'm convinced he's looking right into this shed, the sun rising behind me, a dim light just breaking on his face. I catch my breath, reluctant to move and, though I avert my stare, I feel his all over me. I tuck my chin into my chest and, when I finally pluck up the courage to look back, he's turned away, only the outline of his neck and shoulders visible. How am I going to convince this man I've changed my mind about him if I'm jumpy just looking at him?

Rick walks fast as he leaves his house – about five minutes behind schedule – and my shins burn as I try to keep pace. I follow him all the way to his favourite spin studio – I know him so well – the main area of which is located on the fifth floor of a new-build structure overlooking the Thames. I look up at the glass then across at the near-identical developments on the other side of the river, futuristic homes interspersed with cranes and construction-sites, at the impossibly tall office buildings that dot the horizon in the distance.

Frosty studio windows catch my reflection as I scuttle by and remind me to book a hair appointment. I keep my ombre cut neat and tidy, chopped at my shoulders in one straight line, but I crave the ritual of bleach on my hair, so I go back every six weeks or so to have it topped up. I think it's the smell of it, the fact that it's so intensely clean that I feel my entire head is being cleansed every time it bites at my tresses.

I summon the courage to step into the glossy space, the front desk patrolled by muscular receptionists, air conditioning blasting me as I tiptoe towards them. Rick has already been waved through, handed a towel, so when I reach the front of the queue, I am determined to follow right behind him.

'I'd like to set up a membership. Who do I speak to about that?'

I marvel at the size of the veins on the receptionist's arms as he passes me a form to fill out. 'Here are all the details, we'd love you to join our tribe!'

I half-smile, unsure how to react to marketing-speak in everyday situations, take the form to a quiet corner, and scribble through it. *£200 upfront fee, one year minimum, two months' notice.* I agree to it all, the whole £1,200 I'll end up spending on this place, then walk back to hand it back to the man behind the desk.

'Right on,' he encourages, and slips my details into his computer. 'I hope we can help you on your fitness journey. Is this a New Year's resolution thing? How much weight were you looking to lose exactly?'

How much? I think, my eyes betraying how affronted I am by this question. *What do you want from me? Skin and bones?*

'Oh, it's not really about weight for me, it's more than that.'

'Right on, right on,' he repeats inanely. 'Like a life overhaul thing?'

Why does it have to be about anything?

I mumble a non-committal agreement and wait to be let through.

'I'll put your membership through final checks and then, hey, soon as you know it, we'll have you working out! Your card will come through the post once it's all approved. Looking forward to welcoming you to the tribe!'

I blink at him, breathless, annoyed. 'Can I take a class now? To try it out?'

'Ah,' he sounds, his expression changing. 'Afraid that's against our policy, it's members only.'

'I am a member.'

'You're nearly a member.'

'Right, so what's the difference?' I lean over the desk slightly, put my elbow up on it, stare him down.

'The difference is I need your card so I can swipe you in.'

A man from the queue, building steadily behind me, draws level at the desk, clearly irritated by our elongated exchange. 'Sorry to interrupt,' he bites. 'Can I just grab a towel?'

As the receptionist pulls a towel from the stack next to him, I take a step back, shrinking. I wait until towel-man is at the turnstile, then use the cover of the next person in the queue to pounce, while the receptionist's eyes are diverted.

I hurry through behind him, heady with adrenaline, stealing a glance over my shoulder, relieved to see that no one's chasing after me. I take a moment to catch my breath – I am not used to this kind of risk-taking – but find, somewhat to my surprise, that part of me is enjoying it.

I step into the bright studio bouncing with well-groomed gym bunnies, their beautiful reflections splashed across the mirrors on the three walls that encase us, the peachy rear of a woman in the front row beamed at me from all angles as she begins her warm-up. The instructor, facing the class, wears a light-pink sports bra and skin-tight leggings, her hair sitting in a perfect plait that runs between her shoulder blades. I know immediately why she's been hired for this role: she's the aspiration, she's who all these rich office-workers wish they could be, or be with. I spot Rick approaching, my eyes glued to his well-tuned form as he sidles up to a bike in the front row and latches a towel round the handlebars.

As it's my first time at this class, the instructor pauses her own warm-up to introduce herself to me and to set my level to 'easy', which irritates the competitor in me. I can do this – same as everyone else – and I twist the dial to up the resistance.

I pump my way into the main portion of the workout, breathing heavily, sweating as the instructor demands we climb hill after hill, pedalling faster with each relentless incline. Rick's sculpted physique perspires as he thumps on the pedals underfoot. I'm entranced. I can see what Tabby saw in him once – if you're interested in gym-boys, he's not awful to look at – but, as I study his reflection – the determined bite of his jaw and the dogged look in his blue eyes – I wonder why he looks so angry.

A tear of sweat lands on my chapped knuckles and soaks into my flaky skin. I grip the handlebars of the static bike tighter. I've tried countless home-remedies and over-the-counter lotions to soften the scaly backs of my hands but nothing seems to work. I know what would work: clean a little less, always wear gloves to do so, stop my obsessive handwashing at work, quit the anti-bac. But these rituals are too important to me, so I must rely on lotions and potions and exfoliating scrubs to bring my dead skin back to life.

I analyse the other people in the room to take my mind off the workout: there's a serious Lycra-clad white guy at the front, a curvy brunette to his side, a lithe black girl barely breaking a sweat to my left. I am forced to park my observations just as the instructor takes us through a sprint series; my vision beginning to spin. Rick rides with increased intensity and I watch as his T-shirt darkens under his effort, puddles forming beneath the machine. His body rises and falls as his thick legs pedal, his focus straight ahead.

As the room heats up, perspiration covering the surfaces, my anxiety at being in this close-quartered, germ-ridden environment begins to flare. My heat and my effort and my shortness of breath don't help – I used to be fine with this sort of thing – but, today, my anxiety worsens. Someone won't have washed their hands, will have left infectious marks over the door handle, the water-dispenser. Someone else will be unwell but powering through it, spluttering and sweating their illness into the air surrounding me. My face reddens as I think about it: I'm pedalling in a bath of lurgy, a sea of filth. And then my head is loud with ringing, high-pitched, my vision disintegrating, my heart thudding, each burst echoing in my eardrums. Before I have a chance to slow my pace, to take a break, I can feel myself slipping, the world around me closing in. It swallows me and I drop to the floor, pedal cutting flesh, hand out to break my descent, the whirr of his bike in the distance.

I wake with a start, my vision filled with worried faces, concerned expressions, and agitated voices.

'Are you OK?'

I try to sit up, panicking, remembering where I am, but a pair of hands grab my shoulders and push me back. 'Woah there, take it easy, let's get you some water first.'

A flimsy paper cup is thrust into my grip and I turn onto my side, sipping it gently. 'Thank you,' I manage to bleat. I wish people would stop breathing on me, everyone's so close, the carbon dioxide from their exhalations gusting against me.

'Space,' I stutter.

Disgruntled noises follow; they're probably annoyed I haven't had a heart-attack – that would give them something to talk about at work – but, eventually, they disperse. The instructor stays by my side, pressure round my shoulder. She's not going anywhere until she knows I won't sue.

And him. He's here. I can feel him, close. Though it isn't how I'd liked to have reintroduced myself to him again it's certainly… memorable.

'I'm fine,' I say as I attempt to rise to seated again, a few dots splattering my line of sight as I move. Hand gripping head, pain percolating behind my eyes, I hear him. I know it's him, I just——

'Annabella, are you OK?' he asks.

I open my eyes then take him in. His cheekbones sit high, sharp lines cutting either side of his face. His hair is receding slightly but the colour is bold and brown. One of his eyebrows sits low, concerned, the other higher, alert. His legs are muscular and parted. His blue eyes are locked on mine. My heart shudders. I worry he's about to ask why I've been following him.

'What are you doing here?' he asks. 'I didn't recognise you at first; it's been years.' The mirrors that encase the room reflect my new and improved features back at me. My cheeks are slightly swollen from a recent tear-trough procedure and yet I still appear ghoulish, somehow. I do not like to look at myself for too long; I always find something I need to improve. I've changed a lot since Rick knew me.

'I'm fine,' I insist, my lips in a line, knowing Rick would be suspicious if I appeared happy to see him.

'Do you often faint when you exercise?' he asks.

I shake my head. 'I don't often exercise.'

'You should get it checked by a doctor,' he presses, moving closer, so close that I can smell his deodorant. The instructor shifts to let him in.

I look up. 'I don't think it's anything serious.'

He looks worried when I refuse, lips ajar. 'I'm taking you to a doctor.'

'I'm fine,' I protest.

He moves to standing, holding his hand out for me to take. 'Let's get you up.'

I reach out, his skin on mine. It feels wrong. Dangerous. I'm letting this hand, this murdering, evil hand touch me, willingly letting it clamp me in its grip. I squirm as I feel him, his fingertips warm and clammy, his palm sticky. My anxiety rises again and I reel at what we're sharing, the microparticles, the infections, the germs. My pulse quickens at the risk I'm taking letting him hold me like this, and I can feel my heart beating against his clutch.

'Thanks,' I croak, pulling my hand away as soon as I'm up, the rush dying as we part.

'You're OK, then?' the instructor asks, abrupt.

I nod and she quickly forgets all about me, bouncing behind Rick as he goes to make a call, talking quietly to him so I can't hear. I don't know what they're saying, but they stand close, her hands gesticulating towards his middle.

I don't know for definite what she's saying, but I can guess. 'Who is she? You know her? Why do you care so much?'

★

Rick orders a car to take me to a walk-in centre not far from here. I have absolutely no intention of going but thank him profusely for his concern as we stand in the lobby of the gym, air conditioning fanning from above, flattening a pancake-round circle of hair on top of his head.

'You have to let me know how you get on,' he says, pulling his phone from his pocket. 'Can I take your number, to check in later? I'll be worrying all day otherwise.'

I watch him type his passcode into the screen – 303030. I briefly wonder what the significance is, then commit the number to memory. It could come in handy.

'Sure,' I say, taking his phone, thinking back to all the things Tabby once told me she'd found on here. Not that this will be the same device, but the comparison, the very thought, sends a ripple down my spine. Rick's secrets are in my hands, right now, if I could just take it, I could examine them, find proof, find evidence…

'Promise you'll actually go.'

I nod, then pass his phone back to him.

'It's been great to see you again,' he says, lingering awkwardly. 'You know, I feel terrible about how we left things…' He stops short of addressing why we fell out in the first place. I guess he's right to, it would somewhat sour the atmosphere. 'Would you like to get dinner next week?' he asks, putting himself out there, waiting for me to answer. 'I'd like the chance to clear the air between us,' he adds, pausing. 'Catch up.'

Catch up? I think instinctively. *About what? The way you killed my best friend?* I'm taking too long to answer, his eyes darting nervously to the floor, but I can't help the way my heart thuds when I look at him. My thoughts turn to Mandy, too. Not only have I sent her to hospital, I'm about to book in a date with her boyfriend. *I'm doing her a favour in the long run*, I tell myself. *This is for Mandy, this is for Tabby, this is for me.*

'Sure,' I reply. 'It's been a long time.'

'Five years,' he chimes.

My eyes turn to water troughs in the beats that follow, my head full of Tabby, and how I've let her down. I colour, turning back to him. 'Sorry,' I splutter. 'I'm a little dazed. I just wasn't expecting to see you today. Hearing your voice, it's just... all I can think about is her.'

'You don't need to apologise,' he tells me, as he opens the car door for me. 'I understand. I feel the same.' His eyes look sad as I slip inside, drying my tears, pulling myself together. I clench my water bottle in one hand, the other shaking.

'I'll check in later,' he says, then shuts the door, hitting the roof twice with a closed fist, sending me on my way like I'm in the back of a New York taxi.

I fix my eyes on his silhouette, his sculpted frame occupying the entire rear-view mirror, waiting to wake from the elongated dream I'm having. I feverishly rub anti-bacterial gel over my hands and arms, ridding myself of him, then sit back, letting my heartrate return to normal, touch my hand to my head, feeling a bump beneath.

I did it. Though it wasn't planned, it had worked.

'Excuse me,' I say to the driver, far enough from Rick to be safe. 'Can you just drop me here?'

'Here?' he repeats, quizzically.

'Yes,' I confirm, reaching down to the rip in my leggings, the graze that lies bloody and oozing below. I need to get to work as soon as possible. This won't clean with over-the-counter anti-bac, I'll have to use the real stuff.

I pull my phone from my pocket, looking at the screen, wondering when he'll text.

Kay's voice fills my ears as I play the next instalment of *The Cold Case of Tabitha Rice*, listening as she feeds her hungry listeners with delicious morsels.

'Today on the show I'll be chatting to serial-killer-expert and friend of the show Dr Malcolm Reese about victim profiles. We'll be discussing the fact that most male murderers select a "type" of woman, and that it usually extends to the relationships they have, too. We often see serial killers throughout history repeat this pattern. So why is Rick Priestley different? What does his new partner, Mandy, tell us about him?'

Rick

Fourteen Years Ago – 2006

I was assembling Happy Meals for a bunch of precocious nine-year-olds when my phone started ringing. I ignored it at first but picked up on the fourth call. No one calls that persistently unless it's an emergency.

It was my college president. 'There's been a serious allegation brought against you, Rick. We need to talk immediately. Soon as you can.'

I free-wheeled back to the university, my wheels ricocheting over the cobbles. I took a short-cut that wasn't designed for bikes, it was full of pedestrians, angry pedestrians, and I was jeered as I tore through them, brakes screeching to avoid a collision with a girl and her hula-hoop.

'Watch where you're going, idiot!'

I ignored the cries, pedalled faster, harder, let the blood rush to my head, my brain bumping my skull each time I hit a cobble at speed. Tabby had carved her name at the base of this bike – TR & RP 4EVA – a childish inscription that had irritated me at the time but didn't so much now. She was my safety blanket, my security, my crutch. Thoughts of last night jumbled my consciousness as I sped, the way she'd jerked her body to get closer to mine, the coy look on her face as we'd reignited our fire.

I'd promised I'd call her to work everything out. We needed to talk about what had happened between us, iron things out. Tabby deserved that much, even if last night only ended up being a one-off.

I crashed my bike against the wall and ran, sweat beading my hairline, splinters in my lungs as I tried to catch my breath. Three corridors along was the college president's office and, just outside, a mirror. I groaned when I drew level, realising I was still in uniform. The president wouldn't understand. I pushed my fringe back off my face, cursed at the stubble on my jaw, then took a moment to compose myself before heading in.

The next few minutes passed in a heart-stopping blur. 'A girl has made an accusation of rape against you. The evidence is compelling enough to suspend you immediately. There will be an investigation. Please collect your things.'

'Who?' I managed to say and, though the president hadn't spoken her name, I knew full well. Tabby.

Her revenge.

The memory of what she'd said, 'I'm sorry too,' played from the depths of my mind – but my brain was a fog and the way I'd felt about her – happy, loved, close – stuck to the bits in between. More than anything, I couldn't believe it was happening. Tabby wasn't raped. She was just angry.

It will blow over: that was my first thought. Tabby just wanted to let me know how much I hurt her, her lovesick, childish desire for a reaction from me, acting out to get her point across. But what if it doesn't blow over? That was my second thought. The problem was, if I'd been an important student, the college would have defended me, would have battened down the hatches and figured out a way to prove my innocence. As it was, they were more than happy to feed me to the wolves, haul me up as proof that students from comprehensive schools shouldn't be let into institutions like Oxford in greater numbers, that people like me were liabilities to have on campus.

I left the room sweatier than I arrived and pulled my phone from my pocket, calling her.

I spoke first. 'You have to drop the allegation, Tabby. I don't understand why you'd make something like this up.'

Her foster mother answered the phone. 'Please don't call this number again, Rick.' Then hung up.

That's when I knew this was serious.

I slammed my way back to my room, trying to convince myself this was temporary, a blip, a mistake, some confusion, a misunderstanding – my eyebrows knotted, my muscles tight. But my room still smelled of her and I couldn't escape. Didn't she realise how much she'd upended my life here already?

I thought about what would happen next... going home to Mum and Dad and my moron brother. I couldn't do that. I'd ostracised them, stopped them from visiting, embarrassed. I couldn't slink back, tail between my legs. My brother would laugh from the pit of his rolling gut. 'Not so smart now, huh?'

Also, there was the money issue. I'd paid for my accommodation here upfront with my student loan. I couldn't afford anywhere new, I had about £50 in my pocket from today's shift – that was it. I briefly thought about sneaking into college and sleeping in the bathrooms, of going out each night and making sure a willing girl took me back to hers.

But I couldn't keep that up: where would I keep my stuff? Would I have to find a shed... a barn somewhere? Someone's garden?

This was useless.

There was only one person who could make this right, only one girl who could make this all go away. I had to convince her to drop it. I had to force her to tell the truth. Whatever it took. It was her word versus mine, and I had to silence her.

Annabella

Now

We sit in a white-marbled eatery, a plate of picture-perfect sushi between us. The background plays quietly, the clatter of ice cubes as the waitress fills my cucumber water, occasional shrieks from overexcited women on a table across from us, the chink of cutlery as tables are re-laid for new customers. Blue flowers lie beside me on the light-pink bench I'm sat on, giving off a soft pollenated scent that tickles my nose if I breathe in too deeply and, even though Rick had described this dinner as a catch-up, the flowers have turned the atmosphere from friends to maybe-more-than-friends. It's put me on edge. Does he think that seducing me is the best way to get me on side? He doesn't know me very well if so.

'You haven't told me about your day. Are you still working at the clinic?' he asks, snapping me back to attention.

'I am and, today wasn't too bad,' I reply, forcing a smile, finding it difficult to open up and let my guard down. I've never been good at hiding my feelings. 'The usual.'

I study his face as his mouth half-opens, reaching for something else to say, trying to save us from our awkward pauses in conversation. His hair is thick on top of his head – thicker than usual – then fades as it reaches his ears, his neck.

He catches me looking. 'I need to sort this mop out,' he laughs.

'No, it looks good,' I reply, a little too enthusiastically. 'I was just…'

I swallow a slippery piece of fish as Rick chuckles, my sentence hanging, awkwardness dominating the mood between us. I begin to wonder if Rick regrets asking me here. The only thing we have to catch up about is Tabby and, let's be honest, it's not exactly friendly conversation.

At least the food's good. Sashimi is always my friend at places like this – sitting separate and apart from the sticky clumps of rice and hidden fireballs of wasabi, in neat, slimy slices. One of my stranger personality quirks is that I prefer to eat my meals in clear sections. In my opinion, sushi should be eaten fish first, rice second, seaweed third, not all in one messy, mixed-up mouthful. Rick must have remembered that about me and, I have to say, if it weren't for the uneasy company, I'd be enjoying myself.

'Can I get you anything from the wine list?' asks the waitress.

Rick looks at me and cocks an eyebrow. 'Should we?'

The waitress taps her pen on her pad, she's after a yes or no not a protracted discussion.

'We haven't seen each other for years. How about a bottle of bubbly?'

I nod at the waitress, confirming our order, telling myself

that I'm doing the right thing. That I'm in control. That getting involved in the podcast, that getting closer to Rick, that it's all for the greater good, that it's all for Tabby, and, when I lock my eyes onto his, I feel confident, sure about what it is I have to do.

His voice gets progressively slower as the fizz flows and early evening turns late. His words are heavier, somehow, his shoulders hunched protectively over his glass, spinning it between his thumb and forefinger.

'It's been really hard,' he tells me, midway through chronicling how he still isn't able to live a normal life. 'And, you know, they're bringing it all up again, opening the wounds. It's been years… but the world still won't let me move on. There's a podcast about it now.'

My eyes narrow. *Yes Rick, you're the victim.*

'Have you listened to it?' I ask, thinking back to today's episode and the slightly different direction Kay had taken it in, preparing the listeners if Rick outs Tabby for what she put him through at university.

Who among us can say we haven't made a mistake at some point in our lives? I've made too many to count. So, it strikes me today that our victim, Tabitha, was probably no different. And doesn't that make her more human?

Kay had stopped short of saying that Tabby may have falsely accused Rick of raping her, and I can't say I blame Kay for that. Personally, I believe there's more to the story, that Rick slimed his way out of the accusation and let Tabby take the rap, but I'd have no way of proving that… and neither would Kay, if it came to it. She must be annoyed.

It's far easier to get the public on side when your victim is squeaky-clean. But it isn't very realistic, is it?

'I listened to the first episode,' Rick replies. 'It's always the husband,' he tells me, citing the episode title, knocking back the last of his drink. 'But that line of inquiry: it's lazy. Look how far the police got following that one.'

He sits back, brings his hand to his mouth and glides it down his chin, creases his brow so a determined line carves a path between his eyebrows.

'You never did say sorry for accusing me.'

I swallow, hard. In the days and weeks after Tabby went missing, I made no secret of the fact I wanted Rick's story turned upside down, any false alibi he had searched inside and out.

'I get it, though,' he continues. 'You wanted to blame someone. I just happened to be an easy target.'

You were cheating on her, you wanted her gone, you were desperate for a life without Tabby in it.

'I'm sorry,' I lie. 'I was upset. I just wanted her back.'

He waves a hand at my apology, bats it away, and I'm surprised, honestly, by how flippant he is. If someone publicly accused me of murder I don't know if I could just wish it away with a flick of my wrist.

'I don't want you to think I'm being glib,' he adds, reading my mind. 'But you have to understand, the whole world has thought me guilty at some point. If I held onto the hate, the injustice, it would eat me alive. So, I've been working to let it go. To forgive and forget.'

Not me. I haven't forgotten and I'm not about to forgive.

'That's good,' I say instead, playing along. 'Be careful,

though, next you'll be knocking on people's doors, telling them to let Jesus into their lives.'

'Never say never,' he laughs, gripping the stem of his glass, the muscles tensing in his forearm, changing tack. 'You know what makes me angry, though? Because she's still missing, because she's not here, she's untouchable. She's been preserved in this perfect *image* that was never real and never really her. The press won't bring up anything uncomfortable about her past, about her character. She's missing and therefore she's an angel, end of story.'

I think about the conversation I overheard between him and Mandy in the hospital, about the article Kay showed me. 'If you see it like that, why haven't you said what you need to say?'

'Because I can't,' he replies. 'How can I say anything negative about a woman who's been canonised by the papers? If I said anything negative, anything at all, it would count as evidence that I didn't like her and wanted her gone.'

'OK, so what *would* you say if things weren't so complicated?'

'That she was messed up, fragile, emotionally unstable, sometimes suicidal, but you know all of this, you were close to her too.'

I can't help but speak up. 'She was also kind and generous and fun and brilliant…'

He shrugs. 'But she wasn't perfect.'

'Do you know someone who is?'

I watch his expression frost and I berate myself for pushing him away, for letting my emotions get in the way of the bigger picture.

'You're right, though,' I concede. 'I know she wasn't perfect and that she hurt you when you were together.'

'You don't even know the half of it. You know she tried to get me kicked out of Oxford?'

What happened to forgive and forget?

'She did?'

'She made up a story about us having non-consensual sex. She retracted it, but only after my world had fallen apart. I forgave her, she did the right thing in the end, but it was a horrible process to go through, for both of us.'

'Tell me what happened. I just, I can't believe that she'd make something like that up.'

He rubs his forehead, pained. 'It's a long story. In Tabby's mind, the police and her foster mother had more culpability than she did.'

I lean in, knowing that I can kill two birds with one stone here. 'You should keep it to yourself, Rick. Journalists have not been your friend, and the more fuel you add to the fire of Tabby's disappearance the more, ultimately, they'll want *you* to burn. Not her.'

He looks into my eyes and I search them for answers, realising the questions I have aren't for Rick, but for Tabby. I can't believe she'd accuse him of something so serious unless she had good reason. She wasn't malicious like that.

A few beats of tension build between us and I turn raw-salmon pink, nervous to dig any deeper, fish hook caught in my tongue.

Tabby

Five Years Ago

It's finally here! The day I've been waiting for! And it hasn't been easy to keep my brilliant mood hidden from Rick. He suspected something when I bounded in from work, grinning from ear to ear.

What's got into you? he asked, eyebrows askew, and I had to pretend that I'd had a pay rise.

'Lucky for some,' he said. 'They're working me to the bone at the office.' Rick's an asset manager. He deals with other people's money, which is ideal for him – he's always telling me what to do with mine. 'Going to have to head back there this evening, actually, lots of end of month accounts to finish up.'

I decided not to point out it was the 21st and that 'the end of the month' was still ten days away… *Come on, Rick, at least be believable.*

Still, my stomach fizzes with the possibilities of what's next. My life will be so different after tonight. Will I even come back here again, to this place? What if he's so perfect that we just decide to move in right away, elope, get away from it all. Wouldn't that be wonderful?

No matter what happens, I am not coming back.

Then a dark cloud closes in. What if he doesn't show up? He can barely turn up to a text chat let alone face-to-face. What about his life makes me think he's willing to leave? What if he just wants me as a bit on the side? What if he discards me immediately when he realises I am not quite the 'Belle' he's hoped for?

I push my thoughts to the periphery as Rick steps out of the front door, grinning nervously, his empty briefcase swinging stupidly by his side. When did this become the reality of our relationship? Have we been doomed from the beginning?

When I'm sure he's gone, I dye my hair dark at the roots so I am more Bella-like, I rub the darkest fake-tan I can find over my porcelain skin, I draw thick black pencil over my eyebrows, run red lipstick over my lips. I look different, more like her. I *feel* different.

I scan the news on my phone, hoping Alex will text to confirm that we're still on for tonight, and cook dinner as though this is a normal evening. I watch the clock as it passes, painfully slowly, drink an espresso. I wonder if he's packed a bag like I have, if he's going to be as ready as I am to jump into a new life together. Even though this is only our first meeting, if he asks me to move to Turkey tomorrow – I am ready.

Eventually, it's eight o'clock, and our meeting in half an hour draws close. I decide to send him a message before I leave.

On my way. So excited! x

I don't want Rick to realise anything is wrong when he comes home, so I pile my side of the bed with pillows, shoving them under the duvet, and hope he won't try and touch me – not that he ever does – when he gets back from his night out with his lover. I exhale heavily as I pass a framed photo from our wedding day on the mantelpiece. Something about the twist of Rick's bow-tie, of the neatness of his shoes, of the happiness in his smile makes my stomach cramp and, for a second, I want to abandon everything and sort things out. Then I remember the texts he sent to someone else and regroup.

Our relationship is not capable of being saved. Fuck him. Fuck her.

I wonder what Alex will think of me when we meet. I have to walk across the park down the road, then through the carpark of the superstore, to the bar that sits on the corner of Battersea high street. He'll be there when I arrive, sipping an Old-Fashioned, following a long shift at the clinic. I dream that he'll tell me I'm even prettier in person. That we'll fall in love and, all things going well, he'll ask me to run away with him.

When we're safe, I'll text Annabella to let her know where I am, that I'm sorry I had to leave in such a hurry but that it was the only way. Obviously, Alex can never meet her, so I won't see her again after tonight. Losing her friendship will be a tough price to pay.

I will miss her, greatly.

My pulse thumps in my wrist as I pull the door wide. My stomach twists and turns. This is it. I turn the lock confidently and swing my rucksack onto both shoulders. I check that I have my phone and my wallet in my pockets before I step out into the evening.

The rest of my life starts now.

PART 3

Dog-walker finds body

A report by the London Times

The body of a young woman – suspected to be that of missing South-London woman Tabitha Rice – was found floating in a flooded field at Brimley Farm, Dartford yesterday.

A dog-walker found the badly decomposed body. They said, 'My dog, Barney, wouldn't come back when I called him – which was odd, you know. He's usually very good, like, very obedient. I went over to grab him, and he had this beaten up shoe in his mouth. He wouldn't let it go. He ran off again, back into the field, so I followed him, he was barking blue murder, he was. I saw him in the distance, pulling on something. At first, I thought it was a branch, then I realised it was bone… then that it was a body, floating in the mud. Barney kept digging it up until the police arrived. Maybe he wanted to save them? He's a good dog.'

Tabitha Rice went missing nearly five years ago, but so far there have been no breakthroughs in her case. This latest development is being linked to the missing

Battersea woman as Brimley Farm is owned by Tabitha's paternal grandfather.

The dog-walker, who did not want to be named, continued, 'It looked like she'd been there for a while. The skin on her body was grey, like, swollen. I'll never forget it. I thought she were face down; then they turned her over and I realised… Barney was barking, the police were trying to back me up but I couldn't move: her face was missing, caved in, but moving. Rolling with maggots, it was. Someone said, down the pub, that she'd drowned in the mud, buried alive.'

The body has been sent for identification. More on this story to follow.

Annabella

Now

I meet Kay in Camberwell at an establishment called Tea Time. Inside, the walls are covered in multi-patterned teapots, the tables stacked with loose leaves in glass domes, beside them chests of teabags ordered by tea-type – black, green, white, rose – dozens of options within each sub-category. The aroma of the place is fruity potpourri and, each time a chest is opened, the tea gasps a new scent into the room. For some, I could imagine this place might feel too close and claustrophobic – an unwelcome assault on the senses – but, as I inspect the surfaces, though it is cluttered, it is perfectly clean, so I am relaxed as I head to the bar to order. It feels almost rude to ask for an English Breakfast, so I choose an Earl Grey from the bespectacled server. Black. *The way you're supposed to have it.*

Kay is sitting in the corner, purple teapot to her right, trying to find her way around the ball-strainer she's been given. From what I can make out, it looks as though she's decided to separate it into sections, pulling it apart to better understand how it's put together. Concentration laces her face but, when she spots me, her worry dissipates and she leaps up to greet me, pushing her hand fast into mine.

As we sit, I observe her outfit: a tweed blazer, faded tartan shirt beneath. If I'd just seen her top-half I'd assume her bottom was also Scottish-inspired, a bright blue saltire printed across a denim skirt, or a kilt and sporran. As it is, she's wearing black bell-bottoms and I can't help but smile. Kay's nearly two decades older than me, but her eccentric style is ageless – she'll look exactly the same when she meets someone else here in ten years' time, a new mystery to solve, another podcast to put out.

She's speaking before I've had a chance to sit, steaming pot in one hand, strainer discarded, sitting in a pile of brown water by her side.

'The body is on Tabitha's *grandfather's* property,' she says. 'This has got to be it. *This* is our breakthrough. I might need to fast-track putting the series out, I hadn't realised it would end here.'

'It's not her,' I reply, pouring my tea.

Kay opens her mouth to speak, but nothing comes out and her jaw bobs, slack.

'What makes you say that?' she asks eventually.

'Five years and the body's still fresh with maggots?' I point out, recalling the witness statement in the paper. 'It doesn't add up. I think it's a coincidence.'

'No,' Kay interjects. 'Firstly, witnesses who speak to the media are notorious exaggerators, especially if they've just seen something traumatic. Trust me, I've met my fair share. And, look, if you read the report, the papers says the body was badly decomposed. The man probably didn't even see any maggots.'

I distract myself by stirring my tea, there's no need, I haven't added milk or sugar, but the ritual allows me a second to think.

'Finally,' Kay muses. 'After all these years. Risen by the rainwater.'

It occurs to me, escaped leaves swirling in my cup, that I've spent so long thinking about what might have happened to Tabby and where she might be, that I haven't paid a single thought to how I'll feel when it's all over.

'What do you know about him, the grandfather?' Kay asks, grabbing a notepad from her bag and scribbling something in the margin.

'Nothing,' I reply. 'Tabby didn't often speak about her family. We didn't like to. It was one of the things that bonded us: neither of us had particularly pleasant childhoods.'

'What was it… domestic abuse? Neglect?'

The way she asks the question, pen poised, so matter-of-fact, is somewhat callous.

'Mine or hers?' I ask.

I watch Kay scribbling, our early years about to be confined to a few notes on her notepad, all that we went through dismissed by a couple of inadequate words: *abusive upbringing*. I try not to let it get to me. I remind myself I'm projecting.

'Hers.'

'Tabby lived with her grandfather for a while before she was put into the foster care system. She went through a few different families.'

Kay looks up at me for a moment, her face twisted, as though what I've said about Tabby is a red flag.

'We should go down there, figure her grandfather out, interview him, get something on tape,' she suggests, her leg bouncing beneath the table, the edge of her bell-bottom swinging. I take a sip of tea, the heat burning the roof of my mouth.

'And what's the latest with Rick?' she asks, leaning closer.

'I did what you asked,' I reply, part of me nervous to talk about our 'date'. 'I ambushed him at the gym, then he asked me to dinner.'

Her face lights up. 'That was quick.'

'We spoke about the case – and he knows about the podcast, by the way, says we're lazy for following the thread that he must be guilty.'

'He would say that. Did you ask him about the allegation?' Kay eyeballs me.

'Yes. And it's true, it was Tabby.'

A bubble of tea escapes from Kay's lips. 'Shit,' she says.

'But I think I convinced him to keep quiet. Whether or not Tabby was in the wrong, Rick's wary of newspaper editors – he's right to be – so I don't think we're in danger of the story leaking just yet.'

'I've got previous for having bad instincts with cases like this,' Kay cuts in. 'I always side with the woman, accuse the man, *assume* it's the man. Maybe in this case I should keep a more open mind,' she says, her tone changing. 'AB, can I ask you something? Will you still want to be involved in all this if it doesn't turn out quite as we expect?'

I blink at her, my head full of Tabby's memory. I can't

help but want to protect the person who isn't here to protect herself.

'Tabby's not behind this.'

I feel somewhat child-like in this moment, sticking up for Tabby no matter what. Putting my loyalty for her before everything.

'Listen,' Kay says, reassuring me. 'The sensible money is still on Rick. He was seeing someone behind her back when she went missing and he's been paying someone off for months. He could have used the allegation to exonerate himself five years ago, before the newspapers turned nasty, but he's kept it from the police. You need to keep close to him, make sure he doesn't have a sudden urge to get things off his chest. But first,' she announces, 'we need to go to the farm. We need to speak to the grandfather and, you're my in here, he won't talk to a journalist, he won't understand it, he'll turn me away.'

'OK,' I agree. 'But I don't know her grandfather, he doesn't know me from anyone.'

'It doesn't matter. We just need enough to get us through the front door. Once we're in, we can pump him for information: find out what kind of kid Tabby was, assess whether he has a good enough reason for sending her to foster care, or a good enough reason to bury her in his back garden.'

I slurp up the last of my tea, poke at the leaves that escaped the strainer and sit, gloopy, at the bottom of the cup. I wonder what a tea-leaf reader would make of them; if I squint, I can just about make out a skull.

The body in the bog.

★

Tabby's grandfather's farm is hardly in the middle of nowhere and, though the land he owns is vast, all three sides are flanked by houses. Some ramshackle, some grand, some colourful, some bland.

Kay told me that the farm was built in the 1950s, that Tabby's grandfather was colloquially known as the 'King of Cabbage' when he first set up. His *actual* name is Ernest – Ernie – Rice, but not many people know that. Apparently, the nickname was something of an irony: his cabbages were the only crop that didn't fail that first year. He inherited a small fortune from his father which enabled him to buy the land, but the farm has never turned a consistent profit, so Ernie hasn't managed to do away with his countryside clown reputation. Much to his chagrin.

I'd wager, judging by the belligerent smirk that accompanies each newspaper article Kay's managed to dig up about him, that he's still not over it. I look down at one of the articles, into the old face of Ernie Rice, into his fierce eyes and petulant expression, and surmise that underneath the wrinkles he's still just a boy trying to prove himself, desperate to show the naysayers they were wrong about him wasting his daddy's money.

Ernie has been notably absent in Tabby's story up until now. I didn't meet him at the memorial, Tabby herself never really spoke about him, the police, Chad, even Kay – no one mentioned much about him until a dead woman escaped her grave and rose to the surface, pointing a bloated finger in his direction.

I have to confess, Kay got us here much quicker than I

expected. I thought there'd be a week, at least, to prepare, but Kay Robero doesn't hang around so, just two days after we sipped tea together, brown liquid in our cups, we're heading to Ernest Rice's farm, brown liquid swilling against our boots. She'd called me yesterday to fill me in on the details and hung up midway through saying goodbye. I'd forgotten that about her phone calls and it made me laugh as I'd said a serious goodbye to myself, the line dead in my hands.

Kay and I catch the train there, rolling through the grey of East London, the even greyer bit just outside of East London, then, just as I'm expecting an explosion of green, Dartford arrives: another tinpot commuter town, same big brands lining the high street, same fast-food chains dotted between them. Kay tells me there's a Central Park here. I'm not holding my breath.

On the road out of the station I see something that reminds me, heart-stoppingly, of Tabby. A salon – Nice Nails – that she'd told me she had a Saturday job at when she was a young teenager. It must have been during one of the times she was staying with Ernie, waiting to find her next set of foster parents. My stomach lurches with the memory. I should go in. I should walk into that place and see if anyone remembers her. I should get my nails buffed and polished, then coloured sickeningly pink, just the way Tabby used to.

'Come on,' Kay trills. 'We don't have time for *nails*, AB.'

'She used to work here,' I explain, dozy with the thought of her.

'Ah,' Kay sighs, turning swiftly towards the building to take a photo on her phone. 'Anywhere else she mentioned?'

'I don't think so.'

My reflection glints back at me, rain droplets distorting my features, only one eye visible in the glass, my light hair darkened by the water it's holding. I stare at myself but think about Tabby. She'd told me Nice Nails had been on the cutting-edge of the 'fish-pedicure' when she worked here. That a sweet old woman had been their first recipient, her hair in rollers when she'd arrived, a hearing aid in each ear. *That should have been a warning,* Tabby had said when she'd recanted the tale. When the bowl of mini piranhas – or whatever they were – came out, the lady hadn't noticed at first, her head deep in a magazine; it was only when they started snaffling away at her heels that she'd taken a proper look, screamed, told the entire place she was going to sue them, that she didn't expect the salon water to be contaminated with *fish*, and had stamped on a fair few of them before she'd left. Tabby said she was surprised the pedicure had continued to book out at the salon, what with the fact she'd spent that entire afternoon wiping fish blood from the floors, the receptionist calling each of their booked customers to make sure they understood the fish-pedicure featured *actual* fish.

Kay's hand wraps round mine and she pulls me away from myself. 'We should keep moving,' she says, so we do, away from the drab high-street, zigzagging through the walkways and bridle paths towards Ernie's farm. On the way up, I can't help but marvel at the fields surrounding us: each one is wider than the next, though the dull grass has been drenched by this winter's never-ending downpour. I huddle closer to Kay as we squelch on together, the heavy hum of the rain unsettling as we duck under a fence and dive onto his land. It's the kind of weather you'd expect in a jungle, not on the outskirts of London, and I can tell my black boots – apparently waterproof – will never be the same again. I formulate a plan to throw them in the bins at the front of the flats when I get back – I can't stand the thought of this mud, thick with animal excretion and human remains, treading into the nooks of my wooden floors. It takes a monumental effort to keep going, to plough forward. I know one thing for sure: without Kay I would never have come here. Even with her by my side, I can't shake the feeling that something bad is about to happen. *What else lies beneath this rotten land?*

We climb a slight hill together and, just as we crest, a boggy field comes into view on our right side – blue and white tape taut round the exterior, a tent towards the back. The surrounding plots are yellow-green, so the brown of the field in question stands out. I'd imagined it being further away from the house, but it isn't, it almost backs onto it. *How lazy*, I think. He didn't even walk very far to bury the body, he literally dumped it in his back yard.

Kay raises her eyebrows at me.

'I still don't think this body is Tabby,' I say. 'If this was where she died, I would feel it, it would infect my bones and crawl all over my skin. I would *know*. She would find a way, somehow, to tell me.'

Kay draws to a halt and I feel her ribcage expand as she holds her breath.

'There aren't any police here today,' she says, after a minute. 'If there were, they'd have put a cordon at the foot of the property. There'd have been officers on the gates.'

'They could be inside?'

'No,' she replies. 'They've already searched it. And Ernie's moved back in, I checked.'

We press on, Kay's waterproof anorak blowing in the breeze, the farmhouse a few hundred yards ahead. The exterior is granite, slate tiles on the roof, gutters brimming with rainwater. It's an ancient building and sits in contrast to the much newer barns that surround its north and east corners. It could just be the weather, but even the potted plants, scattered randomly at the front of the property, look downtrodden and depressed: wilted at the stem, missing petals, pooling with watery soil, dirty puddles on the gravel. The windows are mostly covered with curtains, except two downstairs, and the front door is missing large patches of red paint. It looks like an unfit jigsaw that needs throwing away. The smell of the bog, muddy and waterlogged, floats by as Kay lifts her hand to knock.

We stand, crinkled, and wait. Two girls playing at being detectives – at least that's the way I feel about being here. Just as I'm imagining holding a plastic magnifying glass to the splintered front door, the way I used to as a child, I hear steps behind it, then a dog's urgent scamper as it launches towards us, nose stuffed between the gap to the outside, pacing left to right, desperate to greet us. Oh great. As if the mud wasn't enough dirt to deal with. The door opens and Ernest Rice emerges from the gloom within, the flash of a border collie behind.

He's less intimidating than I'd imagined – he's probably only about 5'7" – and his Aran sweater is dotted with holes – just like his front door, and his mind, judging by the far-off look in his eyes. He takes us in, curls his lips into his trademark belligerent smirk and, just as Kay's about to introduce us, he cuts over the top of her, breathing this morning's alcohol into our faces. Whiskey, I'd guess.

'I'm not interested,' he says, then slams the door, the flash I'd seen of his dog disappearing, followed by a sad whine.

'Well,' I say to Kay, turning to go, taken aback but relieved that our run-in with Ernie had ended before it had even really begun. 'We could try the salon,' I suggest, before I'm interrupted by another loud knock at the door.

'What are you doing?' I ask, eyes wide, hand on her arm.

'I have money,' she calls through the door. 'We'll pay you for your time. Just half an hour, that's all.'

I look at her. 'Bribery?' I ask. 'What happened to being friends of Tabby's?'

'Change of plans,' she whispers back. 'This is the in – he needs the money.'

'You really think a few quid will make a difference to this miserable old—'

'How much?' a gruff voice calls back. I curl my lips in on themselves and stop speaking. *Kay knows what she's doing.*

'Three hundred?' Kay plucks, seemingly out of thin air.

There's a pause, and I ride a choppy wave of nausea in anticipation of what's next.

The door swings open, slower this time, and Ernie's collie pads out, nose down, sniffing at our boots. He can probably smell the blood on them. Ernie stands back and makes a *come-in* gesture, his smirk elongated but still every bit as nasty.

Inside, the walls are pale-green and sparse, the furniture is wooden and chipped, and the cabinet we walk past to reach the lounge features more empty photo frames than full. I can't speak, so I am glad that Kay is running the show in my mouth's absence.

'We're recording a podcast into the disappearance of Tabitha Rice and we want to hear your side of the story.'

I sit, tentatively, on the faded brown sofa, tucked into the corner of Ernie's lounge. There's a square television set opposite, a little wooden chair beyond, and a patterned rug underfoot. Apart from these features the room is empty. Even the lightbulb overhead hangs exposed. I can't imagine a young girl living here, let alone Tabby. Kay stands, angular, her anorak dripping wet on to the wooden floor. Ernie's eyes haven't left her, a cat focused on a mouse. He doesn't seem to mind the mess she's making.

'Very well,' he says. 'Half now, half later.' He holds out his hand.

Kay's anorak billows as she pulls her handbag from underneath and counts out £150 in ten and twenty-pound notes. Ernie's eyes narrow and he tucks a longish tuft of grey hair back behind his ear. He's bald on top but the edges are unkempt, pixie-like. When they get too long, I imagine he takes a pair of sheep shears to them himself, slicing erratic chunks off his girly hair. Kay takes three small steps forward and places the money in Ernie's hand. He studies it – makes a pointless and offensive scene about counting it out – then, satisfied, drags the wooden chair from the edge of the room and sits. He motions for Kay to join me on the sofa and I blush, aware I sat too soon, and shuffle to the right, smiling thickly to make up for it.

'Are you two lesbians or something?' he asks, grinning. Ernie Rice takes pleasure in others' discomfort – that much is clear – and he's a championship prick, certainly, but I'm not sure he's brilliant enough to be a killer.

Kay clears her throat, his question going unanswered, and hands Ernie a small microphone to clip to his sweater. She depresses a button on the recording device in her hand.

'Tell me in your own words about Tabitha Rice, your granddaughter.'

He takes a deep breath in, then sprays spittle from his lips as he blows out in a heavy, sarcastic sigh. 'Her mother dropped 'er on my doorstep whenever she felt like it. I was lumped with 'er – feeding 'er, getting 'er to school – and I didn't ask for it, I couldn't look after 'er on my own. I called the social services and got 'er a home that wanted 'er.'

My heart pounded as he spoke so matter-of-factly at sending his granddaughter away.

'Were you ever close with your daughter?'

'With Marie, no.' He shakes his head, rubs his hands in his lap.

'What happened?' Kay asks, pressing him.

'Marie got pregnant at eighteen, she couldn't keep the kid 'ere, obviously, I had enough to deal with running the farm. I told 'er if she wanted to have sex like an adult then she sure as heck could live like an adult. I told 'er she had to work it out herself.'

'She moved out?' Kay asks.

'For a bit. Then kept coming back, leaving the girl with me for longer and longer. Asking for money. Track marks all over 'er arms. I never gave 'er any money, never had any to spare. Do you know how expensive it is to run a place like this?'

I cast my eyes to the damp patch creeping up the wall

behind Ernie, bleeding into the ceiling. Ernie took his vast inheritance and whittled it away into this farming passion-project, turning his back on his only daughter and only granddaughter... and for what? The place is crumbling, oozing from its foundations, his secrets literally rising from their graves.

'What do you know about Tabitha's missing persons investigation?'

'Well,' Ernie balks, a guttural sound erupting from him. 'A right mess she got 'erself into. Just like her mother, I imagine. Nasty, stupid women. I doubt Marie was even mine, 'er mother was a slag too. They're all the same.'

Kay isn't fazed by him, but I clear my throat in a high-pitch splutter to communicate my contempt.

'Do you know where Marie lives now?'

'I s'pose you're going to tell me.' Ernie shrugs, his back curled, his body sagging like a sack of potatoes.

Kay moves on, her silence on the matter telling me that she hasn't been able to locate Marie Rice yet.

'Who do you think they found in your back garden?'

'How should I know?'

'It's your back garden,' Kay fires back. 'You have private property signs all over this place.' I remember the red notice on the gate leading up to the farm but, where I'd largely ignored it, Kay had committed it to memory. 'You're very concerned with your privacy, Mr Rice so, with respect, I'm a little surprised you didn't notice someone trudging into your back garden with a dead body.'

Ernie laughs. 'Didn't stop you two trespassing, did it? And what, you expect me to have eyes in the back of my head? I was probably asleep when they did it.'

'I just find it odd – that someone could sneak in overnight, dig up one of your fields, and you wouldn't notice anything amiss the next day.'

Ernie shrugs again.

'What were you doing on the night of 21st August five years ago, Mr Rice?' Kay asks, changing tack.

Ernie combusts in response. *'Ha!'* He wraps his arms round his middle and shakes with laughter. 'How do you expect me to remember that? What were *you* doing on the 21st August five years ago?'

Kay ignores him. 'If you didn't bury that body. Who do you think did?'

'Could be anyone. Bill from Frattingham Farm, if you ask me. His wife died ten year back. He wants me shut down, probably rolled 'er out of the cemetery to put 'er there. Anything to get me out of business.'

Kay makes a note of the rival farm on her pad. 'Who works here, on the farm, day-to-day?'

'Well, I got my Polish lads and a Romanian lad – think they pick on him for it – and me.'

'Did any of them ever meet Tabitha?'

'How would I know?'

'What did the police ask you when they took you in?'

'Same as you, love. All about the granddaughter I haven't seen for years.'

'What else?'

'What I was doing the night she went missing, you know, all of that.'

'What did you tell them?'

'That I was away.'

There's a silence then and I snap my neck up at Ernie.

Kay presses him on it. 'You just told me you couldn't remember.'

Ernie stands up. 'Well, what does it matter? Old man like me, can't remember what day it is let alone what I was doing any given night in August five years ago.' He brushes his dirty hands against his jeans. 'Half an hour,' he says, then holds out his hand again.

As Kay counts the rest of his money, I consider his story. Ernie has a lot stacked against him: his persistent absence from Tabby's life, an uncaring, unresolved relationship with her mother, a couple of confused stories about the night Tabby went missing and his generally obstinate demeanour.

And, of course, the body.

Rick

Fourteen Years Ago – 2006

I pushed my way into Tabby's bedroom and pressed my finger to her lips. I shouldn't be here, I was breaking all the rules, but I was desperate.

'Ssh,' I whispered, touching her arms. 'I just want to talk to you.'

She looked frightened, but let me in, the pink of her bedroom grotesquely childlike given what we were about to discuss.

'Listen,' I said, pulling the door shut behind me. 'You have to stop this, Tabby. It's not right.'

I watched her eyes fall to the floor.

'You have to retract your allegation.'

I touched her again, fixed her with a meaningful stare. 'I've been suspended from college, but my parents won't let me come home. They're getting threats. They think I'm a pervert, my brother's spreading rumours that I'm into little girls. The things I'm hearing about myself, reading about myself, they're bad, they're really bad. Only you can stop them.'

I couldn't figure out what to do with my limbs, or with the tears that were raging at my eyes. I turned to the right, away from her, then to the left, then sat down on the edge of her bed, flowery duvet flattening beneath me.

'This isn't what I wanted,' she told me.

'I believe you,' I said, meaning it. 'You have to make it right. Take back what you said.'

'It's not as simple as that,' she told me, shuffling back, out of my reach. 'I didn't say yes, Rick.'

'I don't get it, since when have you ever said yes before we've had sex? Why this time? Why is it different? Because you were angry. Because I didn't lie to you afterwards and tell you everything was going to go back to normal.'

I could smell her confusion. Her foster parents and the police had a lot to answer for. Was it best to lie? Would that make this all go away?

'Practically the first name out of your mouth after it happened was hers.'

'Saskia's?'

Tabby looked at me, her anger palpable, and I could tell she wanted to scream at me for saying her name again, for acting as though I didn't know exactly who she was talking about.

I shuffled towards her again, tried to make her understand. 'You know I'm crazy about you, don't you?'

She didn't nod, but didn't move away, let me cover her hands in mine.

'I want you to know that hasn't changed. But you have to understand, Oxford has been such a lonely place for me.

Being with Saskia changed that… for a while.' I paused, held her baby-blue stare in mine. 'But it's always been you, Tabby.'

She shook her head. She was in an impossible situation. 'I don't know if I can even take it back,' she said. 'What would happen to me?'

'They'd understand, Tabbs,' I assured her. 'They'd understand you were just doing the right thing. Do you really want to see me chucked out of university, sent to prison, even, for this? For what?'

She shook out an agreement and my tears came all at once, my cheeks suddenly wet, relief running through me like a river.

'Will you go down there tomorrow and take it back?'

'Yes,' she said. That word. There it was, at last.

Tabby dropped the allegation the next day, the charge against me shelved, the case swept from police desks as quickly as it had arrived. The university issued a statement, designed to show they supported me staying on at Oxford due to the victim retracting her accusation, but their reluctance to do so shone through in the details. *He's guilty, everyone, but our hands are tied. Rick Priestley stays until he strikes again.*

At Oxford, no one forgot what had happened. On the outside world, though, Tabby was bearing the brunt of a furious right-wing response. Everyone had an opinion about us that fit their own agenda. The facts of the matter wouldn't have changed anything. Coming to that realisation was a big moment for me. And for her.

By the summer break, Tabby and I were going steady again, but our relationship turned long-distance from July, when I finished my first year and headed home. Tabby was away with her high school for a week of activities – surfing, I think, in Cornwall. Then I went to Spain with my family, the Priestley summer holiday a week-long exercise in trying not to catch E.coli from yet another dubious all-inclusive buffet. I had essays to write, reading to skim, reams and reams of preparation for second year that barely gave me a moment to myself. In between that and working at the local pub, my summer break had felt less like a break and more like an obstacle course of relentless chores.

When October rolled around and I moved myself into a studio flat out of the city centre, seeing Tabby wasn't far from my thoughts. I expected to pick up where we left off, taking things slow, perhaps I'd even ask her to be my girlfriend if things were still going well come December. What I hadn't expected when I pulled up on my push bike at her foster parents' house was this:

'First of all,' wailed Tabby, loud enough for me to hear through the double-glazing. 'You're not even my real mum and dad, so you can't tell me what to do.'

'We deserve better than that,' her foster dad replied, quieter. I pressed myself against the wall, darted fervent looks at my bike which I'd left a few metres away. I should come back another time.

'Even if you could tell me what to do, it doesn't matter, I'm nineteen now, I can do whatever the fuck I like.'

'Language, Tabitha!'

Yes, I thought, slinking away from the house. I would come back later, this wasn't the right time.

It was then, probably fifteen steps away from the house, that the front door opened and her voice crawled out. 'Rick? What are you doing here? I thought you weren't back till tomorrow?'

I spun, about to tell her I wanted to surprise her, and then I saw it. Tabby's surprise for me. Her belly was gently rounded, poking its way out of her cardigan like a kid playing hide and seek behind a pair of curtains. She ran towards me, flung her arms round my neck, pushed that pregnant belly right up against my crotch.

'It's yours,' she cried. 'I'm sorry I haven't told you yet. *They* stopped me.'

Tabby's belly was rounding by the day and I honestly didn't know how to feel about it. Part of me was excited, part of me terrified, another part proud. My sense of duty, of purpose, of stepping up and being a dad – a man this baby could rely on – kicked in and got me through. I told Tabby I wanted to help, that I wanted to be there for the baby, and she'd kept on saying the same thing. *Well, Rick, actions speak louder than words.* And I agreed. In those first few weeks, I felt compelled to act the right way.

But, before I knew it, everything was wrong.

Five months in and Tabby moved her stuff out of her foster parents' home – she couldn't bear to live with them anymore. They wanted her to get an abortion. They hated me enough as it was for the rape-allegation-incident, but to find out she was pregnant with my baby was their breaking point. It's him or us, they'd told her. And she'd chosen me. As a result, she split her time between a women's refuge and my new studio on the outskirts of Oxford. I didn't really get a say, but standing by her was the right thing to do, so that's what I did. My acting speaking louder than my words.

Soon my study-books were piled in among baby ones, and Tabby was more concerned about arrangements for the baby than my degree. She started spending the money I made at McDonald's on cots and cotton Babygros that we didn't need yet, and I couldn't afford. But, rather than tell her, rather than enrage her, my autopilot brain was still in charge and told me to bury my concerns. More complicated was the fact that, because she was pregnant, it was just assumed that we were back together properly, that we were going to be mummy and daddy, boyfriend and girlfriend. I didn't want to make things any worse than they already were, so I went along with it, outwardly telling her I was thrilled about the baby, inwardly horrified about its arrival.

Six months in and I felt the baby kick for the first time, an alien-foot stretching Tabby's purple-streaked stomach further still. She'd felt it before, but whenever I pressed my hand against her stomach to feel for the baby it stopped. I wondered, quietly, whether Tabby was imagining it. Whether the baby was even alive in there at all. But this confirmation of life had terrified me. This baby was real. *This was actually going to happen.* Things were difficult enough already… I wasn't prepared for night after night of no sleep, night after night wondering if Tabby had planned this, night after night staring at the ceiling wondering how I could ask her to do a paternity test.

Seven months in and Tabby's bellybutton had been forced inside out so it stuck out in front of her like an earthworm wriggling from its hole. Thick, slimy stretch marks invaded the smooth skin that used to be there and her whole body was just... disgusting. Swollen. Sore. Tired. Animalistic. Udders swinging from her chest, fluid leaking from every orifice. She even smelt like an animal. She'd stopped wearing rose shimmer on her eyelids, they were crusty with dry skin instead, the pink-pearl of her lips replaced with snake-skin flakes. The closer we came to the due date, the more I began to find the whole thing repugnant, find *her* repugnant. But of course, I couldn't tell Tabby that. Can you imagine what she'd do if I did? Can you imagine what she'd do if I *left*? Since she'd moved out of her foster parents' house, she was relying on me, the baby was relying on me, she reminded me of it every day.

Eight months in and, maybe I shouldn't have suggested it but, somehow, I convinced her we should see her grandfather, that maybe he could help. My parents were completely useless. My dad had told me in the weeks before I left for my second year that he knew I'd fuck up my place at Oxford by doing something stupid, that he was on standby waiting to see what particular brand of stupid it would be. The baby kind, it turned out.

'When this baby arrives,' I began, 'you need to be with someone who can support you properly.' I watched her heart break but still I continued. 'I can't do that for you right now – I need to study, I need to get a good job after this, for you, and for the baby.'

'If you don't love me anymore you can just tell me,' she wailed. 'I can handle it.'

'It's not that, Tabbs, of course it's not that. But I can't be the dad you want me to be if you're living here all the time.'

'I can't do this on my own!'

'You're not on your own. I'm here, I just need some space when the baby arrives. That's all. You can come back for the weekends, maybe? But you can't be here the whole time. You need to get help from someone who can actually support you: I don't have any money, everything I earn goes to pay for this place, topped up by my student loan, with you here all the bills double and I can't keep it up. Once I've graduated, once I have a good job, I'll take care of you properly, I promise.'

She cried, her yellow hair slathered over hot cheeks. Her hand was on her belly, protective, her boobs pushed east and west either side, framing it like dog's ears. What had I done to her?

'You said your grandfather helped you when you were in trouble before, right? And he owns that big farm... maybe he has some money?'

A few days later we arrived at Brimley Farm and, walking up the muddy footpath, I smiled for the first time since this whole saga began. This wholesome place was exactly the right environment for Tabby and the baby, she needed this, the baby needed this, I needed this – fresh air, fresh start, fresh family.

But Ernie Rice, though he let us in, had other ideas.

'Stupid girl just like her stupid mother.'

I squirmed, tried to find the right thing to say, puffed my developing chest, widened my elbows, tried to appear protective, tried to instil values into Ernie that he was sorely missing: he had to step up and be the dad he wasn't to his wife, his daughter, or his granddaughter, that his *great*-granddaughter – *these Rice women didn't hang about, did they* – needed him.

He laughed like a bulldozer and told us to get fucked.

After that non-starter, we spoke all night about what we should do next and, while Tabby was deep into looking for night jobs for me – in addition to my restaurant shifts and Oxford degree – my phone pinged:

when can I see u again? i miss you x

Annabella

Now

The buzz of daytime plays outside my bedroom walls, the steady patter of rain as it falls against my window, dull daylight crawling through the cracks of the shutters.

Last night, I'd worked late with Caroline, the final phases of her handover taking us to well past ten o'clock and, on my way home, I'd lingered outside Rick and Mandy's, just to see them, but all I'd glanced had been fuzzy shadows against closed curtains. I'd sent a message to Kay when I was there, reminded of someone I'd rather forget.

What if those payments I found were going to Chad? You said yourself Rick might have been paying him off to keep me from discovering anything.

Kay and I had met earlier that day to debrief about our visit to Ernie's farm and, though he was a revolting old man and, though we'd both left him wishing him guilty, we didn't have any more information to go on.

I'd told Kay all our efforts should resume with Rick and she'd agreed.

I laze between sleep and wake, then grab my phone to check for messages. I open the first, it's from Kay.

> You're obsessed! You're worse than me. They could well have been payments to Chad, you're right. Let's talk tomorrow. Get some sleep.

She's right. I am obsessed.

I fling my covers from the bed, swinging my legs to the floor. I push to standing, a headrush dizzying me, blotting my vision for a few seconds, halting my progress. I stand in front of the wardrobe, staring at the rack of perfectly ordered outfits, colour-coded and occasion-categorised and pull my perfectly pressed uniform from within. I follow my routines, clean each surface before I leave, then, satisfied, pound the pavements to the clinic, pushing open the door to my room ten minutes ahead of time. I inspect my tools, make sure everything is just as I expect, and when my first patient knocks, my stomach flutters.

In a few hours, I'm meeting Rick.

He appears, leggings under shorts, padded jacket zipped high, rucksack slung haphazardly over his shoulder. We're here for coffee so our meeting is casual but, personally, I prefer his evening look: shorts swapped for a suit, rucksack for a briefcase, trainers for brogues. I bristle as he draws closer, pepping myself up to see him again, his hand about to make contact with the cold metal of the café door. I feel better this time, more confident, you could say I'm settling into my role.

'Rick,' I say as he comes in, not making eye contact at first, affecting a slightly different voice, one I think he'll like. He greets me with a confident hand to my waist, a friendly peck on the cheek.

'Hey,' he says. 'What can I get you?'

We approach the till together.

'Could I just get a white americano?' I ask – I know from my surveillance it's what Rick's about to order – and I stand a little closer, his body inches from mine. Kay's instructions ring loud as I spot Rick looking at me, a little unsure what to make of my proximity. *'Get closer to him, AB. Blur the lines. You need to pull his guard down with your bare hands, not wait around for him to lower it for you.'*

'Make that two,' Rick says to the barista, smiling wide. She's wearing a grey-ribbed jumper that hugs her torso, faux-buttons down the front, her hair scraped up into a cute messy ponytail, a chewed biro balanced over her left ear.

'Hiya, Rick,' she says coyly, blowing a pink bubble with her gum.

'Hello,' he replies, the barista's bubble bursting as he shoots his eyes away from her and back towards me, instead. *Is it working?*

'I need to get one of those,' I say, turning from the barista and nodding towards Rick's reusable flask, wondering if he boil-washes it every night to keep the bacteria at bay.

'Right,' he says. 'Just doing my bit for the dolphins.'

He smiles at me with a set of dimples I hadn't noticed before and lifts his eyebrows, guiding us to a quiet area at the back of the café.

'Did you see the news?' I ask him first, getting to the point.

'About the body?'

'Yeah, what do you make of it? What do you know about her grandfather?'

'Not much, I only met him once. I didn't trust him but I'm not sure he killed Tabby.'

'You don't think she could have gone to him for help and… I don't know… there was some terrible accident while she was there?'

Rick curls a hand round his flask.

'Maybe,' he replies. 'I guess anything's possible.'

'But you're not convinced,' I say, two hands at the top of his guard, tugging at it.

'Well,' he muses. 'There's something…'

I shift in my seat.

'What?' I ask, pulling harder.

'I don't know how much you know, how much the police told you.' I tilt my head and widen my eyes, waiting for him to go on. 'She was talking to someone before she went missing. Romantically, I mean.' He looks at me, searching my expression for signs that I knew, but I didn't. I honestly didn't.

'How do you know?' I ask, sceptical.

'I found the messages they'd been sending to each other on her phone one night. She was asleep and the blue light woke me up.' Just as I'm writing this off as another of Rick's lies, he says something that catches my attention. 'They were making plans to run away to Turkey together, they wanted to set up a clinic on the beach, I think he was a doctor of some kind. She'd been pestering me to pay for her to complete some qualifications, I guess she needed them before she set off.'

I catapult back five years in a heartbeat, Tabby persuading me that moving to Turkey would be a savvy career-decision. My gut wrenches as I consider the spiel she gave me about moving; the one I've replayed in my head so many times, isn't the whole story.

I move uneasily.

'Do you know if she ever made any real plans to go? Flights, accommodation, a job?' I ask quickly, my heart racing. 'Because she spoke to me about going to Turkey too. She wanted me to come. She asked me the day she went missing. I told the police but...'

Rick looks at me as though I've just given him an answer for something. 'Really?' he says. 'I think that must have been part of the reason they let me go, I guess you corroborated my story without realising it.'

My eyes narrow. *Did I let him get away?*

'You think that's where she is now?' I ask. 'In the foothills of some Turkish town with a random doctor?'

Rick shrugs.

'Did you ever ask her?'

'No,' he replies. 'I didn't want to corner her. I wanted her to tell me when she was ready.' He has a far-off look in his eyes as he remembers. 'The man was rugged and olive-skinned and every woman's Mediterranean fantasy... I doubt it was even a real picture.'

'Do you think she was tricked?'

'Maybe,' he says. 'But then he wasn't the only one.'

'What do you mean?' I ask, picking up on the chill in his voice.

'She wasn't sending real photographs either.'

I crunch my face and wonder why Tabby would do that. She was confident and gorgeous and secure in herself. Wasn't she?

'I don't know how to say this,' he begins. 'I kind of assumed you knew.'

I shake my head.

'The pictures Tabby sent him were all of you.'

Tabby

Fourteen Years Ago – 2006

The sad studio we shared fell silent for a few minutes after Rick sped away to see Saskia. He thought I didn't know, that I hadn't realised, that he was successfully pulling the wool over my eyes. Or perhaps he just got off on the thrill and didn't particularly care if I knew. We'd been on and off since the moment we met, I'm not sure why I thought me being pregnant would change that.

One minute, two minutes, three, then the studio filled with sound from the upstairs neighbours, blaring music down through the ceiling, then shouting across the top of it, bass line vibrating through the walls, marijuana fogging through the air vents. I'd made the mistake of walking out on my foster family and now I was trapped here. It would take a lot for them to let me back in. I had to work to earn my foster parents' trust, the love I had for them conditional and fragile, the love they had for me accompanied by a paycheque.

Money. My foster mother was obsessed with it. *Think*

of the newspaper deals you could get if you dropped your anonymity over this rape charge, Tabby. She had this eBay account, flogged most of the family's Christmas presents on it, along with worn-out clothes and things she'd shoplifted from charity shops. I'd seen her do it. *Are you calling me a thief?* she'd asked me once, hunched over in the charity shop changing room, three extra jumpers lining the gap between her T-shirt and jacket.

It was how I knew she wouldn't have told the council I'd left, she'd still be taking the cheque every month, rubbing her hands, saying she'd put up with me for long enough that she deserved it. That was my only way back, by threatening to turn off the money.

I had to think about it. I'd surprise Rick soon, catch him in the act with his sometimes girl – the one he thinks will make him into a better man – and call his bluff.

Me or her.

Annabella

Now

I call Kay on my way to the bus stop, filling her in on the latest about a doctor in Turkey, fake pictures, a possible killer, someone the police had considered in the beginning but hadn't been able to track down.

'Do you believe him?' she asks, her voice aloof. She's between meetings and doesn't have long to chat.

'Well, Tabby never told me she was speaking to anyone, but, I don't know…' I hesitate, the air so cold I can see my breath as I talk. 'She was sending him my pictures. I can't imagine she ever wanted me to find out.'

'Interesting,' Kay replies. 'We'll try to track him down. Do you have a name? Any more information?'

'I didn't ask much, but I will next time.'

'You need to dig deeper, find out exactly what he knows.'

And with that, she hangs up, my meeting with Rick casting a great, grey shadow across the case. I fidget as I wait for the bus to pull in, trying to keep the warmth in my hands, and wonder if Tabby had valued my friendship as much as I'd valued hers. Why hadn't she told me about the doctor? About the pictures? Was our friendship not as close as I thought? It was true that I was always the one to make plans with her, the one who forced us to stick to our routines and traditions. She was flaky and unreliable but I forgave her for it, I didn't mind. She'd get into trouble and I'd bail her out. She'd persuade me to go clubbing and I'd end up playing her carer for the night. My mood clouds. Was our friendship unequal? How had I not seen it before?

I remember, she came to my place one day, it had been raining and I'd been upset about some relationship or other. It was my first year at Pure You and we were already in each other's pockets. She'd marched through my flat in her trainers, drenched – I remember feeling anxious about the marks she was leaving on the lino floor but hadn't said anything – and she'd flung my bedroom door open, a bottle of vodka bursting in with her. *Come with me, get up, we're going out!* She'd bundled me out of my dressing gown, slipped a sequin dress over my shoulders and pushed me out of the front door. It was gone midnight, but that night we danced together till four. It had ended in a strange room, a slimy creature on the sofa next to me, its whiskered top lip vibrating with each exhalation. Tabby was on the floor. I'd crawled on my hands and knees towards her, woken her up, and we'd run from there together. Tabby had laughed about it, told me she'd spiked our drinks with something to make the night a little more interesting. I'd been horrified, initially, but nothing had gone wrong and we were both OK, so I'd let it go. I'd spent the next hour in the shower, scrubbing at every inch of my skin, trying to rid myself of the germs from that place, from that person, from the strange substance running laps in my bloodstream. I was panting when I came out, exhausted. *Let's call in sick today,* she'd said, knowing that I didn't have that choice. I had patients. I'd left her in my flat with a smile on her face as I'd trudged to work with dry skin and tired eyes.

Rick

Thirteen Years Ago – 2007

Saskia lay in the cool morning light in a lacy nightdress, her hair scrunched underneath her cheek like an extra pillow. Saskia. Even her name was sensual. I imagined her sometimes as a fork-tongued serpent-woman, sent to tempt me.

'Morning handsome,' she hissed, and slithered closer, curling a sleepy leg between mine. I felt, as I always did when I woke up with Saskia at her plush flat, an uneasy combination of guilt and glee: like waking up and remembering a vivid dream about sleeping with your ex – your wife right beside you – then the dawning realisation that it wasn't a dream, after all, but a waking nightmare.

I was cheating on my full-bellied girlfriend and, though I knew I should stop, I wasn't going to. Tabby used to feel like home, but now that she was living in mine, all I wanted to do was run from it.

'What are we going to do today?' Saskia asked, and I wished my life was as simple as hers.

I twirled her dark hair round my fingertips and breathed her in: fire and spice. I wrapped my hands round her body – svelte and skinny – her pelvis protruding like antlers, her bellybutton the right way round. I inhaled Saskia behind Tabby's back, enjoyed her, let the high of not having anything to worry about take me over. It was a pure and indulgent escape. A selfish one, too, because Saskia and I both knew whatever *this* was, wasn't long-term. She hadn't even come back into my life with a bang. She'd just never really left. On and off, we were, like a faulty switch that, right now, showed no sign of a problem. My relationship with Tabby was less light switch, more bulldozer, and she'd ploughed back into my life this year with the ferocity of industrial farming equipment, leaving me no choice but to look after her and her calf.

I pushed Tabby from my thoughts and lazed my way into Friday with Saskia. We ate leftover pizza and made a loose plan to head into town together in the afternoon. Saskia wanted to see an old friend, and I needed to spend time with the pregnant woman who'd upturned my life.

Saskia snaked her hand into mine as we boarded the train together.

'Are you staying at mine again tonight?' she breathed into my ear, wet.

'Course,' I replied, settling into a duo of seats. We nestled into one another, her head balanced on my shoulder, her long dark hair ducking into the seat of my trousers.

'Let's go to the toilets,' she whispered, then kissed me. 'I want you.' Her face frowned and she kissed me harder.

'We have to be careful up here, Sas, people know us.'

She withdrew then, yanked her arm out from behind me,

rushed a hand to her heart. 'You're embarrassed to be seen with me?'

'No, I didn't mean—'

She lurched away, folded her arms, and again I was tired and irritated and... *Why couldn't anything just be easy?*

'Sorry,' I wilted. 'I'm an idiot.'

Those words clung to me and I echoed them because I *was* an idiot. I could feel Tabby agreeing with me, her presence burrowed beneath my skin, calling me an idiot from somewhere deep inside because she wasn't here to tell me to my face.

Why was I doing this? If she knew... it would break her.

Saskia and I alighted the train and walked the short path to town, the station lined with students. I didn't realise this at first, but many of my peers would head home from university for a short weekend here, a long weekend there, Mummy and Daddy paying the exorbitant train fares to allow them to hurtle back to London for a quick get-together. Mummy would iron the collars of their polo-shirts, daddy would take them to the club for a swanky dinner. Saskia was one of them, of course, and she waved to somebody on the platform. 'Have a great flight!' she called, and the girl nodded back, her shoulder weighed down by a Louis Vuitton holdall. 'Her parents have moved overseas. Typical, right?'

I didn't know what she meant, I just smiled as she grabbed my hand and we walked out of the station into the wind, ice dropping from the sky. I helped her with her hair as the arctic breeze whipped it across her face. We were close then, our noses Christmas red, and though I knew I shouldn't – *people knew us here* – I pulled her into me, her hair flowing free, batting against my cheeks and, I don't know why I did it then, in that moment – maybe because I wanted to self-destruct – but I kissed her just as I spotted Tabby walking towards us, the rhythm of her waddle familiar, drawing close.

I closed my eyes. Hoped she'd see. Hoped it would be enough to end us once and for all.

Actions speak louder than words, Rick.

Annabella

Now

Rick Priestly looks like the perfect man. Tonight, for example, he's dressed exactly as you'd expect, in a white shirt and dark jeans, a grey pair of trainers tied neatly to his feet. I wonder what terrible truth he's going to reveal this time about the girl I thought I knew so well. Kay's words from an earlier conversation play loud between my ears. 'You need to try and get hold of his phone, if you get the chance. But be careful, AB. Promise me.'

He stands under the orange glow of a streetlamp across the road, his hair tidy in his familiar side-swiped style. I recall the times I followed him from a safe distance, watched him from metres away, scared to get too close, and, for old times' sake, I pause, taking him in. I observe him undo his top button, adjust his shirt, check his watch, blow his breath on his hand, smell it, press mouth-freshener into his tongue, check his watch, check his phone, sigh. Then, just as he's been debating texting me something simple, but curt – *I'm here, outside the bar*; the implicit message clear: *Where are you? Why are you keeping me waiting?* – I smile and head over. It's an almost out-of-body experience – because now I am walking straight for him, about to say hello, placing myself willingly into his clutches. He hears me approach, heeled boots striking pavement, then looks up, my camel coloured coat breezing behind me. He throws his arms wide and angles his head back.

'There you are,' he beams.

I press my cheek against his and his hand presses firm against my back. I close my eyes, a queasy cocktail of excitement and horror bubbling in the pit of my stomach, as though I'm riding a rollercoaster but have suddenly discovered the safety bar isn't locked into position.

'Let's go in,' he says. Hungry eyes, red socks.

We sit at a two-seater table at the back of the bar. Vibey music and dim lights twinkle behind the heads of other couples on very different kinds of dates and the smell of expensive small plates – caviar canapes, sun-dried bruschetta, feta-stuffed grilled peaches – whizz by. Rick's back is to the room and I recall the elaborate dance he'd performed to get me into this position. First, he'd turned down every table in the house except this one – the one at the very back – then, when the waiter had pulled out my chair, the one Rick clearly wanted to sit in, Rick acted quickly to usurp him. He'd pulled out the other chair, then chastised the waiter.

'You're showing me up here, mate,' Rick joked, and the waiter blushed and pushed the chair back in. I probably wouldn't have picked up on the way he'd done it, if I hadn't known. But I'm fake-dating a man I can't trust, so I look out for these things. It's interesting, that I'm saying the word 'date', it's not as though Rick and I have discussed it – it's too taboo to bring up – but neither of us could deny that our frequent meet-ups have taken a turn, the place Rick's chosen for tonight's meal decidedly romantic. I'm blurring the lines, just as asked, surprised at how easy it's been.

'Shall I get us a bottle?' he asks, and I can't help but notice the stretch of his shirt against his arms.

'Sure,' I reply. 'Your choice.'

He flashes me a grin with wide, white teeth then heads over to the bar. In the meantime, I familiarise myself with my surroundings. A woman with a sharp face sits by herself at a table across. Black strands of her hair are stuck to the backless gape of her top and she's eating a tiny portion of steak, blood pooling from the meat onto her plate, chewing away at it, engrossed. It annoys me that she's not more alert, that her focus is entirely on her food. I might need a witness after tonight, I might need an alibi. Rick clouds my view of her as he returns, retaking the seat across.

'I Googled you the other day,' I tell him, a bottle of red wine reaching our table shortly afterwards.

'You did?' Rick asks, tentative.

'I wanted to read about what you've been through these past few years. What you've had to put up with.'

Rick takes my wine glass and pours me a large glass, filling his with half the amount. *Interesting tactic.* I will have to drink slowly, I won't let him top me up again. I won't go to the toilet in case he puts something in my glass.

'I read about a break-in…'

'Mmm,' he replies. 'I thought you might find out about that.' There's a brief pause before he speaks again. 'You've probably been wondering about me and Mandy.'

I bring the wine to my lips. 'You let me assume you were single.'

'Mandy and I have an arrangement.'

My mind flashes back to the bank statements I'd held between gloved fingers in the middle of the night, of the separate bedrooms they slept in.

'What kind?'

'It's complicated.'

I cock an eyebrow.

I think back to my months of surveillance. It would certainly explain the look he gives the spin-class instructor as she ups the resistance on her bike, how the barista at his favourite coffee shop flirts with him, the way he acts in front of me now, lusty eyed and hard jawed.

'What would happen if Mandy knew where you were tonight?'

'She wouldn't care,' he replies. 'We can see other people, we just have to be careful.'

'Is that what you'd say we're doing?' I ask. 'Seeing each other?'

Rick crosses his legs and laughs nervously to cover his embarrassment. 'I'm not sure what I'd call it. Do you have any ideas?'

I tuck my lips and look up at the ceiling. 'It's been nice.'

'You want to be careful, giving me compliments as gushing as that,' Rick jokes. 'But seriously, whatever this is, meeting up, catching up, why do we have to define it? We're enjoying each other's company. Why don't we leave the subject of Tabby alone tonight? Why don't we just pretend we're normal?'

We talk long into the night, the numbers in the bar thinning, the bubbles from the prosecco Rick's just ordered bursting behind my eyes. I learn that Rick's family haven't forgiven him for the rape charge Tabby filed against him at university, that people in the small community he comes from still call him names. Apparently, his younger brother was scouted for Norwich City Football Club when he was fifteen but, when headlines about Rick's rape made the papers, the club dropped his brother in favour of another rising star. 'That's the real reason they've never forgiven me,' Rick says. 'I go home once a year, for Christmas, deposit a load of shiny gifts then leave as quickly as I arrived. Behind my back they accuse me of "trying to buy their love" but when the shiny gifts aren't shiny enough, similarly accuse me of being "cheap" and "not caring about them anymore." It's lose-lose and one of these days I'm going to have to stop trying.'

I tell him I come from an unhappy family too.

Later, the bar grows rowdier, and he leads me outside, his palm wrapped tight to mine.

'I really like you, Annabella,' he says, curling a hand round my ear, bringing it down to my chin.

My stomach clenches and I take a moment before I reply.

'I've had a wonderful night.'

He breathes out, smiles at me, and I notice the way his cheekbones catch the light.

'Me too.'

He loops an arm behind my back and pulls me closer

and, though I know I should be scared, because of the wine I find that I'm not. I lean into him, holding him in return and, as our bodies press into each other, I feel the outline of his phone in his jacket pocket. The zip is sagging open, the phone within my reach. He looks down at me and lunges for my lips and, though my initial instinct is to pull away, in the rush, in the distraction, I use it to my advantage and press my fingers into his jacket and sneak his phone into the sleeve of my coat. I hold my lips against his for a second longer then release.

'Sorry,' he says, breaking away. 'I shouldn't have done that. I don't want to make this more complicated than it already is.'

'It's OK,' I reassure him. 'Life's complicated. Let's just take things slowly.'

He smiles at me, a sigh of relief leaving his puffed-up chest as I tell him not to worry, as I convince him that I feel the same way he feels about me. We part ways and I watch him walk into the night, his taste on my lips, his phone up my sleeve.

I know how this must look: late night following date night, four glasses of prosecco and half a bottle of wine down, sad mid-thirties woman installing a spyware app on her would-be lover's mobile phone round the corner from the bar he's just left her at. My mind spins with questions of whether I'm doing the right thing – but this will confirm it. If Rick isn't lying, he'll have nothing to hide.

I must be quick. I key in the code I'd memorised the day

I'd gone to Rick's spin class and watched him type it in. 303030.

Annabella never forgets.

I install the programme Kay suggested – *i-Spy* – and click through the various approvals, then I hide the app in a folder marked 'iPhone programmes' alongside a whole trove of apps Rick clearly never uses – Assistant, Watch, Voice memos – then I go back into the bar. I curl my hair up into a scruffy bun and take off my jacket – just in case someone remembers me – then head up to the manager whose finely-trimmed facial hair follows the curve of his jaw in rigid, right-angles.

'I found this on the table at the back,' I say, wide-eyed. 'Thought I should hand it in.'

I take a seat at the far end of the establishment, the opposite side to where Rick and I sat. I order a sparkling water from the server. I haven't been drunk for a long time and I need to sober up quickly, I must not let the alcohol get to me.

Fifteen minutes later, Rick appears, drizzle stuck to his face, vein pulsating over his forehead with the stress. I wonder if he'd been thinking about texting me and had gone for his pocket to pick up his phone, his brain running draft messages, the words clumping together, replaced with worry when he found it wasn't there. I sink lower into my seat and angle my body behind a group in front of me, my eyes glued to Rick as his powerful arms gesticulate towards the manager.

Before he can finish his sentence, the man with the finely trimmed beard bends beneath the desk and, between the menus and the extra cutlery, fishes for Rick's phone. He hands it back to him with a wide smile.

'That was lucky,' I watch him mouth, over-excited.

I wait until I've finished my water and, just as I'm swallowing the dregs, a plum-faced early-twenties ex-Rugby boy with drowsy eyes makes his way towards me, slamming a half-swigged pint of lager on my table, his mouth halfway to opening. *'What's a girl like you doing all alone on a night like—'*

I leave.

The rain is coming down harder now and I let it soak me, sumptuous drops splashing my face as I stride home. I can't stop thinking about Rick. We kissed. I didn't pull away. Then I betrayed him. The solid lines I'd drawn between the real me and the me who sees Rick are blurring, the rain running the ink together so it's impossible to see where one ends and the other begins. *What do I think about him now? Who do I trust?*

I power down the final home-straight, cars blinking, the wider London skyline sparkling to the East, high-rises glittering through the darkness.

I push my palm into my key, twisting it to the left, then open the door. My phone buzzes in my pocket, a message from i-Spy, sent to Rick's phone then forwarded to mine, glows:

Stop what you're doing, Rick. Trust me, this path doesn't end well for you.

Tabby

Thirteen Years Ago – 2007

I locked the door to my bubble-gum bedroom and sat in the dark by myself, the baby kicking up against my ribs. I felt young here, childlike, far too young to be carrying a baby of my own.

I'd gone to a refuge when I'd found out I was pregnant, stayed with Rick in between, then came crawling back to my foster parents when it all imploded. At first, they weren't interested in helping me. They saw it like this: now that I was pregnant, I was an adult. Now that I was pregnant, I was bringing them another mouth to feed, another burden to bear, another problem to solve, more forms to fill in. Then, when I threatened to tell the council that I'd been living away and that they'd been claiming their allowance fraudulently, they let me back in. Said I could stay for a few nights while we worked things out.

It had only been a week, but they'd made their feelings clear: they wanted me gone. They'd called my bluff, spoke to our local authority, and told them I'd been in and out of their care for the last few months, that they hadn't known that I was pregnant, that I'd run away and come back more times than they could keep up with, that I was behaving erratically and that they couldn't cope anymore. They needed me gone. As soon as possible.

My biological parents. My grandfather. My boyfriend. My foster parents. All of them have left me. And, even though it's not here yet, the baby will too. The baby will be taken away as soon as it arrives, and I'll be alone.

I imagined Marie, my real mother, coming to me tonight, turning up on the front door with a giant teddy bear, a bag of sweets, and the news that she'd won the lottery.

'Sorry I abandoned you, baby,' she'd whisper, and I'd hold my head, blurry-eyed, against her body, warmth radiating from her. Home.

Knowing that would never happen pushed me to a darker place. I never asked for this life and, honestly, I was sick of it. No one wanted me here.

I sifted through the boxes under my bed, looking in all of my old hiding places for something I could use. In the first box, I found a pen knife. I unfurled it, a little rusty, and pressed the blade against my skin, poking holes in my hand, wincing as I dared myself to dig in and draw blood. I kitten-yowled as a perfect ruby appeared beneath the tip of it, pricking the end of my index finger, testing the limits of my bravery and coming up short.

I stuck my hand in to the next box and pulled out a newspaper article. *Marie Rice, 38, is wanted in connection with a number of robberies in the East London area, but has skipped bail and is on the run.* I clutched it and red glistened beneath my grip on one side, spoiling the article. I threw it down and jammed my finger into my mouth, blood on my lips, rolling down my chin.

In the next box, I found an ancient bottle of vodka, the label flaking away. I opened it, brought it to my lips, then chugged it, brightening as the liquid roared at the pit of my stomach.

'What are you waiting for?' my foster mother hissed at me, her long, wiry hair curling round my neck like a boa constrictor, tying me tighter, my face changing from pink to blue. A hallucination. It must have been.

I staggered to standing, dribbling on my sweater, the vodka rushing to my head. I pulled open the drawer beneath my bedside table and retrieved a packet of pills I'd been given for my acne when I was a teenager. I'd stopped taking them a year ago and there was a warning on the front. The first thing you saw when you picked this medication up: *Roaccutane can seriously harm unborn babies. Women must use effective contraception when using this drug.* I pulled out some other pills from underneath, painkillers, mostly.

I burst the seals, took the vodka, wanting to escape, wanting all of this to end. I dialled Rick after it was done.

'I'm sorry,' I slurred, or texted, I can't remember which, maybe both. Then I downed the rest of the bottle and closed my eyes, waiting for someone to lead me out of this life and into a better one.

Annabella

Now

'Someone's threatening Rick,' I rush to tell Kay, breathless into the mouthpiece as I catch a cab to see her.

'What? Slow down. Who?'

'I just got back from drinks with Rick and... *shit*.' I swear, not a particular habit of mine, but it's hard to find the words.

'Come over,' Kay told me. 'Quick as you can.'

She hangs up and I try to steady my breath, the cab driver's eyes twitching over me. My mind rushes to Rick and I think about calling him to check he's not in trouble. I steady myself. That's not the right thing to do.

'You OK?' the taxi driver asks from the front, the intercom system clicking on and off.

'Fine,' I tell him, rubbing my hand against my forehead. *Am I OK?*

Drained of energy, I head inside Kay's home for the second

time in as many weeks. Ever since Kay had taken my hand and pulled me deeper into this case, my perceptions have tilted, shifted on their axis, and I'm beginning to wonder if this is going to end the way I'd planned, the way I'd hoped.

Sitting at Kay's kitchen table in the middle of the night – sweater sleeves pulled into my fists to avoid touching its surface – I show her the message.

Her sleepy eyes fall to the screen in front of us and she pushes highlighted articles and overfilled folders out of the way to bring it towards her. Kay's always working on a million projects at once – commissions, consulting for TV documentaries, sniffing for stories for her podcast series – but still she finds the time for me. She's a good friend, and an even better detective.

'It's very threatening, isn't it?' Kay marvels. 'Though I hate to say it, death threats aren't uncommon in these types of investigations. We should take it as good news; it means we're getting closer. Have you run the number?'

'No,' I tell her.

Kay takes the phone from the table, squinting at the number, then runs it through an online database. A few moments later, she scowls at the screen. 'Nothing,' she says. 'Not that I'm surprised.'

'On my way over, I was wondering, what if it's the same person as the doctor? What if he's out to get them both?' I can hear the panic in my voice. 'What if Rick had nothing to do with Tabby's disappearance? What if this message proves it?'

'Slow down,' Kay tells me. 'Let's be logical,' she says. 'And I want you to bear something in mind: we only know about the doctor in the first place because we're taking Rick's word for it.'

I squeeze my eyes shut. 'He didn't know I knew about Turkey. That's how I know he's telling the truth.' I can't believe I'm sticking up for him, but here we are.

'Let's rewind for a moment,' Kay says, focused on the message in front of her. 'The night you found those bank statements. What if the payments Rick made have something to do with this message? Whoever he's paying could well be blackmailing him in other ways.'

I jump on the thread, filling Kay in with the details from our dinner. 'Rick told me something,' I say, recalling his words. 'He was cagey with the details, but admitted that he and Mandy have some sort of arrangement.'

Kay scrawls Mandy's name on her notepad. Her image comes to me then: the damsel who I'd distressed, crushing her petrified face in on itself the night I broke into her home. I can't stop thinking about what I have done to get here, flashes of myself that night play in maddening loops. When I open my eyes, Kay's partner Tom is standing at the threshold of the kitchen door in navy blue pyjamas.

'Sorry, I'm keeping you both up,' I rush to say, embarrassed by my presence in their home at this time of night.

'No not to worry, you're doing important work, don't mind me,' he says reassuringly, moving towards Kay to say goodnight. She doesn't lose her focus as he leans in to kiss her forehead, but mumbles something to him about being up in a minute. When he pulls away, I notice his fingernails are dirty, black crescent-moons on each tip. My stomach loosens, but I bite through my queasiness to wish him goodnight, reminding myself that he likes to work in the garden and that I'm one with the problem, not him.

Kay looks up at me. 'This is what I think,' Kay says, pouring herself a glass of water from the cloudy pitcher on the table – goodness knows how long it's been there. 'I think Mandy knows what happened to Tabby and Rick's paying her to keep quiet. What if they were together for a while, then, I don't know, Mandy found something Rick couldn't explain away. After that, he had no choice but to tell her what happened. He couldn't kill her, that would be too obvious. So now he pays for her silence and their relationship is... well, like he said, it's more of an arrangement.'

The tips of my fingers ice.

'And now she's worried the pipeline's about to be switched off,' Kay says. 'Because of you.'

Kay flips back to the first page of her pad, drawing a circle round Mandy's name. 'All roads lead to Mandy. We need to find her.'

There's something acutely embarrassing about going to dinner alone.

'Table for one?' the waitress asks, purely in the hope I'll correct her as I loiter by the *Please wait to be seated* sign. It's not as bad at lunchtime, completely acceptable over coffee, but dinner by yourself is, frankly, indulgent. Suspicious. Why would anyone choose to sit in a sweaty mass of people if the other option is a home-cooked meal and a night in front of the TV? Unless you're travelling, of course, in which case... why not get room service? There must be something very, very wrong if what you've decided to do with your evening is spend it isolated in the noisy company of strangers. All these thoughts run through my head as I reply to the bespectacled waitress, cursing Kay for being at some 'concert' she couldn't miss. I like the idea that the concert isn't her choice, but her teenager daughter's, and that Kay's catatonic in a mass of squawking girls, each screaming slightly different lyrics at the top of their lungs to a clutch of baby-faced popstars. Kay loves these missions, if it wasn't something like that, she'd have dropped everything to join me, even though I only asked her thirty minutes ago.

'Yes, just me,' I reply, forcing a smile and following the waitress inside. 'Actually, could I take this table?' I ask, hopeful.

I withhold the fact that I've been loitering outside the restaurant for half an hour waiting for this *particular* table to become available.

'Sure,' she says breezily and clears the lipstick-stained glasses and dirty tableware from the table-for-two behind Mandy and her friend.

This is why I am here.

I'd paid a visit to my favourite Battersea residence after work today, arriving just in time to see Mandy shooting out of the door. I'd noticed the lights were off in the rest of the house which meant Rick wasn't home yet. I'd wondered where she was going, all dressed up, hair straightened, the bruises I'd given her painted over, faded skinny jeans seemingly sprayed to her legs, and had thought, just for a moment, that she might be meeting another man. I was wrong, though. Tonight was just dinner with a girlfriend. 'Table for two', one of them will have said to the same waitress earlier on, her request met with a nod and silent social acceptance. Dinner with a friend is good, really good, the sign of all being well, of normal adults enjoying one another's company, the waitress would have wanted Mandy and her pal to think she was one of them so she'd have smiled, joked with them, asked them how they were doing tonight. She'd frowned at me, of course, she'd wanted me to know that she wasn't a table-for-one kind of girl, not like me. I imagine she's already bitching about me to another waitress.

I sit facing them, Mandy's back to me and, as soon as the waitress leaves, I edge the table closer so I can overhear their conversation. I check my face in my compact mirror: I've probably overdone it on the lip fillers recently, but the doll look is in fashion, so I'm lucky. I've drawn my eyebrows in long arches across my brow bones and parted my hair centrally, so I look a little different. I imagine my name would be something like Jodie, or Josephine. I duck my lashes to the mirror as I close it, hide half of my face behind my sweeping, two-tone hair, and lean on my palm, elbow on the table, as I edge closer, hoping I'm not too late for the gossip. I note that they've already eaten, their main courses cleared, but a half-drunk bottle of wine sits expectantly on the table.

'It's one thing after the next for you, darling,' says Mandy's friend, chocolate corkscrew curls looping down her back. 'You just can't catch a break. Poor duck.'

As I listen, I'm handed a menu and told the specials are tikka turkey, lamb rolls and pork stew.

'I'm pescatarian, actually, do you have anything?'

I don't mind the idea of eating fish, swimming in fresh water most of their lives, but the thought of ingesting pigs and chickens and cattle, forced to live in cages ridden with their own excrement, is just, frankly, revolting. I struggle with vegetables from manured fields, too. I refuse to buy organic. I'd much rather my vegetables grow thanks to chemical intervention than being coated with faecal matter.

'Oh yah, of course, the grilled cod is good or, the black bean potato bake?' replies the waitress, her pseudo-posh accent jarring with the rest of her look: tattoos, pink hair, large-framed glasses.

'Great, I'll get the cod.' I hesitate for a moment, but know I have to ask, 'This is an odd request… but, could you make sure the separate parts of the meal don't touch?'

She pauses for a moment. God knows what she's thinking. Then she replies, saying far too much to reassure me.

'Absolutely, no problem at all. Separate, like, cod one side, lentils the other, kale at the bottom. I get it, believe me, I've had much stranger requests than that.' She hasn't.

'I'll get that going for you right away, miss,' she says, pity in her eyes.

'Thanks so much,' I reply, embarrassed, unwrapping my scarf from my neck, static buzzing in its fibres.

I wonder what Rick's doing for dinner tonight.

I turn my attention back to Mandy and, now that I'm able to get a proper look, I can see she's emotional about something.

'There's nothing I can do to change your mind?' Mandy pleads, her sleeve under her nose, slimy trail left behind. 'I just want to go back, you know, undo it all.'

Her friend grabs her hand and I look away, close my eyes, focus only on what she's saying to Mandy, doing my best to drown out the background noise. 'I'm sorry, Mandy, but the feedback has been the same for a while. Production companies won't touch you with your association to a suspected killer, especially with this podcast blowing up.' *This is her agent, not her friend.* 'You've been standing by him since the break-in and all it does is make you look culpable. Times have changed, bad publicity isn't better than no publicity in 2020. My advice is to get out, move abroad and start again somewhere else. Canada, perhaps, there's good work to be had over there. I'm sorry, Mandy, but I can't help you anymore.'

I follow Mandy home, the patter of rain against my umbrella, and hang back when I reach her cul-de-sac, taking a moment to let her get ahead – women are far more aware of people following them, so I have to be careful. Once I'm confident she's inside, I power-walk along the pavement, check the couple at number 50 haven't returned from holiday yet, then head determinedly for their garden. I creak their shed door open to shelter from the weather, careful not to attract any unwanted attention, hit by the faint smell of moss, then settle down to the perfect view of my favourite house.

I watch Mandy flit between rooms, curling her hair into a twisty bun on the back of her head, pouring a glass of water, snacking on something small from the refrigerator and sighing as she picks up her phone, reading something on the screen with increasing irritation. I can only imagine what it might say: *Sorry. Working late tonight. And tomorrow. Don't wait up. R.*

Rick

Thirteen Years Ago – 2007

The ambulance sped through the centre of Oxford to the hospital, the roads cramped with people and vehicles, Tabby gurgling from the stretcher, me rattling in the jump seat by her side, my hands pressed hard against my head, trying to keep it in place.

Tabby was punch-drunk and pill-filled, her cheeks covered with bile, her legs covered with blood. I wanted to hit her, shout at her. *Are you fucking crazy?* Not that I needed the answer.

I'd arrived at her foster parents' place, breathless. She'd sent me a strange text, then a voicemail, and, as soon as I heard her slurring, I ran over to make sure she was OK. The spectacled face of her foster dad eyed me up on the way in. Ever since Tabby fell pregnant, the milk was somewhat spilt, so they'd given up trying to keep me from her, but it didn't mean they had to like me, or let me in. I didn't give them much of a chance when I arrived, barging past her father and taking the stairs up to her bedroom two at a time. I'd thumped on her door to shouts of, 'What on *earth* do you think you're doing?' behind me. When she didn't answer, I tried to force it open, and, when that didn't work, I tried to kick it down, shouting at her slack-jawed parents to call for help. The wood splintered under my heavy shoe and I didn't have to step into the room to know something was horribly wrong. It almost hummed, a silent chant of foreboding that linked with the dark orange glow of her bedside lamp. I poked my head closer and what I saw sent a jackhammer scream from my body. I froze, for a moment, with the shock.

Tabby was leaking ruby-red blood, some of it thick and black, onto the carpet, empty packets of pills by her side, a bottle of vodka in her hand. *Drip, drip, drip*, it went.

'What have you done?' I half-screamed, half-cried at her burbling body, and the angry, protective father that had been developing somewhere inside me wanted to strangle her for hurting our child. Instead, I picked her up, twitching and urgent, a vein throbbing over her foster father's temple as I'd shouted at him to *move!*

Her head had lolled backwards as we'd passed him, then jerked up, spraying blood all over me in vengeful protest as I'd carried her outside. I'd waited on the pavement for the ambulance, Tabby fading in my arms, my shirt stained in her mistake.

I watched the Oxford lights fade into the distance, the blue from the sirens overhead the only thing I could see, that and miles of tarmacked road stretching out ahead.

'Your girlfriend… she's going to be OK,' the paramedic said, her luminous jacket too big for her body. Tabby groaned in the bed as we lurched over a bump in the road – clumsy and confuddled.

'What about the baby?' I asked.

'We'll have to wait for the scan,' she replied, smiling bravely at me. 'You be strong for her, OK, lad?'

She took in the blood splatter all over my top and read me wrongly, thought I could handle this, that I was someone who'd be strong enough to step up. Actions speak louder than words. She saw me faltering and drew close. 'Listen, lad, people don't try to kill themselves because they want to, they do it because they feel as though they don't have any other choice. Go easy on her when she wakes up.'

Was she right? I look at Tabby's milk-white face and imagine what she'd say if she could speak. *You chose Saskia once, I accused you of rape. You chose Saskia twice, I killed our baby.*

How long did she want to keep doing this dance?

How long did I?

Annabella

An alert flashes bright on my phone screen, barely morning outside, the blue light making me squint. *Breaking News, Live Episode*.

'Good morning, everyone,' Kay says, her tone solemn. 'Further details about the body found buried on Brimley Farm in Dartford have been released.'

It's Kay's first live episode, and I have to say I like the immediacy of it, the up-to-the-minute reporting that ensures her show isn't left behind.

'Police say the victim's hands and teeth had been removed before burial, they believe this was a deliberate effort to obscure the victim's identity. The body itself is in a bad state of decomposition and police can only identify the victim as a white female with a small oval-shaped birthmark on her stomach.'

My heart pounds, pushing blood from my head to my gut. I try to remember if Tabby had a small birthmark on her stomach but can't be sure. What had the killer done to her face that meant it couldn't be identified?

'In a further development, a police dog team are in action at Brimley Farm this morning… I suppose the authorities are wondering if this is the only body on the property.'

After the broadcast, I send a Kay a message.

> Do you have any more info that you couldn't say on air?

> That's it. But the gambler in me guesses the body is Tabby's mother. We haven't been able to track her down and the way Ernie spoke about her… it still chills me.

There's a brief pause as Kay types out the second part of her message.

> While we wait for more on the body… I have news for you.

I sit up, awaiting my instructions.

> Mandy's a member of some running club in Battersea. She goes every Saturday. A decent number of them belong to the run club's Facebook group. Anyway, I spoke to a few… Mandy's been out of acting work for a while, apparently. And, according to the people I spoke to, she keeps her private life very private. They know she's in a long-term relationship but, from what they were saying, she doesn't speak about Rick. At all.

I read Kay's message wondering where she is. I can never imagine her calming down enough to sleep so, even though it's early morning, I struggle to picture her in bed. I suspect she lies there every night, for a while, then has an idea too good to forget so springs out again, grabbing a scrap piece of paper from the myriad littering the floor to jot it down. She probably repeats the process until the sun rises and she can get going all over again.

You found all this out from a Facebook group?

Don't sound so surprised! I know how to get information from people… it's what I do. Anyway, you're going there today. You have two hours. Grab your running shoes.

I scroll down to another message, from Rick.

Dinner this week? X

The run club's Saturday jog loops a series of pretty parks in South London. Green open spaces, tree-lined and grassy, the vista slightly frosty in the winter air. Mandy's figure is all muscle in front of me, save for a crazed halo of hair, pulled scrappily into a ponytail. She wears full-length leggings, svelte over her angles, and a money belt that bobs in time with her strides.

Though Kay had thought about joining us on the loop, she'd decided that taking part in physical activity might blow her cover. '*I haven't exercised in years,*' she told me. '*I don't think I could run for five minutes let alone five kilometres! You stick with her, but not too close, give her space, but talk to her, let her know you like her shoes or something, or ask for help. Tell her you work in TV – so she thinks you might be able to help her career – and that you're newly single – make sure she knows you're single, she might reach out to you about her failing relationship – but don't leave her with the impression you're hitting on her.'*

I'd ended our conversation a little confused and told Kay I'd try my best. She clearly didn't think that was good enough so she told me she'd sit in a car at the start/finish of the loop so we could catch up afterwards. I imagined her now in her burgundy Volvo, a near-PI-parody pair of dark glasses covering most of her face, baseball cap pulled low to her nose, fiddling with the wind-down windows, adjusting her shirt, unable to sit still.

Mandy and I, along with twenty or so other runners, pound the tarmac back to the starting point and, though I'm almost last, I am proud that I have manged to keep up with them. An older man whose shorts are white and nappy-like, with droopy skin that's slipped down his face and gathered at his jaw – gravity from the constant up down, up down, of running pulling hard at his features – accosts me as I pace over to Mandy.

'Has anyone ever told you how beautiful you are?' he asks, sweat fizzing across his forehead.

'Oh, that's sweet, thank you,' I reply through a quarter-smile, wondering, genuinely, where he thinks this conversation will go next. And then I have an idea – use it to my advantage.

'You know, my boyfriend used to, but he dumped me

four months ago so...' I almost shout the line, hoping Mandy will hear.

'Why would anyone get rid of a pretty thing like you?'

My skin crawls as the man draws closer, his words sticking to me like blood-thirsty leeches. It's then that Mandy turns – her features finally facing me – and I assess quickly that, in addition to the Botox, she's had a nose job. It doesn't suit the round of the rest of her face – it's too tiny and pinched and it unbalances her. She should have come to me for a consultation, I'd have advised her to keep more width, personally. Her eyes are dark and she's wearing false lashes – even for a run – and, if I wanted to sum her up after this second first impression, I'd go for... insecure.

She turns to me, looks me dead in the eyes, and – just for a second, I think she's going to intervene, to ask if I need any help – but instead she looks horrified and walks away.

I hesitate, my legs stuck for a moment before gathering myself to race in her direction, nappy-man bleating something about catching up next week. I can't let her slip through my fingers; Kay would be furious.

'Hey,' I pant, running after her. 'Do you mind if I join you for a moment? That guy...' I gesture behind me. 'He won't leave me alone.'

She doesn't make eye contact. 'Sure,' she says, though I can tell she's uneasy about speaking to me. She'd be even less keen to speak to me if she knew how much time I'd been spending with Rick.

'I was actually hoping to talk to you earlier,' I blurt, my mouth moving before my brain has a chance to engage.

'You were?' she asks, audibly surprised. 'About...?'

'Your leggings, I wanted to ask where you got them from. They're gorgeous.'

We look down at her black leggings simultaneously. They're nice, sure, but they're not particularly special. They're certainly not *gorgeous*.

Kay's voice rings between my ears: *Make sure you don't come off like you're hitting on her.*

Mandy shrugs, the breeze fluttering at her ponytail, and I can tell she's trying to figure me out: lesbian, true-crime fan-girl, psycho, or... hopefully just a nervous newbie? My brain plays me an unhelpful reminder of the last time we were stood in such proximity: the night I'd caved in her skull and left her bleeding on the carpet. If Mandy knew all that I had done to her, she would wish me dead.

'Nike,' she replies curtly, revealing the obvious white swoosh on the right side of the design. This only serves to make me look more stupid and I realise I have to think on my feet, like Kay does, find Mandy's weakness, feel my way into the corners of her mind.

The problem is, if it is Mandy behind the messages, as Kay suspects, then what if she followed Rick the other night and saw me? If I'm not honest about who I am and what I want, I could well lose my chance to speak to her.

'Listen,' I begin. 'I know this is going to sound bizarre, but I'm part of a team making a podcast about the disappearance of Tabitha Rice.'

Mandy's expression completely changes when I say these words, her anxious half-smile replaced with one hard line, and she takes a step backwards. She wants to get away from me.

'I don't want to scare you, I just think we could use your

DO HER NO HARM

help. We've found some things out about Rick that might interest you. Our lead reporter is just around the corner. She'd love to talk to you.' Mandy's eyes dart to the corners of their sockets as she looks. 'What do you say?' I ask. 'Do you want to meet her? Do you want to help?'

I add an extra incentive, learning from Kay, and the image of Mandy's agent dumping her looms large in my mind. 'You know, we're in talks with a Hollywood production company. They want to make this whole thing into a film. You could be a part of that if you join us.'

Her false eyelashes flutter and, after a moment of weighing up her options, agrees.

We home in on Kay in her beat-up Volvo and I watch her twitch and turn, moving up in her seat as she spots me, then shrinking down when Mandy comes into view behind. She paws at her cap, pulls it lower when she thinks I might just be passing by and don't want her to be seen, but then I call her name and her face creases like wrapping paper.

'It's all right,' I tell Kay. 'I told Mandy about the podcast. She knows who you are.' Kay's eyes slide towards Mandy and she plasters a false smile on her face. 'And about the Hollywood production company.'

'Does she now?' Kays replies, picking up on my meaning, our brief eye contact not a million miles away from an exchange of elongated winks.

'What is it that you want from me, specifically?' Mandy asks nervously when we're all inside.

Kay and I sit straight in the front, our bodies facing forward, and Mandy's in the back, as though we're a couple of police officers who've just arrested her. Her eyes tennis-ball between us as we speak, my gaze fixed on the rear-view mirror, the smell of pear-drops and dust crowding my nostrils.

'We just want to ask you a few questions, that's all,' Kay begins softly. 'And, listen,' she continues. 'AB and I were both shocked to hear about the break-in and your head injury.' Mandy touches her hand to the area. 'How's your recovery going?'

Mandy smiles like a survivor might smile. 'I'm getting there.'

'Rick told the police, and the papers, that nothing went missing that night. What's your theory – that you caught the intruder before they could nab what they'd come looking for?'

'I have no idea, it was all such a blur. I'm just thankful I'm still here to tell the tale.'

I shift in my seat.

'Do you mind if I ask you a few questions about your boyfriend?' Kay asks next, a few short-hand notes scribbled across her pen and paper.

'Sure,' Mandy replies, timid, and I observe her body language: her arms are crossed over her middle and her strong shoulders are hunched inwards. I wonder if we're in quite the right venue for Mandy's guard to drop. She's a clean, Farrow-and-Ball kind of girl, the pantones of today's dark running outfit carefully curated. Death's Whisper on her upper half, Pagan Grey on her feet. I think we need to take a different tack, be less combative. I shuffle round in the chair so we're facing each other. I want her to relax, I want her to feel safe. I want her to trust me, to let me in.

'Tell me about him, Mandy,' I say gently. 'What's he like as a partner? You've been together for a little while now…'

She brings her hands up to her triceps and squeezes them absent-mindedly. 'He's great,' she replies. 'I love him.'

'Really?' I probe. 'Things can't have been easy. You've had a spotlight on your relationship for as long as you've been together.'

She half-smiles in return, her eyes angled towards the floor of the car, a couple of Kay's discarded energy drink cans and a splattering of crumbs littering the footwell. 'We do our best.'

'We know about the arrangement, Mandy,' Kay interjects, snapping her neck to the rear-view mirror to analyse Mandy's immediate reaction. Fireplace Red splashes Mandy's face.

I swallow hard. *What's the plan here, Kay?*

'Tell me about it,' Kay presses.

Mandy sighs, moves her hands to her face, visibly weighing up her options, years of tightly woven secrets about to unravel.

'He'd kill me if I told anyone,' Mandy says, wiping the perspiration from her forehead with the sleeve of her running jacket. 'But, honestly, I just want it to stop,' she mutters, her admission hanging in the cramped space between us. 'I should go,' she says, grabbing at the door handle, the panic clear in her voice.

'Listen,' Kay says. 'Why don't I give you my number?' Kay fishes for something in her wallet, overstuffed with receipts and loyalty cards and a couple of loose notes. 'Here you go,' she announces proudly, passing Mandy a business card, coffee ring on the front.

'Think about it and, if you want to tell us anything else about your boyfriend, or the night Tabitha Rice disappeared, you give me a call.'

'What about the production company?' Mandy asks, her soft voice hardening. 'Can I meet them?'

'Only if you talk to us first.'

Mandy nods, pulls the door handle, and makes to leave.

When the door's shut behind her, her strong figure disappearing into the distance, Kay and I exchange a look.

'Good work,' Kay tells me, revving the engine. 'I think she's going to talk.'

Tabby

Thirteen Years Ago – 2007

Imuttered a ring of sorrys as the doctor hurried towards the door, and then Rick was in the frame instead, bringing in the freezing air from outside, his eyes blinking back cold tears. Between blinks, he tried to find the right thing to say.

'You're awake.'

He shut the door and curled his arms up to his chest, his young hair brushed to one side. He looked like a teenager in a sulk, but the people here knew him as the man who'd lost a child today.

'Are you OK?' he asked.

He looked at me, then looked quickly away.

'I'm sorry,' I said, then fell asleep.

I drifted in and out of consciousness, the medication I was on shifting me from one blur to the next. When I woke up later, Rick was scooting away from me, padding out of the room. I could hear him rustling, the bed creaking every time he resumed his position by my side. I liked having him there, and I wished he wouldn't keep getting up.

'Don't leave,' I groaned, the next time he moved, a pair of too-big brogues on his feet.

'Tabby?' he asked, moving bloodshot eyes in line with mine. 'What you did last night, Tabby –' I raised my hand, interrupting him. I didn't want to hear it.

'I'm sorry,' I told him again.

'Why didn't you call me earlier? If I'd known you were planning something like this, anything like this, I could have helped. You could have spoken to me.'

I lazed my eyes shut once again, machines bleeping beyond, and tilted my tired head away from him, the relentless sway of his verbal tango dipping me backwards.

I could feel the void left in my belly, the emptiness. For the first time in months, I was alone, just as I knew I would be, except—

'Rick?' I asked, my voice scratchy.

'What?'

'Thank you for being here.'

Rick shifted, moved closer. 'You know I'll always be here for you, no matter what.'

'That's not true.'

I tugged at the cannula on my hand, it was itching me, sore, and I wanted it off. Rick's hand wrapped around mine and I felt him move the cannula back into position, relieving the pain.

'Why are you still here?' I asked. 'Don't you hate me?'

His grey-blue eyes misted once more. 'Never,' he said, wrapping me into him.

Annabella

Now

The i-Spy app twinkles and I read the message that's just been sent to Rick from the same unknown number.

You can't hide who you are forever. Your truth will out, Rick.

The message weighs heavy in my hands and, as my mind whirrs with questions, I decide to pace the pavements to Rick's house and capture his mood first-hand. I have a plan, I need him to talk, and I know what to use to make him sing. Kay would be proud of me, her protégé striking out on her own, acting on instinct. The wind gusts as I close in, blowing my hair from my face. In the frosted glass of a passing window I see that my nose is pink at the tip, my cheeks reddened from exertion. Crisp air fills my nostrils, propelling me forward. Around me, the breeze combs the tops of the trees to one side, smoothing the branches to a capital-wide side-parting.

I press the doorbell and wait for Rick to answer, noticing that I'm dressed in the same outfit as when we met at Rick's spin class all those weeks ago. I pull out my phone to text Kay, to let her know where I am, then decide against it, knowing she'll want the full story in one go rather than in two halves. Dewdrops of perspiration dot the Lycra stretched over my limbs, uncomfortably warm beneath my puffy winter coat.

Eventually, the door creaks open and a thicket of tawny hair appears in the gap, Rick Priestley's smiling face below it.

'Annabella!' he exclaims. 'What are you doing here?'

'We need to talk,' I tell him, and he stands aside.

My eyes bounce over the muted colours of the hallway, stairs leading to the second floor and the cream carpet I well remember. For a moment, I replay taking those stairs two-at-a-time as I'd fled the scene, Rick's voice bouncing off the walls behind me, *Mandy…Is everything OK?* but I force myself to move on and scuff my feet into the hallway doormat.

'Drink?' he asks simply, coiling a hand round my waist, moving me towards him, leaning in to kiss me.

'Sure,' I smile, letting his warm lips touch mine. Again. This situation is a mess.

We part and, just as I'm about to follow him into the kitchen, my eyes zero in on someone in the pictures, a woman with light blonde hair looping either side of her face in soft curls. Her face is round and red and, what arrests me first, is how much this person looks like Tabby.

'Hey,' I call out. 'This girl here…' I squint closer. 'Is that Tabby?'

Rick moves back this way, a pair of orange socks on his feet. 'Ah,' he says. 'Yes. I love that picture. I took it on one of the morning shifts at McDonald's.' My eyebrows raise, he hasn't mentioned this before. 'I used to work there at university, Tabby would keep me company on the quiet days.'

He hands me a glass of white – I won't drink it – but I take it with thanks and find myself loitering at the frames a moment longer than I should. 'Is something the matter?' he asks.

'No, I just...' I begin. 'It's nice.'

'What do you mean?' he asks, moving closer.

'That you keep her here. And that Mandy doesn't mind,' I say, gesturing towards the picture.

I look away from the frames and over at Rick, shrugging his shoulders to his ears. Why would he keep a picture of Tabby on display if he killed her? The story behind it seemed genuine too. The devil's advocate in me weighs in: *He's bluffing, Annabella, why can't you see it? You're falling for every trick in his book.*

'Sorry,' I reply. 'I'm prying – I shouldn't have said anything.'

'Don't be silly. Do you want to come through?' he asks, smiling to cover the awkward moment I've created.

I sit gently into one of the sofas, pulling my arms from my coat.

'Can I take that?' Rick asks, and I hand him my jacket, watching him pace out of my eyeline for a moment as he hangs it up. I cross my feet, my legs, then my arms, twitching nervously as I try to clear my head.

'Tabby,' he sighs, when he comes back in. 'When am I ever going to get out from under that girl's shadow?' His eyes grey. 'It's not as though I want to forget her, or what's happened, it's just... exhausting.'

'Sorry,' I say quickly. 'I didn't mean to upset you.'

He creases his features as he sits on the sofa opposite.

'What did you want to talk to me about?' he asks.

I wiggle into the sofa cushion and recite the sentence I'd rehearsed on my way over, knowing it's what I need to do to make him talk. 'I don't think we should see each other anymore.'

I watch as he falters, hurt and surprise twisting together across his face. 'Why?' he manages to ask. 'Because of Tabby?'

'No,' I reply. 'Because of Mandy,' I say, avoiding eye contact. 'You told me you have an arrangement and that's fine – I don't want to push you to tell me the ins and outs of what it is, because that's between you – but I don't feel comfortable seeing you until your arrangement is done. How do I know you're not telling me one thing and her another? She lives here, her pictures are on the walls, her pyjamas will probably be tucked under her pillow upstairs. It's not right.'

Rick covers his face with his hands.

'Until it's over, and I mean properly over, I think we should call time on whatever this is between us.'

'I understand,' Rick says after a while.

He looks at the floor, pulling his thoughts together, and I can tell he's going to talk, that he's going to tell me about his and Mandy's arrangement, my first attempt at using reverse psychology working wonders.

'Mandy and I...' he explains. 'Our relationship isn't real. She's an actress. I hire her to play a role.'

The separate bedrooms. The payments. It's her they're going to. Kay was right.

'At first it was temporary. The media had been on my back, another day another story about my killer instinct, another friend-of-a-friend-of-a-friend-of-a-friend filling column inches with lies. I needed someone to change the narrative, to prove that I was capable of being loved, that there was someone who'd chosen to be with me despite what the papers were saying. Despite what everybody thought about me at the time.'

He gives me a look, and I can tell he's talking about me, about the way I'd turned my back on him.

'The problem was, I didn't want to date anyone new, I wasn't ready.'

I sit up a little straighter, not sure if I'm impressed or horrified. I understand, in a way, why he did it. The media were relentless. They still are. And now I'm one of them.

Kay was right about the payments, but not the motivation. Rick's not paying Mandy to hide from the press, he's paying her to be seen.

I swallow the fleeting guilt I feel, this recurring feeling of getting Rick wrong all too familiar. What he's done with Mandy is duplicitous, certainly, but it's not murder, and it's not as though she's been an unwilling participant.

'How did you convince Mandy?' I ask.

'I met her at a theatre club and, yeah, I took a gamble, guessed she'd need the money.

'It's probably a lot to take in,' he says, stating the obvious. 'Mandy and I have been talking for a while about ending the arrangement, but then the break-in happened, this podcast came out, and now I'm back to square one.'

I cast my eyes to the side.

'If I had my way, the arrangement would continue until the noise dies down. If she leaves me now, the papers will hound her for tell-alls and I don't have the money to match those kinds of deals. But Mandy is desperate to get out, and I understand why: she's losing work, she's been fired by her agent. We're not in a good place. She wants compensation, she's threatening legal action.'

An alarm sounds on my phone. I have to be at work in twenty minutes.

'I'm sorry, Rick, I have to go,' I say, silencing the alarm. 'But thank you for telling me the truth. It means a lot that you trust me to keep your secret.'

'Wait,' he says, reaching for my hand as I get up from my seat. 'I need to tell you something.'

I turn towards him, my ears pinned back, animal-like. 'I want you to know that, without you standing by me, well, I'm not sure if I'd have coped. Knowing that *you* trust me, that you, the closest friend in the world to Tabby, have changed your mind about me, it's more than I could have hoped for.' I think I see his eyes water, but he looks away, embarrassed by his sudden outpouring of emotion, his guard in tatters. 'If you never want to see me again after this, I'll understand, but I didn't want you to leave without telling you how much reconnecting with you has meant to me.'

I am floored, unsure exactly what to say or how to say it. This story, this arrangement, proof that Rick has been leading a double life, tricking the public into thinking he's one thing when really he's another, is dynamite. I can just imagine Kay rubbing her hands together. *We've got him, AB! The public will hate this! Soon there'll be a petition to reopen the case, his home will be searched, and finally, after all these years, they'll get him.*

Funny then, that I feel for Rick. That I believe in his struggle and the lengths he's been pushed to by the press. Strange that, because he trusted me with the truth, I feel protective over him. Surprising, certainly, that, as I leave his house, I know that I am not going to tell Kay Rick's secret until I am certain that it needs to be told. Only if we can prove his guilt beyond doubt.

I push open the surgery door eleven minutes late and the receptionist shoots me a look, pigeon-necked patients craning forward in the distance, the waiting room full already – Saturday afternoons are always the busiest – but, before she can speak, her mouth half-open, I interrupt.

'Busy morning. Just give me two mins, then send my first down, OK?'

I bustle into my bright space, take off my running clothes, and replace them with my uniform, smoothing the creases in the black cotton against my skin. Have I been wrong about Rick? Is it possible? Am I really going to keep what he's told me from Kay? I wipe away the sweat that's trickling from my hairline, then press my face, armpits and chest with tissue and pedal open the noxious-yellow waste bin. There isn't a shower in the office – and I didn't have time to go home to have one – so that's exactly what these tissues are: Toxic. Disgusting.

Are my memories wrong too, then? When Tabby disappeared, Rick had seemed almost... glad... and everything spiralled from there. Ever since Tabby told me he was happier with someone else, that he and Tabby were struggling to find a way to end their relationship, that her disappearance meant he didn't owe her half of his assets, I've been convinced of his involvement. But a hunch isn't enough. Every time I see him, he throws doubt on what I thought I knew. My guard's still up with him, certainly, but I'm not sure whether I need protection from Rick, or he from me. What am I doing? What have I done?

I hear a flurry of footsteps from the stairs – my first patient of the afternoon – my breath coming quick as I rush to get ready. I hurriedly inspect the rest of the room – all clear – then turn my attention to my desk, then to the instruments on the side, checking that everything is in its place. I need to get ready. I need to calm down. I need to focus on my job. I run a cloth along the skirting boards, rub at a stain on the cornicing, then move my gaze up to the mirror above. That's when I spot it: a handprint. Clear as day. My eyebrows close in and I step towards it. Whose is it? I inspect it for a moment – it's a handprint all right, with five fingers that run long, as though whoever left it had tripped and tried to grab the mirror for support, the palm-print much smaller, just a faint and foggy stain below the finger-marks. Who's been here? The person threatening Rick? Do they know about me? About us? Am I in danger, too? I rub at the mark, coating the mirror in tiny bubbles, cleaning it, my thoughts wrapping in knots. I shiver as I think about someone being here, touching my things, reordering my carefully placed items, my precisely labelled implements.

A knock at the door severs my nightmarish daydream.

'Come in,' I say, trying to imitate a breezy tone, but I'm fogged with thoughts of the handprint behind me, and

Rick's parting words, and I can't keep up the pretence for long. After a few too many beats of silence, my patient takes the initiative to tell me she's here for a consultation and that she's interested in facial rejuvenation. I force myself back to the present and take her in, head to toe in beige, with small eyes and a sunken complexion.

'I want cheekbones,' she tells me. 'I want them to look natural, but also noticeable.'

'Certainly,' I say, all too familiar with this contradictory request from my patients.

I half-listen to her as I trace round the cupboards, glancing up at the mirror as I move. Then I spot something else that's not right. On the metal dish next to the patient's chair is a scalpel. What's that doing there? I grab it in my unsteady grip. This isn't mine. Who's been in here? Whose is this?

I inspect it, my breathing ragged. *Deal with it later*, I repeat internally. *Don't do anything rash,* I tell myself, forcing my hand to release it. I look away. I double check my items in the drawer beneath my desk: gloves, plasters, bandages. They're all there, in line. Just as they should be. I glance over at my patient, who's rabbiting on about something.

'To be honest, I think it's what's always been wrong with my face.'

I'm only half-listening to her, trying desperately to silence the noise in my head that's telling me to turn this place upside down and check what else has moved, to scream at her to get out, to tell her the only person I want to talk to about the confusion I feel in my head, is my friend Tabby, but I can't because she's not here anymore and, more than that, I can't because I don't know if I ever really knew her.

I breathe steadily – in and out – going into autopilot. I've done this job for thousands of patients and all I need is a cannula, rather than a needle, to go deeper under the skin to create the illusion of cheekbones. *It won't take long,* I tell myself. *It will be over soon.* I trace back to a CBT class Tabby had taken me to, and practise the technique of acknowledging my anxious thoughts, then casting them away.

'I'm going to use this blunt-tipped cannula,' I tell her, acknowledging the anxiety I have that I've been betraying an honest man. 'Because I need to go deeper under the skin to give you the look you want.' I try to cast it away, forget it, but how can you forget something like that? How can you just forgive yourself for something that terrible? 'First, I'll create small injection sites at your cheeks, then slide the cannula under the skin, along the bone, depositing the filler once it's in place.'

I hold onto the anxiety I feel with two hands and say a silent prayer that the patient will recoil as a result of my graphic description and tell me she wants to think about the procedure in more detail. The scalpel glints at me from beside her. To my dismay, she isn't fazed, and nods enthusiastically.

'That would be great,' she says. 'The sooner the better. I have a wedding to be at in two months.'

'No problem,' I reply with a begrudging smile. 'Let's get started. Could you lie back for me?'

I offer her a drink as I mark-up her face, selecting the areas to fill, but she refuses. 'I'm in a rush,' she says, and, just as I'm setting up the injectable, I notice a fingerprint on the errant blade by her side. What the... Why do these marks keep appearing where they shouldn't? I grab a wipe, put down the needle, hurried, and rub it feverishly over the metal, blurring the print but not removing it. Stubborn. I need to anti-bac it again. I rustle about grabbing extra lengths of tissue, cleaning materials and towels, busy scrubbing, wiping and buffing when my patient interrupts.

'Sorry, but, I'm in a bit of a hurry – like I said – and we're already running quite late…'

I look up at her from my position bent over the blade, aghast, and realise how I must be coming across. I take a deep breath, though it leaves my lungs in raggedy exhales, my anxieties at fever pitch now, crawling over each other maddeningly quickly, taking turns to reach the top. I put down the scalpel then press down on the patient's cheek but I'm in a rush and I'm distracted and everything's out of line and, too late, I realise I haven't given her any numbing cream and, as I slide the blunt tip deep inside her cheek I hear her scream.

'Ow!' she cries, recoiling, her hand dashing to the spot, ripping the cannula from its position under her skin, causing a deeper incision and a messy ejection from the site. 'Don't you numb it, first? *Jesus.*' She presses her hand in front of her face, blood smeared across it. 'What have you done to me?'

I shake my head in near disbelief, but the patient in the chair starts to morph into someone else. Me, as a child: scared, angry, eyebrows curled upwards.

I look away, try to compose myself, but the mirror and the scalpel and Rick and Kay and Tabby crowd me and I am frozen in place. It's been a long time since I've made a mistake like this – *was it a mistake?* – and my eyes widen as I watch the blood running down her cheek. I don't know what to do.

She rubs her hand across her face once again, a renewed layer of shiny, sticky blood coating her fingers as she pulls it away.

I watch as she pales, her eyes rolling back into her skull, her body limp.

She's about to faint.

'No, no, no,' I repeat, the image of her falling off the chair pulling me back from the edge. I kick into gear at last, recline the chair, get her head in line with her heart, then wait for her system to re-boot. What have I done?

As I wait, I wipe the blade clean with a wipe and press a towel to the area on her cheek, applying pressure.

'Are you OK?' I ask softly. 'Sorry about that.'

Her eyes fall from the back of her head. She's confused, a little dazed.

I push a wet wipe into her hands, so she can clear the blood for herself. I think of the other night, of hitting Mandy over the head, blood trickling into the carpet. What else am I capable of?

'Did something go wrong?' she asks, dizzily, when she wakes a few moments later.

'No, it's fine, you just didn't respond to the numbing injection,' I lie. 'But I'll give you a bigger dose and we can try again.'

'Absolutely not,' she puffs, and leaves the room a few minutes later with a blood-stained tissue stamped to her face.

I already know, as I hear her footsteps slap the staircase, that I haven't heard the last of this.

Rick

Thirteen Years Ago – 2007

My dissertation tutor, Ken, leaned forward in his seat, the faded leather of his elbow pads on the desk.

'You have the highest mark in the year group, Rick. You should be really proud of this work.'

My face was literally glowing, beaming with pride. Ever since we lost the baby, I promised that I would do everything in my power not to find myself in a situation like that again. If I was ever lucky enough to have a child in the future, I wanted to be excited about its arrival, confident of my place in the world, able to provide for its future.

My tutor asked me for the second time if I'd had any help with my work, reminding me about the seriousness of plagiarism, when my phone rang. Ken lowered his spectacles, scraggly white whiskers on his cheeks, his shirt over-ironed, the creases in his trousers severe. He looked as though he smelt of musty corridors and tea but, to be honest, I'd never leaned in close enough to find out.

'Can't talk right now,' I said into the receiver, then hung

up the call from Darren at McDonald's. I'd handed in my notice earlier in the day and I guess he was calling to try and convince me to do just one more Friday night shift. It felt good, hanging up on Darren. Graduating from his management. My degree had already opened doors, I had an internship at a top city bank lined up for the summer – they'd paid for my rent, they'd organised my train fare from Oxford. I didn't even have to go back to Norwich to say goodbye to my family, I just sent a quick email outlining my plans. *Good luck*, was the reply I got back from my parents' joint account, almost as though their work with me was done. I didn't mind, not really, this was the beginning of the rest of my life. I could see a future now, one I didn't think I'd see after everything that had happened at university.

I locked my phone as Ken called our meeting to an end, not getting anywhere with the plagiarism accusation, the entire Economics department silently furious that the comprehensive schoolboy they'd tried to oust on a false rape accusation was going to be honoured at this year's graduation. I smiled. Wondering if Darren would call again. But I couldn't have worked the Friday night shift even if I'd wanted to. Tonight was a big night. I had something special planned.

I waited for Tabby to come into the kitchen, a rich bottle of red wine breathing on the counter, her favourite dessert – chocolate lava cake – bubbling and molten in the oven, the smell of it lapping at the back of my nose. I pressed my palm into my courds and willed myself to be calm. It was my favourite time of the day: dusk, the sky a patchwork of pinks and oranges, a slow-setting sun in the distance. And then she appeared, a silhouette in the doorframe.

'What's going on?' she asked casually, as I dropped to one knee, a nocturnal bird singing in the distance.

'We've been through so much together,' I said, and noticed how she'd pulled her hair into a long, blonde plait. Over dinner it had been loose, flowing over her shoulders, the way she usually wore it.

Her pearlescent lips parted and she dropped to her knees too, hugging me before I'd even asked the question.

'Yes!' she shrieked, and the trauma that we'd been through together flashed behind her eyes. We'd got through it. Together. And that was what was important, that was why we were here today. No matter what, no matter how bad things were, Tabby and I found our way back into each other's lives.

Tabitha Rice and I were meant to be together. Forever.

Annabella

Now

When I was younger, my mother crafted me in her own image. She'd tell me stories about dirt and dust and grime and germs and make me believe terrible things would happen if we didn't expel them from our home. As an adult, I look at it differently, and realise that she was obsessive compulsive in a way that I am not. She'd gargle with diluted cleaning products – *toothpaste and mouthwash are about as useful as sucking on a mint when it comes to ridding your mouth of bacteria.* She'd make us live in one room of the house if the others didn't feel right, she'd only go outside if every inch of her skin was covered – citing that pollution and particulates could land on her and burrow inwards. I used to ask her how it was possible other people survived if the germs were all so dangerous and she'd look at me, dead in the eyes, and ask me to explain why else the cancer rates keep rising, why else antibiotics were becoming less effective, why else our olden-day diseases were on the up again? My formative mind soaked up this information like a sponge and, though I know none of it is true now, I haven't ever been able to let it go. But I can live, I can function. I exist in a way my mother never could. Even when things are bad, I can keep going, I can push through.

I catch the bus to Kay's. She wants to talk about the next episode and, to be honest, I'm grateful for the distraction. I need to stop thinking about the woman I butchered, about the man I might be betraying, about the friend I don't know how to help anymore.

I skate my shoes across the icy pavements to her house; the rain doesn't usually bother to freeze properly in the city, but it's just about cold enough this morning and the grey slabs glisten underfoot.

'Hi,' Kay says in the threshold of her front door. 'We need to go to the shed.'

'OK…' I reply, and she interrupts before I can speak again.

'I have something to show you.'

Kay's shed is as ramshackle as her home, and objects grow plant-like through others in order to reach the light: a lawnmower tilted sideways, an old bike missing its front wheel, a collection of brooms, some with bristles up, some down. Out of the window, weed-geysers bubble and spew across the back lawn; at my feet a woodlouse scuttles by, searching for the dark. I reach into my bag for my anti-bacterial gel and squeeze it – liberally – into my hands. My mental health is suffering and, when I'm like this, everything is junk and clutter and mess, the lens I see the world through magnifying the chaos around me.

'I invited Mandy here,' Kay announces, her voice ringing like an ominous bell.

I want to object. Why has Kay brought Mandy here without discussing it with me first? She is not someone we can trust yet. She is not someone we can bring into our inner circle. What is she thinking?

Mandy stands just behind the door, playing the same doe-eyed damsel as the other morning. She wears a black leather skirt, her hands in big mittens, her face stretched into the same expression she always wears on account of the bad Botox she's had pumped into all the wrong places. I flash back to the patient from yesterday; no doubt her cheek will be bruised this morning, purple and raised, yellow round the edges. Mandy fiddles with the zip on her jacket, nervous.

I bite my tongue, my face hard, as Kay catches me up.

'Mandy and I had a chat on the phone yesterday. I, er...' Kay pauses, giving me reason to squirm. 'I told her about you and Rick.'

My stomach clenches and I stare straight ahead, straight at Kay, unblinking, aware that Mandy's eyes have locked onto my position, sniper-like.

Mandy's going to tell Rick about my double life. I should have told him my secret yesterday when he trusted me enough to tell me his. I have to get to him before Mandy has the chance. Why didn't Kay warn me? Does she think I've been getting too close? Does she know that I have? Does she sense that I'm starting to have doubts about him?

'She knows it was just a honeytrap,' Kay runs to explain.

'Keep your enemies close,' Mandy says to me, deadpan. 'And I don't care, he deserves it. He used me, he should get it back,' Mandy sniffs.

It's a while before Kay speaks, but when she does, it's dynamite. 'Mandy's here today to talk. On the record.'

★

I am stiff and stilted as Mandy positions herself on the edge of an ancient chest of drawers tucked into the front corner of Kay's shed, readying herself to speak into Kay's recording device. A dank stench hangs in the air and I wonder, as Mandy curls her mittens together, whether I should try and convince Kay that Rick should be the one to tell this story, that, in Mandy's hands, what he's been doing is going to seem even worse. That we're burying him with this before we know that burying him is the right thing to do. Then again, hearing Mandy out will be useful – she might reveal a completely different side to this story. I need to give her a chance, I need to hear what she has to say.

Mandy fiddles with the leather edge of her skirt, jittery, and bends to perch on an old lawn mower, then, when she can't find a comfortable position, stands up again.

'I don't know where to start,' she says, timid, laughing gently after she speaks.

'Why don't you start at the beginning, Mandy? How did you meet Rick?'

'We met at a theatre club about six months after Tabby went missing. I was anxious at first, to date him, I mean, but I tried to put what I'd read about him to the back of my mind and judge him for him.'

I sit back, taking in Mandy's version of events, noting where her story diverges from Rick's. He said there was an arrangement from the beginning. She says otherwise. I'm inclined to believe Rick, Mandy's just protecting her reputation.

'It was difficult, at first, the media really hounded our

relationship, but when I moved in things began to settle. They backed off, left us alone.'

'I see,' Kay says. 'And how have things been recently?'

Her eyes shoot upwards and her lip wobbles almost on cue, a single tear running the length of her cheek. 'Really hard, to be honest. Really hard.'

'And why's that?'

'The truth is,' Mandy says. 'He did this to me.' Mandy pulls back her hair to reveal the marks I branded her with the night I broke into her home.

Kay darts an uneasy look at me, then back at Mandy. 'What?'

'There was no break-in,' Mandy explains, tears pooling. 'He attacked me.'

Kay and I share an awkward glance.

'Why, um...' Kay pauses. 'Why didn't you tell anyone this at the time?'

'He'd kill me. And, to be honest, I'm still scared that he might.' Mandy wipes the steady stream of crocodile tears from her cheeks with the sleeve of her coat. 'I'm so tired of his lies,' she mutters, her hollow sentence hanging limp in the cramped space between us. 'And, I have to say this because, even if it makes me look bad, it's the truth.' Her performance continues, a new round of heavy breathing and fast tears for our delectation. 'He paid me to keep quiet. He knows I need the money. I didn't have a choice but to take it.'

Kay depresses the button on her device, stopping the recording, and I step forward.

'We know you're lying, Mandy,' I say.

'What?' she asks, feigning ignorance. 'I'm not,' she insists.

'What's he told you? What lie has he spun this time?' she squawks. She's panicking, now, that she's too late, that she's going to lose Hollywood if this doesn't come off.

'It doesn't matter, Mandy; what we don't need is any more of them.'

I turn to Kay and consider that now is as good a time as any to fill her in. 'I met with Rick yesterday. He hired Mandy six months after Tabby went missing to play the role of his partner. He did it with the intention of calming the media storm and public scrutiny against him.' I watch Kay's eyes bulge. 'And it worked, as soon as he and Mandy were in a stable relationship, the pressure on him eased. He's been paying her to play the role ever since, but Mandy wants to end things, she's lost acting work because of their association and she wants compensation. I'm guessing what we heard today was something of an audition. A new career direction.'

Mandy wiggles her nose. 'I really don't understand why you're saying all of this... it's, it's just, it's crazy. I thought you brought me here with good intentions, not to tear me down.' Guilty tears brim her eyes.

I set my jaw, determination and drive locking it in place. 'We're not going to air this, Mandy. I understand that Rick's put you in an impossible position but that's no reason to lie to the world about the kind of man he is.'

Kay clears her throat. 'AB,' she says. 'I should have told you, sorry.'

My chin curls round to face her.

'We were live.'

Tabby

Ten Years Ago – 2010

My eyes were stinging when I woke up, and I rubbed at them with clenched fists. I must have looked like a bad actor playing at crying and, as the image struck me, I wondered if it was prophetic. Rick was already up, inevitably, the shower in our ensuite sending steam under the door. If you'd told me a few years ago that I'd end up living in a place like this I wouldn't have believed you. Rick had really lived up to his promise. He'd made a good life for us here, a world away from where we both came from.

Downstairs, I could hear bustling in the kitchen, the faintest smell of coffee in the air and bread charring in the toaster. Today was the second day in a row my new colleague had stayed over. Her name was Annabella and she'd recently started working at Pure You; she was young, about my age, and, from the moment we met, we clicked. She liked to make breakfast when she stayed here, she'd always unload the dishwasher and clean the countertops, I once found her wiping down the inside of our fridge. 'There was a mouldy lemon,' she'd told me. 'At the back.' Her expression had been deadly serious, as though a mouldy lemon called for a hazmat suit and urgent action rather than simply throwing it in the bin. 'Mouldy,' she'd repeated. My lips had twitched at the corner and she'd started to protest, laughing in between telling me why mould was a serious business, the apple of her cheeks flushing pink. I really liked Bella. She made me laugh, even when she didn't mean to.

I pushed myself to seated, slid my slippers onto my feet and worked my toes into the wool. As I stood, the sound of Rick singing in the shower whistled through the bathroom door and I walked over, opening it a crack, 'Mr Brightside' in full swing from within. Our song. It had blared in the club the night we met, recited by a live band to accompany our first dance. I thought back to our perfect wedding day, to the way Rick's bow-tie had restricted his breathing during the ceremony and I'd thought he was really nervous, about to leave me at the altar, the reality becoming clear as soon as we'd walked down the aisle and he'd ripped at the material, begged me to loosen it. *Who did it up?* I asked. *I did!* he puffed. *I thought it was supposed to be tight!* I close the door, smiling, as he serenades himself, *It was only a kiss, It was only a kiss!*

Amazing, really, that Rick and I made it here. To this house, to this life. For the first time I can truly say that I'm happy.

Annabella

Now

'What?' I say, teeth bared, firing on all cylinders. Mandy had been ejected from the shed, sent on her way so Kay and I can have it out.

'I heard you, you stopped recording immediately after Mandy said she was attacked by him, that he was paying to keep her quiet. Why did you do that? Why did you put it out live? You had no idea if she was going to tell the truth – and she didn't – you know she didn't! You have to erase it, Kay, you have to get rid of it!'

'I can't do that, AB,' she says calmly. 'For your own good. I'm protecting you, no one can know what happened that night. We're both implicated and, listen, isn't this the objective? You want to catch Rick, don't you? Who cares if Mandy's caressing the details into place, we're all striving for the same goal here, AB, the same outcome… aren't we?'

'My goal was the truth, Kay, not a show-trial.'

'You told me you were willing to do anything to put him away. Well, here we are. This is it: this is the anything.'

I hold her stare. 'I can't believe it,' I rage. 'I thought you were a good person.' The condensation on my breath looks more like steam. 'Screw you and your fake show,' I growl. 'I'm done.'

Adrenaline loops my body as I pull out my phone on my way back home. Two new messages. The first is from the surgery, from Anya.

Annabella, can you come in this afternoon? There's a… situation. The woman you saw yesterday, the one who left in a hurry, she's written a terrible review online. It's been getting some attention.

The second, from Rick, is much harder to swallow.

Don't you think I had the right to know you were investigating me as well as dating me?

My heart thumps. Mandy must have got to him already. I open the message fully, the weight of what I've done pulling me down so far that I sink into the pavement, dirt on my hands.

You've been playing me from day one.

PART 4

I

What do you think when you look at yourself in the mirror? Which emotions stir? Whose voice do you hear? Is it yours?

Mirror, mirror on the wall.

I hate you, want to change it all.

I touch my hand to my cheek and pull it back, stretching the skin so the line that traces my nose to my lip disappears. I do the same on the other side. The lower half of my face would look better if my skin were tighter, I decide. My jaw would look stronger. I could do with lifting some of the skin from beneath it, too. A nip here, a tuck there.

I hold my make-up brush firmly and paint furious shades on either side of my nose. Light down the middle and dark at the sides. I create a shape that's not there and hold my face at an angle for the camera that's completely unnatural. My make-up looks good, but my face is still not right. My nose ruins it; even with the shading it looks too big.

My brain concocts an insult before I have the chance to stop it. *Witch*.

I touch up my lips, draw bigger strokes of lipstick over the skin around them. I make them look passable, but the reality is they sit, skinny, on top of each other like a lost section of railway track. They don't curve when I smile. They don't bounce when I laugh. They aren't sensual, they aren't kissable, they aren't good enough.

I am sick of my own reflection.

I don't want to look like me anymore.

Annabella

Now

There's something wrong with me, something wrong with the way my head's been put together. Lobotomise me and I'm sure doctors would find something abnormal among the coils and curls of my brain matter, black red and beating, dripping blood onto the surgery floor. This dark part of me, though I try to suppress it, infects everything: when I am low, everyday tasks become intricate, obsessive rituals; when I fall in love, I love so deeply that I suffocate those I am with; when I am manic, I am reckless with it, changed.

A psychotherapist once wrote three scribbled words across the top of her page after an hour's analysis of me: *obsessive, possessive, manic-depressive.*

And she was right, but sixteen-year-old me wasn't interested in having my personality defined by labels or being seen as something to be fixed. *I am who I am*, I'd told her and, in response, she'd been careful with me, kind, and, when I'd stopped attending her sessions, she didn't force me back, but let me go.

Without a professional to ground me, I quickly developed my own coping mechanisms and constructed the parameters that still make me feel safe today. At school, I cut off my hair and starved my young body when exam-pressure consumed me, invented a new personality to provide a layer between my old self and my new: if I failed it wouldn't be *me* failing. My reinvention was written off as teenage exploration and, when I got fantastic grades – that was all that mattered – and went off to university to study nursing, nobody would have thought there was anything wrong with me. I certainly didn't.

With hindsight, though, I can piece it together. Pinpoint the exact moment my preoccupation with reinvention began, then took hold. At university, when my roommate kissed my boyfriend, I gained four stone and stopped colouring my hair, swore off relationships, decided I'd be a career woman instead, started calling myself Annie, then Annika. I specialised in cosmetic nursing after my degree, used my connections in the industry to create a different look and, with each new procedure, came a new face to meet: Ann, then Anna, Bella, then Belle… But, like the stubs that sit beneath my veneers, I have created only the illusion of perfection – not that most people seem to mind. My shiny, seemingly perfect coat still compels passers-by to stop me in the street. They always say the same thing, eager to let me know that the light of my eyes and the dark of my skin is striking – beautiful, even – as though my reflection might come as a surprise that day if they don't warn me about it first. I look at myself now. My lips are bee-stung, the bones of my face carved to perfect symmetry, my once-embarrassing E-cups lopped to perky Bs.

But what lies beneath remains unchanged: an unstable teenager with trust-issues, a pocket-faced little girl with obsessive tendencies and manic outbursts. So, when Tabby went missing and I wasn't able to help her, my coping mechanisms kicked in once more, and the obsessive little girl in me resurfaced. Now, though, I am running into problems: with each new mistake I make, with each new layer of protection I create, I move further away from the person I was at the beginning. Now, rather than take a leap away from the person I was, I am struggling to recall who she was in the first place. The girl I want to protect is missing.

I try to remember; but her face is blank.

I angle the last of my implements in line, go through the cupboards beneath my work desk, check the mirror for handprints, then make sure everything's in its correct position; the very thought of not being able to perform these tasks breaking me out in a sweat. Even though I am here, now, doing it, I am consumed with the thought that I might not have been able to. I can't stop thinking about Rick, about how many people I've let down, about how disordered everything is.

Anya – one of the other nurses – comes in to talk to me. Her spindly frame is drowned by her baggy uniform – even her bra gapes at the cups – and her hair's tied loosely behind her head, her ponytail crimped and streaked with red highlights. She looks at me, her eyes big and bland, the colour a depressing Coke-brown, no longer fizzy but left to go flat on the countertop. She puffs her cheeks as she settles on a white stool across from me and scratches her chin. I picture her moping about at home, falling into the settee every night, clawing her laptop from the space between the cushions and writing irritating updates, sadfishing for sympathy. *Why are my Tuesdays always so awful? Crying face emoji.* Her voice drips out of her in the same way, all wet and wearied.

'Annabella,' she begins, then pauses with the effort. I hate to bring you in on your day off… but, like I said, we have a situation.'

The window in the corner of the room is open and winter fans a much-needed breeze into the space, the attached blind ruffling in it.

'We have a troll,' she explains, her voice slow.

Anya's the type to turn a molehill into a mountain, but in this instance – to some extent – she's not wrong.

I bite the inside of my cheek. My problem has gone public.

Anya clicks into the review section of our website and reads out loud. 'One of Pure You's barbaric practitioners cut me open last week. She scarred me for life.' Though the sentences are enough to pound my heart into my stomach, it is a relief that she doesn't name me. 'Watch out for this place. Their techniques are more medieval than medical. Zero stars if I could.' A gruesome picture accompanies the article and even I'm surprised by how bad she looks.

'What do you suggest?' I ask Anya.

'Oh,' she noises, her lips parting. 'Sorry.' She sits up.

I raise my eyebrows. Something the matter?

'It's just,' she puffs, wrinkling her nose. 'I was rather under the impression that *you* were running this place now that Caroline's gone to LA – *not me* – so it's kind of your problem to figure out. Plus, it happened in your appointment, not mine.'

'Right,' I reply curtly, realising then that Anya's not to be trusted, that she's after my job.

She peels herself from the stool laboriously, a sarcastic *You're welcome* sounding behind her.

I wait for the surgery door to click shut then bring up the review It's attracted dozens of retweets on Twitter, and I know I have to take control and shut it down. I make a set of extreme decisions: I create a fake profile, Sharon White, who inserts herself into the discussion and accuses the reviewer of being bogus, that she's out for revenge because she works for a nearby competitor and isn't a genuine customer. *Don't believe this woman!* I write. *She'd rather post negative reviews about her competitors than concentrate on improving her own salon. Bitter, bitter, bitter.*

After it's done, I breathe deeply and hope that Sharon's fake story is enough to change the tide. *More lies*, I think to myself. *How easy it is to get caught in them.* My thoughts turn to Rick. How am I going to make amends? How can I explain? It's impossible. But I must try. I have to try. I unlock my phone and type a message.

I'm sorry. I can explain everything. But you can't trust Mandy; listen to the latest podcast episode, she's lying to the world about you, Rick, but I know you're telling the truth and I want to help. I will help.

I turn my attention back to Twitter, Sharon's tweet gaining traction. *This will blow over*, I tell myself. We'll ask every satisfied customer who comes through the door to post us a positive review and, before we know it, this incident will be confined to a blip in the clinic's history.

2

I hold my nose in a straight line to even out the crook. Someone online offered to break it for me to get rid of the bump. Said a good punch to my ugly face would do it.

It's not a bad idea.

I am not beautiful, I'm not pretty, I'm not even average. Even as a girl I was aware of it. I'd spend hours in front of the mirror, comparing myself to the women I saw online, trying to work out why I'd got so unlucky.

A thin waist, big boobs, chiselled features and thick lips: that's what I need. That's what I want. That is beautiful. That is what people want to see. Everyone would call me it – beautiful – if I changed. And wouldn't that be wonderful? To be adored and admired?

'You don't get self-esteem from a scalpel,' my mother snaps at me.

But she's wrong.

Annabella

Now

I'm a blur, a dizzy punch-drunk version of myself, as I stare at the home page of the *Mail Online*, refusing to believe what I can see. My mistake is the top story and, when I click on the headline, a long article appears about the unregulated nature of the cosmetic industry, complete with multiple mentions of Pure You, accompanied with a veritable gallery of hideous images of my former patient.

I click back to Twitter; our profile is being bombarded with noisy demands for compensation and watchdogs and I just wish I could make it all go away. Don't these people have anything better to do with their lives than wait around all day for a negative internet wave to catch?

Just when I think today couldn't end soon enough, a notification arrives from Zoom. *Caroline Mahler is calling you.* What am I going to say? Everything's wrong, everything's a mess, everything's –

'Annabella,' Caroline announces as the call connects, her voice bouncing off the walls. 'Can you hear me?'

I fix a smile across my face. 'Yes.'

Caroline comes into view, her eyes darting from side to side when it becomes clear she can't, however, hear or see me in return.

'Hello?' I call, turning up the microphone and restarting my webcam.

'There you are,' she says, my face filling her screen.

'OK,' she tells me, solemn, a worried finger heading to her lip, picking at a flake of dry skin. 'What the fuck's going on over there? I'm seeing this story and I'm telling people – you know – that it's not real but... what happened? Is this something to do with Anya? I heard she lost a few regulars last week?'

I look at the floor and for a drawn out and agonising minute, try hard to avoid the bait, to ignore the great big carrot Caroline is dangling before me. I love my job and I do not want to lose it. More than that, I *can't* lose it. I crave ritual and routine; the very thought of having to start again somewhere new, of having to organise a new space, navigate the intricacies of a new company... it's unthinkable. My heart beats faster with the thought.

'Well, I wouldn't want to get her in any trouble,' I say, blushing, my teeth biting down on the orange surface before I have a chance to stop myself. It's her word against mine.

'You need to tell me what's going on, Annabella.'

My hands close in on Anya's back, who's about to find herself under a double-decker bus.

I keep talking.

'Anya denies it, but the patient says Anya cut her cheek open with a cannula. I'm sure it was an accident, but the patient left in pain, I think she fainted. I don't know how it was dealt with afterwards – Anya kept it to herself – but obviously the patient's decided to go public.'

A sharp inhalation follows from the computer as Caroline noisily sucks in the air through her teeth.

I sit, staring at the camera, my legs bouncing up and down as I shake underneath the table, desperate to rid myself of this build-up of nervous energy. It's very possible my lie won't stick, but I have to hope that it does.

Caroline shakes her head, mutters, 'Unacceptable. Absolutely unacceptable. Why didn't you tell me as soon as this happened? We could have terminated Anya, got out in front of the bad reviews, stopped this from reaching LA.'

Again, I'm forced to scramble. 'I'd planned to sit down with Anya this evening to understand exactly what happened. Then I was going to talk to you about it. As it is, I didn't get the chance and now, well…'

'OK.' I watch Caroline bring her palms either side of her face and bury her head in them. She breathes deeply again, clearly frustrated. 'Right,' she exclaims after a moment. 'I'll release a statement and explain the staff member involved has resigned from our practice following an internal investigation. You need to tell Anya we're letting her go. We might need to rebrand. This might be the end of Pure You.'

3

I knock on the front door, my nail varnish chipped at the top, shaking slightly at the thought of what it is I have come to do.

At least the location is nice. For the price, I'd expected worse.

A pretty woman opens the door and smiles wide, greeting me. My hands sizzle and I am gripped by an urgent desire to flee.

'Do you want to come through?' she asks, beady pupils focused on me.

I follow her into the room, jittery, able to step forwards because I've detached from my own body. I tell myself that I'm not here, that this isn't me.

The patient-chair is a kitchen stool and a bundle of needles sit in a Tupperware to its side, next to a bag of unpacked groceries and a bowl of cereal.

'Take a seat,' she tells me, so I do.

I look around, the window blinds are pulled tight to the top of the frame, a little patch of rust in the corner, the cord bunched in an ugly mess at the side. I look away. If it weren't for my nerves this place would probably look entirely normal, but I can't stop staring at things and convincing myself they're not right.

I catch her looking at me.

'Sorry,' I say. 'I'm a little nervous.'

'Of course,' she replies. 'But there's nothing to be worried about. Trust me.'

I colour beneath my cheeks, falling silent.

'What were you after today, then? Fillers?'

'Yes,' I reply. 'I've always hated my lips. And I want Botox. I just want to look different. Here,' I tell her, pressing a photograph into her hands. 'I want to look like her.'

My hands itch at the thought of how different my life will be after this, how much better I will feel, and my mood begins to lift.

She nods, runs her eyes over my face, cat-like, and I watch as her manicured fingers select a needle from the stash to my side. She selects a tube of dermal filler, then paces out of the room.

Something's not right.

Maybe the needle's too big, or the filler's ingredients are in another language and she doesn't understand it. My hands shake as I wait for her to come back. Should I leave?

'Sorry about that, just had to dip into the overflow. I've had so many women like you over the last few days.'

Knowing that calms me down and I smile in return.

She snaps on a pair of latex gloves and the satisfying thwack of each being pulled into position signals the gunshot start of my procedure. She swipes her fingers across my face, then over my lips, checking for any natural lumps under the surface. I spot a drop of my saliva on her thumb as she pulls it away. She snaps off the gloves, selects a new pair.

'I think we'll start with the Botox,' she says.

She holds my face back and then struggles to find the right position, I can tell I'm too high up on the stool, so I shrink slightly, round my spine. In turn, she raises herself onto her tiptoes to get a better vantage point and, at that moment, I ask if she wants me to move to a different seat so she can get the best angle. She tells me no, that the light's good right here and that she'll just stand on a box. I look up, squinting into the overhead spot, the light illuminating my stretched features in bright-white radiance. This is all wrong.

'Are you ready?' she asks, her kitchen clock ticking towards nine o'clock.

'First injection going in now,' she says, and the thick needle punctures my skin. I feel her depress it, my mind's eye imagining the fluid pumping into place, gathering in lumps, forming tumour-like mounds under the surface of my skin. My arms begin to shake, my nails digging into my skin.

'And another,' she says. I wince beneath the light, can feel the beginnings of a red-purple bruise emerging beneath my forehead. She pulls the needle out, but I can see only half of it has deployed, a lousy dribble landing on my top lip as it retracts. She wipes it away with a stack of shaking tissues.

'And another,' she repeats, but there's an uncertainty to her voice and she's working faster now. She's scared, I can see it.

I want to ask her if everything's OK, because my vision has doubled, and my right eyelid feels as though it's drooping down my cheek, but I'm scared to move while she's injecting me in case I put her off. My skin feels tight, feels as though it isn't reacting well to the injections. I bet it's turning darker the more she tries to make it right, lumped and large and painful.

'Is everything OK?' I mumble when she finishes with the next needle, my heart fluttering in my chest, my breathing shallow. I imagine the scene in a few minutes time, as she hands me the mirror to take a look at the dream-face I'd imagined.

I squeeze my eyes shut when she doesn't answer my question, the room spinning. They blister with hot tears when she does. 'I'm sorry,' she says. 'The injections, they're…'

I leap from the chair, unsteady on my feet, trembling fingers moving to my swollen features, and scream as I see my reflection in the reflective glass of the microwave.

'What happened?'

She doesn't reply and, as I take a shaky step towards her, she points her needle out in front of her like a weapon. My eyes grow wide and fearful.

I break into a staggered run, twist the front door handle beneath my grip, and race from her home, broken.

Annabella

Now

I stop at a fruit stall on my way into work, the morning sky still dark, and buy a punnet of raspberries, impulse-buying a reduced six-pack of apples at the counter, feeling optimistic. I emailed Anya last night, told her that, on account of a few unhappy patients she'd seen recently, and the fact the clinic was losing customers on account of the Mail article, her role was now redundant. It wasn't a million miles from the truth, Anya had lost a few regulars recently and I just had to hope she'd be too lazy to fight me on it. As long as I'd known her, she hadn't seemed to particularly enjoy working at Pure You, so perhaps I was doing her a favour.

At the surgery, I wash the ruby berries, tucking into their crevices with gloved fingers to wheedle out any mud remnants, my idea of *washed and ready to eat* predictably different to that of the average raspberry packer. Once I'm finished, the result is a plate of flattened, water-logged fruit, but I eat them anyway, the pips lodging in the cracks between

my back teeth, fruity aroma floating from my mouth. The
sky, peeking through the window now, is similarly pink,
the snowfall and cloud-cover of last night long-vanished.
Today will be especially cold. I rotate the radiator dial to
maximum in preparation.

I check my phone for a message from Rick. I'd sent him
a few more, apologising, asking how I could win back his
trust, but they'd all gone unanswered. I have to give him
time.

I set about completing my morning checks and panic
flutters in my chest, a nervous rush rising, when I look
inside my cupboards and find that all of my things are gone.
I push my hand within, as though my eyes are deceiving me,
and wave it around but touch only air. I leave the doors
open, shaking now, and move to the next set – perhaps
someone's moved them? – but I'm greeted by a similar void.
Where are my things? My heart thuds as I contemplate
the chain of events that may have led to this, my fingers
fidgety. 'You're overreacting,' I say out loud and then shiver
because I know I'm not. Even though I can't connect the
dots, I know this is bad.

Anya?

Would Anya have the patience to do something like this?
The motivation? The desire for revenge? The crime doesn't
fit her persona and, thanks to spending so much time with
Kay, I find her intuition rubbing off on me. It wasn't Anya,
this was too much work. I could imagine her going to the
extent of planning it, bitching to the receptionist about
the way I'd set her up, cackling at the thought of putting
me off my game by messing up my space. Her parting blow.
But she wouldn't have had the fire to actually go through

with it, the smallest thing would have distracted her: a comfortable position in her bed this morning, the fact that it was a bit too chilly, the thought that she might be walking to the tube later and wanted to save her energy.

'Where are all my things?' I hiss at the pumped face working the reception desk today.

'Err, Annabella,' she replies, not looking at me. 'What are you doing here?'

I stare back at her, blank. Then I hear a voice; I think I'm imagining it at first, because it's Kay. *Tell us, in your own words, how the attack happened.'*

'It's the Tabitha Rice podcast,' the receptionist says, catching me looking. 'You must have been listening to it. You knew her when she worked here, didn't you? They've had to get Mandy Evans in for a special episode, the last one was cut short.'

'Ah,' I say, heat rising, knowing I have to get there soon, that I have to do the right thing.

'But I thought Caroline spoke to you last night…'

My mind grasps for an email I haven't read, for some event I must have missed.

'She knows it was you,' she says solemnly. 'You attacked that patient, not Anya. I told her the truth.'

I wonder what it means for my career: the end, probably. I am one of those horror-nurses you're warned about online, the ones who butcher instead of beautifying, the ones who should face criminal charges but walk away, often able to practise again, thanks to the unregulated nature of the industry, a graveyard of body parts behind them.

She looks at me through guilty eyes – she snitched on me and I loom closer, about to yell. I take another ferocious footstep towards her, my palm in the air, ready to plant it against the side of her face, but stop myself. The familiar feeling of my world being upended begins, consumed by the desire to transform into someone new.

I grab my bag, the sky bruise-purple as I flee the surgery and jump into a taxi, directing the driver through the backstreets towards Kay's house to avoid the traffic. I've lost my job, I've lost Rick, but I still have a chance to save Tabby's story. To put the podcast right, to make sure Mandy isn't able to infect it with her lies. Sleet splatters the windows as we drive, growing thicker, freezing on the glass. A question – what am I going to do when I get there? – rises and remains in my head, twisting around itself the longer I fail to answer it.

I ram my headphones into my ears and listen to the broadcast, playing live. Kay's speaking. She's calm and measured and slow and I know I won't be the only one who wants to hear what Mandy has to say. I wonder how many people are listening to this rubbish.

'So, you see,' rattles Mandy. 'I was with Rick because I genuinely liked him.' She coughs, clears her throat. 'And I'm sure I'm not the first woman to be let down by her partner. I trusted him, I believed him and the abuse, you know, it was small at first and then... that night.'

'Thank you for being so honest.'

Sweat soaks my clothes and there are dark patches under my arms and across my waist where my arms have been tightly crossed. It's freezing outside but I crack the window open beside me, the driver eyeing me with irritation from the front, an arctic breeze fanning the cold sweat on my forehead.

'Here's fine,' I insist as we approach. The driver hits the brakes just as I open the door, spinning from inside to out before the car has come to a complete stop in my haste to reach her.

Though I'd been hot inside the cab, suddenly I am chilled, the wind drying my sweat, turning my smooth skin bumpy. I press forward, clutching the sleeves of my cardigan beneath my coat. The sweet smell of incense and old bags of lavender breathe from Kay's home. I raise my hand to knock at her front door.

I hold up my hand, curl my fist, but, rather than knock, rather than interrupt the broadcast, I back away.

I walk to the side of Kay's house, looking for a window, but don't find any, the mural – the ruby-red face of a woman and her child – takes up the entire side-wall of the house, the windows here bricked in, an eighteenth-century feature you still see all over London. I pad a few steps further. Kay's back garden is marked off from the road by a run of wooden fencing, rotten holes eating into it, waist high weeds growing through the cracks. I stalk its perimeter, moving insistently, until I find a gate. I grab it, rattle it, my eyes falling to a padlock on the door, jingling against the cheap metal bar it's looped around. I take stock of my situation for a moment, my hand curling around the wooden slat that holds the padlock in place, knowing it's so decrepit it won't take much force to pull it free. My paranoia is on overdrive after what happened at the clinic and, before I know it, I'm breaking into Kay's garden.

I pull two of the ancient slats away, cobwebs dragging behind, a cluster of dazed woodlice racing down the planks, eager to find the dark again. The smell of wood parts my

nostrils as I push my body through the gap, and a stran
of my hair catches on an old nail as I thrust myself int
the overgrown garden, waist-high shoots swishing my leg
To the right of the gate, an old gravel path winds towarc
the back door and down towards the shed, another, muc
bigger overgrown patch at the far end of the space. I stead
my feet and trace the little-walked path towards the bac
door, raising my arms above the grass-line to my left, m
legs brushing against the weeds encroaching on the patl
Overhead, the sky is draining itself of colour, the purpl
turning grey, blues turning black, and I realise I'm talkin
to myself. *Everything's going to be OK, you can wash a
of this away, the germs on your hands can be dealt wit
as soon as you are you are done here, you are not goin
to die.*

Obsessive.

The bricks of Kay's house are within touching distanc
now and I fall to my hands and knees to crawl the rest c
the way. Dew coats my knees and my palms as I move an
I am starkly reminded of breaking into Rick and Mandy
home not so long ago, the feeling of sneaking up on m
target, lioness-like through the grass, rushing back to m
in anxious ripples. *This is my story, my friend, it's not fa
that two people who didn't even know her are claiming h
as their own.*

Possessive.

When I reach the house, I press my left side firmly int
the bricks and crawl towards the voices, hovering under tl
kitchen window. An empty packet of crisps, colours lor
faded, is stuck in the weeds to my side. I wonder ho
long it's been there. I wonder how long it will stay. *If I fa*

to find out the truth about what happened to Tabby, if Rick ends up going down for it, I won't know what to do. I'll have no one, nothing, there'll be nothing left to live for.

Manic-depressive.

I hear their voices rise again – they're recording in Kay's kitchen – and I sit back against the wall, lower myself to the floor, flattening the grass around me.

'That's OK,' I catch Mandy saying. 'I just want to get everything out in the open.' She inhales. 'Plus, I have a theory: I think I know what happened to Tabby.'

There's a small beat of silence before Mandy begins talking again. 'Before she went missing, Tabitha Rice was in communication with a doctor – someone in Turkey who she hoped would change the course of her life.'

I crunch my fist. She's saying it as though it's a revelation but then I realise, actually, for the listeners, that's exactly what it is. Kay and I didn't want to spin a thread about a doctor we'd never be able to find.

'Rick spoke to me about it – Tabby's messages with this doctor – and I saw the photos she was sending him. But they weren't of her, they were all of Annabella, her colleague.'

'You're saying Tabitha took her colleague's photos and shared them with an online suitor, pretending they were her own?'

'Exactly,' Mandy agrees, her voice more confident than I've ever heard it. 'She took Annabella's photos, went to meet the doctor, and then, I think, when the doctor realised he'd been short-changed, he rejected her.'

I can almost feel the delight in Kay's voice as she oohs and ahhs through Mandy's aero display of half-truths and full-lies, the twists of this episode coming thick and fast.

'At the time, Tabitha was at her lowest ebb. She and Rick were in trouble, both of them were having affairs, Tabby was desperate to run away from it all, but the doctor let her down. I think she flew into a jealous rage, killed Annabella, then assumed her identity. I think she went to plastic surgeons she knew and trusted and went through a variety of procedures, using Annabella's money, to look more like her.'

Mandy pauses, lets it sink in.

'I also, I don't know if you know, but have you seen this?' There's a short pause as Mandy fiddles with something. 'Top story on the *Mail Online*. Horror surgeon butchers young woman in South London surgery.'

'Oh God,' Kay exclaims. 'We'll post a picture to our Instagram so everyone can see this but, my God, it's a real hatchet job.'

'I've been looking through the comments, trying to get to the bottom of it, and that's when I found out: It was Annabella who did this. A top aesthetic nurse. A qualified, well-trained, highly respected practitioner. It got me thinking, well, what if it wasn't Annabella? What if it was Tabby? Tabby's no aesthetic nurse, she's no expert, she's a receptionist, and not a very good one at that. She must have watched the original Annabella perform hundreds of procedures. What if she's been living in her shoes for five years?'

Kay cuts in. 'I don't want to pile in here, this is quite a leap, we need to hear Annabella's side of the story too.'

Took her a while.

'Except,' Kay continues, just as I'm expecting her to back me up, 'I like your theory.'

I jerk my neck towards the window, my face bunched with confusion.

'Not many listeners will know this,' Kay continues. 'But Annabella and I have been working on this podcast together from the very beginning. I found the case and reached out to her because she was the only person – as far as I could tell – who had spoken in defence of Tabby in the early days.'

Mandy gasps. 'It's true, then. It's her, it's Tabitha.'

How does that prove anything?

'But – what I want to know is – if Tabby altered her looks via plastic surgery to look more like Annabella, why did she then draw attention back to her case by getting involved in it? Why did she agree to this podcast? How could it end in any other way than complete exposure?'

Kay's just playing devil's advocate, I tell myself. *She doesn't seriously believe Mandy, how can she?*

Mandy ploughs in, twisting the knife. 'I think Tabby felt short-changed that everyone had given up on her, that everyone just wanted to move on and forget. I think your podcast offer was too tempting to pass up. And, with Tabby at the helm of her own investigation, she could steer the case in whichever direction she liked, as long as it was away from her own guilt.'

'You think she's successfully pulled the wool over my eyes?' Kay asks, heat rising in her voice.

'I do.'

'Another thing,' continues Kay. 'Annabella hired a private detective.'

'I didn't know that.'

Kay tells Mandy the rest of the story. 'His name was Chad – American guy – and he didn't uncover anything of real interest. He was so useless, in fact, that I thought it was possible Rick had paid him off to keep quiet. Why would Tabby – now living as Annabella – hire a professional to look into the detail? He could have found her out then and there.'

'Well,' Mandy replies, deep in thought. 'What if she hired him to figure out what other evidence was out there? Maybe she wanted to know how much the police knew, how much they *could* know, and whether there were any loose ends she could do with tying up? I think she'd have killed Chad if he'd found anything that pointed the finger in her direction. She did it once…'

'Right,' Kay muses. 'There's something else,' Kay says.

I look up towards the sky, clouds forming in black barrels.

'Go on…' encourages Mandy.

'Annabella,' Kay begins, then falters. I already know what she's going to say. 'Annabella was the one who broke into your home that night. She was the one who attacked you.'

I squeeze my legs close to my chest. Is this really happening?

I hear a theatrical shriek fly from Mandy's lips, imagine her flinging the back of her hand to her forehead in dramatic fashion.

'No,' Mandy proclaims, groggy as she thinks it through, replays the scene with my face behind the mask. 'It was Rick. It was him, he was in a mask but… I was sure.'

'The listeners might remember from the live episode that our recording ended abruptly when Mandy accused Rick of attacking her. What was happening behind the scenes was that Annabella killed the recording. When you told us you were sure it was Rick, Annabella took it as proof that you were lying, but you weren't lying, you were sure it was Rick.'

'Oh, absolutely I was, absolutely sure.'

'It just happened you weren't right. When you left, I pushed Annabella to tell me why she was so sure that it wasn't Rick behind the mask, how she could possibly know with any certainty that you were lying. And that's when she came clean about that night. She'd broken into your home to find evidence, to get something that, I suppose, she planned to bring to me. I fired her from the podcast, obviously, hence why she's not here today, and that's why I got back in touch with you to come and tell your side in more detail.'

'I can't believe it was her. She hit me so hard...' Mandy continues. 'She fractured my skull! I could have died...'

'I know,' Kay says. 'Isn't it awful?'

Covering her tracks... Smart. Kay doesn't get her hands dirty, and it makes sense, she's planned for a moment like this. She knows what she's doing, Kay, this podcast isn't her first rodeo.

'So, what's next for Annabella... or should I say Tabby?' Mandy asks Kay.

'We need to find her,' Kay replies. 'That's what's next.'

In the thick of the overgrown grass a few feet away, I spot something twitching. It's a squirrel, over-fed and grey, bushy-tailed and bright eyed in the distance. If Kay comes outside now to grab something from the shed, I'll be seen – I have to move – so I scramble into the overgrowth, the squirrel darting away, to buy some time to think about what to do next. This area is relatively vast and nettles sting at my ankles, exposed, as I venture in. The grass rises tall around me, skyscraper strands at least five feet high and, then, my hand touches something. Metal.

I keep moving, deeper and deeper, willing myself around the object, and, at some point, I complete the circle. Just as I'm worming my way back to take it in, to be sure of what I can see, a series of noises erupt from the house and doors slam like drumsticks striking timpani. I shuffle myself in the thicket like a field-mouse, sniffing for a hiding place from the circling birds.

I watch the kitchen window through the grass. Kay comes into view and rubs her hands, washing them under the tap. Then, inexplicably, she begins to laugh. I can hear the gargling sounds she's making, her shoulders shaking by her ears. The kitchen light glows around her, illuminating her features, casting the purple bags beneath her eyes an even darker shade. Piles of rubbish climbing the walls at her sides: old toasters that no longer function, defunct fridges, ancient microwaves, piles and piles of Tupperware, cracked china crockery and, in among them, never-opened appliances like bread bins and ice cream makers, still sitting in their packaging waiting to see the light of day. Her eyes focus on the middle-distance and she runs her hand under her nose, then wipes it on her jumper.

I reach my hand out towards the object, touching the rusted edges. It's a car. I cover my hand with my sleeve and swipe away the green dirt that clings to the number plate. As soon as it's revealed, I immediately wish I hadn't. An EU flag at the side, PL underneath. I take a picture with my phone, my hands fighting an insatiable itch, my throat struggling to contain my fear.

4

I am a freak, a Frankenstein, my face is part paralysed, part pumped. I've locked myself in my bedroom because I can't let anyone see me like this. I'd rather die.

And that's when the thought hits and there's hope once more. The world spins colourful and iridescent and I log into my computer and start Googling what it is that I have to do.

Later that night, I sneak into the woods. I feel as though I'm experiencing everything in crystal clarity – the world is vivid and magnified and perfectly clear. It is so obvious to me that this is what I have to do. No doctor will be able to reverse what's been done to me and, even if something could be done, I wouldn't be able to afford it.

The woods loom overhead, tree branches like fingers blocking the moonlight from the path below. I grimace as I pace forwards, leaves beneath my trainers, a river nearby. I listen to it burble and cry. The smell of soil rises as I take a deep breath in.

My gut clenches as I climb the first section of the tree and loop the rope around the branch. The wind chills my cheeks, buffets my hair against my face. I tell myself to be strong: this is the only way out of this mess.

I vomit on my feet, bile and water, when I climb back down and look up at the rope, swinging. I am immediately reminded of haunted house images, of Victorian children hanging at awkward angles from their necks at the edge of their childhood garden, brought to their end by a possessed demon.

In a way, I can relate. I feel possessed by myself, by my own mind, somehow.

I climb the ladder, the wet of my trainers squeaking against each rung. My eyes leak as I near the top and the scared part of me tries to talk the determined me out of it. There will be another way, just step down. But the louder voice wins out. Just put it around your neck and take a step. Then it will be done. Two actions to end all of this.

I take the rope, it's so much heavier than I expected, and poke my head through it. It hangs round my neck, sweeps my collarbone, the most morbid of accessories. The tears come faster, my cheeks suddenly sodden, and I mutter to myself that I can do it, that I must be brave. Then, from somewhere in the darkness, I hear the faint sound of footsteps.

I panic, step, then swing.

Kay

Five Years Ago

I drive way out past the edge of the capital, the tarmac roads turning to dirt, a loose can shaking in the footwell of the backseat, my hands pressed tighter to the steering wheel as the road turns bumpy beneath the tyres.

I feel psychedelic this evening, my head jarring with how lucky I am. I've found her: the woman who killed my teenage daughter. I am pleased.

I have shed real blood, sweat, and tears to get here.

This woman, this untrained charlatan, a receptionist at a salon posing as a professional nurse, pumped my girl's face with unlicensed poison simply to make a bit of extra money. My daughter killed herself because of what Tabitha Rice did and yet there's been no justice. Suicide, the coroner ruled. End of story.

I take a drag from the stick in my hand, the smell of grass puffing around me. I am high, not much, just enough that my teeth hum and my neck feels loose, like it used to when

I was younger and things weren't as complicated as they are now.

The lights of the city fade in the rear view, miles of dirt and field in front, my headlights like torches in the great outdoor expanse, molehills jutting from the dirt, the occasional tumble of barbed wire stuck in the ground, but mostly nothing-ness, just dirt and mud and grass, and the further I drive, the freer I feel. An hour or so later, I take a ninety-degree turn off the dirt path and follow the signs for the dual-carriage way back to the city, the names of towns I don't recognise shining back at me. The road is treelined and it swallows my car as I speed through. I like to lose myself, to unwind in the great wide nowhere, be somewhere else for a change. Someone else.

Soon, I will follow her to the meeting place.

She knows me as the doctor.

And because of that she trusts me. Just like my girl trusted her.

There she is: at the side of the road, staggering in drunken steps off the pavement and back on it again. I slow the car and trundle closer. A minute later and she's there, at the window, the murderer, her face covered with too much make-up.

My daughter, Orla, made contact with Tabitha Rice via an Instagram page offering a range of cosmetic procedures 'in the comfort of a home setting.' *Perfect for those who are scared of hospitals and clinics,* Tabitha had written in the bio. When Orla died, I'd believed the story the police had fed me – death by hanging – and the coroner had confirmed it soon afterwards. Months later, I was granted access to Orla's social media accounts, and I'd landed upon the last thing message she'd received: an appointment confirmation offering Botox with 'Tabby'. Suddenly it all made sense. My girl's face, so badly bruised when I'd gone to identify her, had been disfigured by this Instagram clinic. Whatever had happened in the 'comfort' of that woman's home had been the catalyst that had sparked Orla's suicide. I was sure of it.

By that time, though, Tabitha Rice had shut-up shop, deleted all traces of her practice from the world-wide-web and, with it, all hope of convincing the police to follow the lead, to bring her to justice. They'd humoured me, the officers involved with the case, but the reality was, in the eyes of the law, Tabitha Rice was just one of hundreds of fraudulent Botox practitioners across the UK, working through loopholes and hoping no one would notice. I'd did some digging, had become obsessed with finding out more about this woman. I Google-image-searched the screen-shoots that Orla had taken and saved on her account and, shortly afterwards, linked the original images to Pure You. I'd assumed they'd been stolen but then, there she was, the smiling face of Tabitha Rice on the screen before me. The clinic's receptionist. I wagered it was more than a coincidence that 'Tabby' was the name behind the woman on the Instagram account, too. And so the picture of what she'd been doing began to emerge. Tabitha Rice had stolen Annabella's pictures – Annabella was a qualified aesthetic nurse with hundreds of procedures under her belt – passed them off as her own, and used them to convince vulnerable young women on a budget, like my Orla, to go to her directly.

Tabitha Rice might have ended up with a fine, if they'd even bothered to investigate, and she'd probably have lost her job, but she'd almost certainly have been spared jailtime. In my eyes, she deserved the death penalty. And, in all my years of reporting, I've come to realise that if you want justice, you have to exact it yourself.

I call out to her from the car window.

'Do you want a lift?'

Tabitha spins in my direction and I watch her relax when our faces meet and she realises I am a woman and not a prostitute-seeking scumbag or a murderer with mummy-issues in a stained baseball cap and egg-smelling sweatpants.

'Oh thank God,' she wails. 'Yes please.'

She's too stupid to see past the stereotype – *women don't hurt women* – so she grabs the door handle with eager mitts, blowing steam from her mouth and nose, animal-like, as she exhales with relief, nostrils panting. I take her in. She has a sweet-looking mouth. It's overridden by her plastic-looking face, though, and her pale expression sits beneath a mop of dyed browny-blonde hair. Not content with stealing Annabella's work, she'd sent the doctor Annabella's pictures too, and I deduce her latest hair colouring must have been an attempt to look more like her colleague. Her eyes are dark-rimmed with make-up which only serves to make them look beady.

'I'm Tabby,' she says as she sinks into the seat beside me, bringing a number of different scents into the car with her: hairspray, white wine, cheap perfume. My eyes shoot to the low-cut of her top, her waist filling the new pair of white jeans she's bought for tonight – I guess she's gone for a size smaller than usual, judging by the way her body presses against them, every detail of the jeans undoubtedly stamped into her flesh in red markings and yellow depressions. When I look back up, she's grinning at me with wide teeth.

'Kay,' I reply.

I lock the doors and windows as soon as she's inside, the sound of five locks thwacking into place thudding through us both. Tabby ruffles in her seat, her guard suddenly up, a flurry of nerves rippling through the claustrophobic space between us.

'Do you mind?' I ask. 'Sorry, I just don't like to drive at night without the locks.'

She relaxes. 'Oh no, of course not. You can never be too careful.'

Because I'm a woman she thinks she knows me, thinks she understands my motivations.

I give her a weird, frenetic smile in response. I want to scare her, just a little bit. Her blue eyes narrow and I watch the cogs in her brain whir, imagining her inner monologue: *there's something off – but this crazy woman is doing me a favour, I should be grateful. Judging by the smell of the car, she's probably just stoned.*

'Bad night?' I ask, pressing down on the accelerator.

'The worst,' she sighs.

'Where are you heading?' I keep my eyes in front, mesmerised by the way the car sucks up the white lines of the road in repetitive, rhythmic fashion.

'I don't know,' she replies. 'Wherever you're going. I'll figure out what to do tomorrow, right now I can't think straight.'

My pupils dilate.

'You want to talk about it?' I ask.

She shrugs her shoulders to her ears.

'Go on,' I encourage. 'Start with tonight. What happened?'

'Uh,' Tabby groans. 'Well, I was *supposed* to meet someone. A man. A doctor. But he didn't show up.'

'Who was he?'

'A plastic surgeon I met online.'

'Oh!' I remark.

'I was going to move to Turkey to be with him.'

'Really?' I repeat, the tone a little different.

'I know – even saying it out loud sounds ridiculous. I'm so stupid. I just, I guess I let my imagination, my optimism, run away with itself.'

She laughs gently, though I'm not sure why, it's not very funny.

We drive, air cooling around us, for a little longer and I listen carefully, mentally taking notes, listening to her story, an idea formulating.

Annabella

Now

I cower next to the car. It's the same one, I'm sure of it, from the CCTV photos.

My mind plays something that Kay had once said to me: *If there was a way of getting into Rick's home, I know there'd be something. Even something small. Killers, or kidnappers, always leave mementos, little trophies reminding them of what they've done and of how clever they've been. Mark my words: there'll be something in that house.*

She hadn't been wrong; I'd just been looking in the wrong house, or garden, for that matter.

I am stuck in the dark of the grass, the insects getting used to my presence now, woodlice and spiders scurrying across my hands and feet, and I feel them occasionally – or imagine them – climbing up my trouser legs. I can't move until Kay leaves and, at the turn of the next hour, thankfully, that's exactly what she does. The kitchen lights disappear, and I hear the tell-tale thuds of her front door slamming, a lock twisting into place behind.

I wait for a few minutes longer, just in case it's a trap, eyeing up one of the ground-floor windows. It's open a crack, but it's small, no bigger than my head, and I assume it backs off a bathroom. Moving from the grass awakens a cacophony of shooting pains and pins-and-needles fizz at my feet as I stand. When I get to the window, I tiptoe up and push my hand through the gap. From here, I'm able to turn the main window's lock open and push it wide, the space just big enough to squeeze through. My coat catches on the latch as I pull myself into the bathroom, a single feather attached to the mechanism as I turn back to check the damage. I pluck it off, push it into my pocket, and observe where I've just landed.

The bathroom is predictably worn, the grout between the beige tiles murky-brown, giving the impression that muck keeps them together rather than cement. Black mould furs around the shower cubicle and the toilet churns out a constant trickle of water, stagnant paper wedged in the bowl. I avert my stare: I don't want to look any closer. I pull my sleeve to my mouth, terrified to take a full breath in. I decide not to explore the downstairs – I've seen these rooms before – and instead head up, climbing the carpeted stairs that wind upwards.

I daren't turn on the lights, cream wallpaper just light enough that I can see where I'm going, my eyes adjusting to the dark. The first door peeks into a bedroom. I step in, it's colder than outside, a thin slither of a window open in the corner. Kay's bedroom floor is covered in clothes, the bed a jumble of sheets and bare pillows, yellow stains on the surface. I press on, find another bathroom – equally as grotty – then a spare bedroom, though it's more of a storage room – they all are – a single bed buried somewhere beneath the stacks of rubbish that sit on top. The air is dense and dusty, my lungs tightening the deeper I go.

Behind the penultimate door, my breathing ceases and my hand drops to my side. Behind it, photographs are splattered on each wall, runs of thread connecting pieces of paper, maps, smaller photographs, scribbled notes. The place is teeming with investigation and, as I move inside, I find the entire back wall is covered in Tabby. Her face provides the central point from which the threads tentacle out, my own face at the top, a picture I took for Pure You's website. On the opposite wall there's the face of a girl I don't recognise, her name splashed below. *Orla Robero, 1999-2015*. I step closer, look into the details, and quickly piece the puzzle together. I trace back, memories of Kay talking about a teenager daughter fizzing at the back of my mind – but I'd never met her. This is why.

Kay Robero's teenage daughter is dead. Tabby must have had something to do with it.

Kay

'You want some?' I ask Tabitha as we speed along, nodding towards the bottle of water between us.

'Is that OK?' she replies. 'I'm really thirsty. You don't mind sharing?'

'No, no, you go ahead,' I encourage.

'Not a germaphobe then?' Tabitha asks, giggling to herself as though it's a private joke. When she sees me raise my eyebrows she elaborates. 'I have a friend who struggles with it,' she says, bringing the bottle to her lips. 'Where are we going, anyway?'

She sips, a circle of moisture ringing the her cupid's bow

'I'm taking you to my house, I figure you can stay the night, then make your way home tomorrow.'

There's just a flicker in my eyes, a hint of menace, my plan of attack packaged as an invitation, hanging between us, trying its best to stay in character.

'Oh no,' she coos. 'You don't have to do that, you've been kind enough as it is.'

She slots the water bottle back into the drink's holder, just a dribble left, and a plan forms as the moonlight glows against my face. I open my mouth to smile, blackness within, eyes ahead, and I feel the anger bubble in me, ready to launch, my fingers tight to the steering wheel.

I slam the brakes. The sudden stop propels us forward, our bodies continuing at sixty miles per hour, the sound of rubber on tarmac screeching hyena-like into the night.

My dark hair balloons around me as we fly, just before we're caught by our seatbelts. My body clenches as it stops, my lungs robbed of air, my chest compressed, then lands hard into the seat, my spine cracked into its shape, the car spinning to the side – uneven brakes – straddling both lanes as it comes to a stop, a sitting duck.

'*What did you do that for?*' pants Tabitha, and she groans with the shock, twisting her seatbelt in her hands, trying to free herself, a trickle of sweat on her forehead.

We're both still for a moment, only the fast gasps of our breath between us. From frantic, ear-splitting action to complete silence in a matter of moments. And, though I know I'm probably in shock, I don't feel it: I feel electric, invigorated, and my eyes glow as I tell her.

'If you don't want my help you can get out.'

I smile again in that same, perturbing, way I know everybody hates. I remember mine and Tomasz's wedding photographer saying, *Relax, don't try so hard! Think of something funny! Say cheese!*

Tabby laughs nervously.

'No need to be like that,' she says, trying to placate me. She thinks I'm a lunatic, so still she has me wrong. I notice her hand crawling towards the door handle and, a second later, she tries to open it, the empty thwonk as the lock initiates loud as a gunshot.

'It's locked,' I remind her calmly, and she closes her eyes and nods her head, moisture pooling her eyes. I press the accelerator, smoke from the tyres still hazing the air outside, the smell of burning rubber trickling through the gaps in the car's exterior.

If she hadn't done that, if she'd fought me, she might well have got away. I'm a thinker not a fighter. If she'd grabbed my hair and pulled it from my scalp, whacked my head into the steering wheel, then lunged across my lap for the central locking, things might have been different.

But Tabitha Rice isn't a fighter either. She whimpers in the passenger seat and wraps her arms round her legs, brings them up to her chest and rocks.

'What was in it?' she asks me, head nodding towards the water bottle.

'Just some sleeping pills,' I reply, reaching for her handbag so she can't call for help.

She doesn't even try to stop me.

Outside, it's cold. Clear-night cold, the wind howling, and we don't pass a single vehicle on that road. It doesn't take long until Tabby's eyes are rolling into the back of her head and her breathing is slowing. There were about six tablets in the water and I'd been lucky she'd drunk so much. If she hadn't I'd have had to persuade her a little more, befriend her, drop the scary-act and convince her to stay with words only.

My house arrives an hour or so later. I loathe and crave my house in equal measure, an oddball on the street with

huge female mural on one side, each room stuffed with
nk I've never been able to throw away. I know why, I
n't need an expert to tell me: it's the direct result of losing
y daughter and not being able to throw anything away
om her past – but, despite all that, the place is worth
most a million. The fact that I live here would probably
flate its value. People like a story. People like a house with
ersonality. Even one as horrible as mine.

I drive up to the space outside my front door and send a
essage to Tomasz.

Can you come outside?

There's no way I can shift this woman from car to house
n my own and there's always the chance, of course, that
e's bluffing, that she's waiting for me to unlock the car
o she can run. I fold my body over hers, hold back her
velids, her pupils like pins, and reason this isn't an act.
omasz appears at the front door and approaches cautiously,
eyeball every window on either side of the street, check
or lookouts, for witnesses, and find nothing but the night
flected in each. I unlock the doors, get out, close it again,
ather-quiet, then pace round to the sleeping woman on
e other side. The yellow flash of our Polish number plate
rikes me; I must tell Tomasz to hide his car as soon as
ossible. He brings her up out of the vehicle, then pulls her
ght arm round his shoulders, leaving me to take her left.
'e manoeuvre her towards the house together, her body
eep-drugged but not entirely unresponsive, her fingers
old, clutched to my neck. For a fleeting second, I think it's
weet that she's holding on so tight.

The smell of cooking oil and decay hit me as we open the front door – opening the windows only does so much, so the smell can't be helped. I need everything in this place, cannot function without it – and we drag Tabitha upstairs.

I watch Tom tie her to the chair in the room at the back of the house, looping rope round her wrists and ankles in silent acceptance that this is the right thing to do. She drove his daughter to her death. I prop the window open in the corner – I want her to be cold – and light a cigarette. The yellow walls in here are ancient, old wallpaper peeling from top and bottom, the tassel-edged Victorian lightshade in the middle of the ceiling marked with giant rings of brown. The things I store in here – saws, knives, rope, clamps – most of them are rusted and overused, a few are newer, shinier. Sharper. But what Tabitha Rice doesn't know about me yet is that I don't intend to kill her with these things; these props are merely here to frighten her into staying put.

'Are you sure you want to do this, Kay?' asks Tomasz, his steady hand on my shoulder. 'She's younger than I thought she'd be.'

I turn sharply. 'You can't be serious?'

'I'd imagined her differently.'

'Yes, well, looks can be deceiving,' I counter. 'And think about what she did. Hold that in your mind: do you think she thought about Orla, about the rest of her life, about her future, when she injected her? No. She was focused on money and profit and greed and… that's why she's here.'

'I'm going out,' he tells me and, honestly, that's OK. I have more than enough brain and more than enough brawn for the both of us. I will do what needs to be done. Tomasz understands.

ie room is musty when I return with the botulinum toxin
id I notice Tabitha's feet have turned a strange purple
lour, zombie-like. She cries when I come in, terrified of
e. She shouldn't be. In a way, I'm freeing her. She won't
ve to worry about anything anymore, won't have to
awl into work tomorrow and stare at another saggy face,
ndering if she'll ever escape the monotony. I'm freeing
r from her husband, from the day when he'll come to her
id ask for a divorce. I'm freeing her from the credit card
lls she's run up and won't be able to pay off. In a way,
n freeing him, too, so he can start over again with the
man he's been seeing behind her back, do it right
is time. She won't have to worry about her best friend
nabella either, about the day when the guilt finally
nsumes her and she has to admit to using Annabella's
ctures and credentials to ensnare victims and men online,
e disappointment on Annabella's face as she slashes their
nd in two. Annabella's kind face tilted away, *I'm sorry,*
bby, I just can't trust you anymore.

It will be my job, instead, to tell her story. I'll begin by
inting her as a victim. If you want to bring someone down
the media, you have to start by building them up.

I lean over Tabitha with the needle and snap a pair of
ex gloves onto my hands.

'I'm going to make you famous,' I tell her, and her eyes
bble with horror.

But, before she can speak, I push the needle into the
ase of her forehead, and whatever she was going to say
me to make me change my mind evaporates.

'Everyone's going to know your name,' I whisper in her ear, two gold studs in each.

Her eyes are baby-blue, child-like fear trapped within them. Her eye make-up long melted, flecks of black dotted like gunpowder residue across the purple-tinged skin above and below each eye. Her lips sit like two dead slugs, artificial, and, rather than shake in flesh-like ripples, bounce with trampoline-jump movements. I lean into her once again, pressing down with the needle, letting the poison take hold. She twists her neck to get away this time, and the needle scrapes her skin, a gem of blood appearing, stopping me for a moment.

I do not like blood, so I let go, I wait in the corner of the room to see if what I have done is enough and then, when I am sure the toxin has paralysed her heart, caught it in its clutch mid-beat, I cross my arms and breathe out, properly, for the first time since I was told my daughter had taken her life.

Annabella

Now

'Annabella,' Kay calls from behind me, her furry eyebrows crossed. She's holding the wooden plank pulled from her garden fence and her mouth bobs open when I turn to face her. 'What are you doing here?'

'I heard the recording,' I tell her. 'Listened to Mandy reveal the *truth* about me.' I pause. 'Then I found the car, the one you used to abduct Tabby. Then I found this room.' My mind flits briefly to Tom, her husband, but he isn't in the house. I wonder how deeply he's involved in all of this.

Kay leans casually against the doorframe, belligerent.

'I feel badly for you, AB, I really do,' she tells me, finally. 'This series could have ended so many ways. Rick being guilty: that was the obvious ending. Then I'd have put in a bonus episode that suggested Tabby took her own and framed Rick for all of it. But this is much more interesting… Tabby's been living as you this whole time and I've been dead for years! And wasn't Mandy convincing? She really thinks she's figured it all out and, to be honest, people have latched onto it. It has everything: assumed identities, betrayal, rivals, lovers, secrets, surgery... and I'm happy because Tabby still gets what she deserves. It's just unfortunate, I suppose, that you got caught in the cross hairs.'

'It won't stick, Kay, people won't believe it. Plastic surgery can only change so much.'

She looks at me through hooded eyes and that's when I realise: she's not going to let me leave here to prove my innocence. She's going to kill me too, this time for the sake of a good ending.

Kay doesn't move, remains diagonal in the doorframe.

'Why did you do it?' I ask.

'Tabby killed my daughter.'

My face pales. 'How?'

Kay blows out.

'Orla.' She points to the wall behind me. 'Killed herself after Tabitha Rice mutilated her face and lips with black market Botox and cut-price dermal filler.'

My mouth sags open.

'Tabby was pretending to be you, she used your credentials to trick unsuspecting teenagers into parting with their pocket money.' My breath catches in my windpipe. 'Judging by your reaction, I'm guessing you didn't know she was doing that.'

I shake my head.

'Well, at least you know the real Tabby now too.'

I've spent years trying to get to the bottom of this mystery and, now I finally know, a huge part of me wishes I didn't.

'What happened that night, Kay?'

'I offered her a lift in my car after the doctor stood her up.

I cut in. 'Were you the doctor, too?'

'Orla got in touch with Tabby online. Orla trusted Tabby and Tabby let her down. I thought it was only fitting for Tabby to know what that felt like.'

'She got stood up and then just accepted a lift from a stranger?'

'She was drunk. I'd arranged our meeting miles away from the nearest train station. She saw I was a woman and trusted me to look after her – just as my daughter had.'

Kay runs her fingers over a picture of Orla as she speaks. I drove Tabby back here and Tom guarded her. She told me everything about her life on the way over – it's funny what some people are prepared to tell a perfect stranger. She filled me in on her hopeless young mother Marie, who'd given her up for adoption, an evil foster mother, a grotty grandfather. She told me about Rick's affair, about her relationship with you, and how gutted she was that she'd broken your trust on so many occasions.'

'But, if you're to blame… Why are you investigating? You could be found out. Why would you risk it?'

Kay sighs as though it won't be easy for me to understand. Because killing Tabby was one thing. An eye for an eye. But her story captured my imagination. If it had been banal and boring, I would have left it there… but I couldn't.'

I crawl with unease, I itch with it. I have an awful vision of Tabby fighting with Kay, of Kay's furious frame pinning my best friend here against her will.

'How did you do it?' I ask feverishly. 'How did you kill her?'

'Botulinum toxin,' Kay answers.

'You killed her with Botox?'

'Well, it made sense,' Kay continues, matter of fact. 'It's one of the deadliest toxins on the planet.'

'How did you get it?'

'I ordered one vial of pure botulinum A neurotoxin, to be delivered to a pick-up point in a corner shop with no cameras and a relaxed attitude to signing for packages. It was destined for a laboratory, so the preparation was incredibly potent. Tabby ordered this stuff directly too, she had it delivered to Pure You and intercepted the packages – against all regulations – then diluted it herself at home. Isn't that horrendous? It's not even that unheard of. Did you know a couple of teaspoons of the stuff could kill everyone in the UK? And yet Tabby used it every day, pumped it into people's faces as though it was as innocuous as saline solution.'

Kay stopped for a moment, watching my reaction, then continued. 'I estimate I gave Tabby 2,859 times the human lethal dose by injection. I put it in her forehead, for obvious reasons, so it could be explained away as an accident at her own illegal practice if it needed to be.'

My voice roars, incensed by Kay's twisted justice. 'You played God, then took Tabby's story and used it to make your podcast series a hit.'

Kay smiles. 'Painting Tabby as the victim, raising her profile, then revealing her for who she really was, outing what she did – and worse – all of her secrets. That was my revenge. First, I killed her. Then I killed her legacy.'

'I see,' I reply.

'She had a rich, brilliant, story and the journalist in me couldn't resist. Everyone's doing true-crime podcasts nowadays... and if I was behind the story, able to contro

ery aspect of it, I couldn't see how it would go
rong.'

My eyes flare.

'And you really think people will believe your final
isode? That I'm actually Tabby… that I'd go to the
ngths of starting a podcast about myself? Even if you kill
e there'll be plenty who won't buy it.'

'And plenty who will,' Kay replies. 'Stranger things have
appened.'

'But no one will ever be able to put me on the scene, there
on't ever be any evidence.'

'The public won't mind – they believe what they want to
·lieve – since when has *evidence* got in the way of anything
owadays?'

I run my fingers through my hair, anxious, talking before
inking.

'You're a bad person,' I level at her.

'Oh AB,' she whines. 'That really hurts my feelings,' she
ys, mocking me.

I feel the glare of Tabby's face from behind me. I am alive,
:an still do something to stop Kay, to out the truth.

'You told me once that killers always want people to
now how great they are at killing, well, no one knows
hat you've done, they just think you've swooped in to
ck up the pieces. They think of you as a vulture, Kay, a
avenger.'

'You're wrong, people know what I have done because I
ll them, every week. And what's better than telling them
being so clever that I've pulled the wool over their eyes
o – it's not just the authorities I've fooled, but the entire
orld. Better still, I can obsess over Tabitha, I've spent

months digging into her dirty secrets, further justifying my surety that killing her was the right thing to do. I love what I do because I can talk about it, what breaks most killers is that they try to take the secret to their grave, never discussing the case, never saying their victims' names out loud. Not me.'

'Where is she, Kay? What did you do with her body?'

I think about the hordes of junk lying around and I wouldn't be surprised if she'd kept pieces of my friend all over this place. A locket of Tabby's hair in an old microwave in the kitchen, her jewellery in an old biscuit tin stacked tall in the lounge. This whole house is teaming with the trapped gasps of Tabby's life. No wonder Kay's always burning incense to hide the smells that must cling to these old, cream-paper walls.

She looks me in the eye, then her gaze falls.

'Tomasz got a job on Ernest Rice's farm five years ago. There were a couple of other Polish men on the team and Ernie was grateful for the extra labour.'

My memory recalls Ernie telling me about his 'Polish lads' when we visited his farmhouse, and I'm irritated I didn't put the number plate together with this clue. We should have asked to see their identification; we should have interviewed them.

'After I killed Tabby, Tomasz and I buried her on Brimley Farm, in the field behind Ernie's farmhouse. Tabby had told me he was a horrible man, that he abandoned her when she was young, left her to rot in foster care. In a way, he's to blame for what happened to Orla. If he'd looked after Tabitha, she wouldn't have turned out the way she did.'

While Kay's distracted, revelling in outing her secrets fo

the first time, I take the opportunity to lunge towards her. I know she's not a fighter, and she's almost two decades older than me, so I have an advantage. But she spots me as I reach her, my body coiled, about to explode with one great, twisting hit and grabs my arm, catches it mid-flight, her strength surprising me, and we struggle round the perimeter of her investigation walls, sending paper and notes and thread to the floor as we fight, my fingernails digging deep into her shoulders, hers digging deep into mine. I catch a flash of fear on her face and it emboldens me. I curl my head backwards then thrash it towards her, landing a giant blow against her forehead, a hooligan-worthy headbutt that sends her staggering backwards.

It takes me a second to realise my freedom but, when I do, it is quickly taken away. I race to the door, twist the lock back, and run in a straight line for the exit but, too late, I realise I have doubled back, ending up at the back of the house, at the threshold of a tiny room. I hurry inside and slam the door behind me, but there's no lock, just a window, so I start hauling a crate of junk in front of the doorframe to block myself in. I can just make out the sound of Kay's footsteps and then, silently, she disappears.

I pivot in mind-numbingly stupid loops, not sure how long I have before Kay comes back, trying to find a way out. I crack my fists against the tiny window, but even if I followed it out, it would not be helpful: the frame is too small and, even if I did get out, I'd break my legs in the fall. *Better than dying.* The space is full of tatt but this time I pull at it, looking for – I don't know – a weapon, or a place to hide, a magic door to another room, a secret fire escape leading me out. I sift through an entire box of keys

– I empty them onto the floor – I find an old bicycle, collection of ancient suitcases with broken handles. I pa in the space, ready to face an absent enemy, casting my eye over the piles of rubbish around me, tricking me into seein her in them, jumping at the mannequin on the far side wal its head between a deconstructed drum-kit, its arm windin around a cymbal. But it's not here and, beyond, the hous is quiet until—

Whack! The door screams, splitting in two, a foc crushing through the wood. I hiccup a mouthful of bile the grab for something, anything. *Thwack!* Another hit crashe the house and the foundations themselves seem to roc with the impact. Dust and debris confetti the room and close my eyes to stop the splinters from blinding me, an it's in these eyes-shut, body-frozen moments that I lose th fight. Kay breaks down the door and, without hesitatio rushes in and spears my neck with a needle. I hear her man laughter in the background, somewhere behind my splittin headache, and she's talking to herself, saying something, bu I'm on the floor before I know it, clawing for the stairs, m vision blacking and, at that moment, I realise she's injecte me with a sedative of some sort.

'I'm sorry,' Kay repents. The blindfold she's tied tight t my eyes squeezes them back into their sockets and I ca only see a blue-black colour, a *you'll-never-see-the-light-o day-again* shade.

Kay

Now

'Rick,' I stutter, surprised to find his cool stare and tall frame on the other side of my front door.

He looks distracted, jumpy, and I brace myself for an interrogation about Annabella's whereabouts. It's the first time I've met Rick in person, and I wonder if he's as fascinated to meet me as I am to meet him. A dark leather jacket hugs his shoulders.

'I want to talk,' he tells me, then looks over his shoulder. 'On your show, I mean, an interview.'

'You do?' I ask him, hardly believing my ears.

The journalist in me salivates. It would be my most-listened-to episode, the scoop I'd need to take this podcast to the big screen, to make it the most successful true crime series of all time.

But the killer in me hesitates. Annabella's upstairs, heavily sedated. I weigh up the risks and rewards but, as my dark eyes twitch in their sockets, Rick makes it hard for me to decline by letting himself in.

'Where do you record?' he asks, not making eye contact, a hint of men's cologne reaching my nose as he steps past.

'Through here,' I say, gesturing with my free hand, mind made up. Rewards don't come without risk, I think to myself, closing the front door. I imagine picking up a heavy, gold-plated trophy for my efforts. *And the award goes to… the most pioneering podcast of the decade… Kay Robero's* Cold Case of Tabitha Rice*!*

I direct Rick through the cream-coloured walls of the hallway into my kitchen and set him up at the table. I offer him a glass of water, which he declines, his nose slightly upturned, and I think that he and Annabella have more in common than I thought. *Uppity, judgemental, rude.* Annabella never liked coming here, either, I could see it, I could smell it, she felt uncomfortable in my home. Where I lived wasn't up to her standards.

'Are you sure about this?' I ask, taking the seat opposite him, setting up the microphones, checking the sound. 'What is it you want to tell the world?'

He straightens up and looks at the floor, weary with the weight of whatever he wants to get off his chest. He runs an absent hand through dark hair.

'I listened to what Mandy revealed on the show,' he says biting at his back teeth. 'And I want to put my voice behind it. Tabby, the things she did when we were together, I'm not surprised this deception was the latest twist in her horrible tale, nor that I ended up being the punchline.'

My immediate reaction is a combination of amusement and horror. Rick *must* know that Annabella isn't Tabby… and yet, this is how far Mr Rick Priestley is prepared to go to clear his name, to shift some of the blame from his back

to hers. Not that he knows it yet – not while this is the
mplexion of the story – but Rick's making a big mistake.
e police will be able to match the DNA of the body on
e farm to Tabitha before long and, though I'm certain
nie will take the rap for it, it will take a while to convict
n. Who knows, he could even end up having some sort
alibi? That's when I plan for the second series to come
t: *The twisted truth about Ernie Rice*. DNA profiling
ll confirm the body is Tabitha Rice, that Annabella was
lly Annabella and, gosh, how horrible that she fled the
untry as a result of the allegations Mandy Evans and
ck Priestley made against her.

Given that Rick's here, adding fuel to this fire, my
cond series will have to focus on his guilt and Mandy's
lpability. People will wonder how they were both so sure
at Annabella was Tabby, when she wasn't, and will realise
t how willing he is to lie about this case, will question
y he jumped on this red herring so quickly. They'll be
iting it in the papers before I can say it myself: *There's
way Rick Priestley's not, at the very least, complicit.*

I can't wait for series two. But, for now, I look at my
erviewee.

'You're really brave to do this, Rick, to speak up. I know
s can't be easy.'

ll my listeners, thousands of them already listening live,
t I'm joined, for this special episode, by Rick Priestley.

'Hi,' Rick croaks into the microphone, clearly nervous.
wanted to thank you for giving me the chance to speak.'

My listeners will be sceptical; they tune in every week

for the regular episodes, eagerly awaiting the next live instalment which always signifies a major development. They chatter about it on Twitter before, during and afterwards, #TheColdCase often trending worldwide after each live episode. Do you know how many people have to be listening to your show for it to trend worldwide? My winning formula: fiction dressed as true crime.

'Shall we start at the beginning?' I ask him.

'Sure,' he replies, his features hardening.

'You met Tabitha Rice while studying at Oxford University. Correct?'

'Correct.'

'How would you describe your relationship? Because, on this podcast, we revealed that she wasn't your, sort of, official – shall we say – girlfriend at that time. Were you embarrassed by her? What was it about being with Tabitha Rice that meant you had to hide her?'

'I liked Tabby a lot and we dated for a few months. decided, pretty early on – because of my problems, no hers – that she wasn't the right person for me. I met Saskia moved on, but Tabby was persistent. She wouldn't let m give up on her.'

'The theory we had on the show was that she must hav had pretty severe abandonment issues. She grew up in foste care because her mother couldn't take care of her and he father was... well, no one knows. Her grandfather didn want anything to do with her. Her foster parents, by a accounts, weren't particularly kind to her. And then she me you and she couldn't bear to let you go, she wasn't prepare to let another person desert her.'

'I think you're right,' he says.

'There's a pretty uncomfortable story we uncovered while researching the show. An alleged rape accusation against you. We didn't air the details at the time for a few reasons. The first was that Annabella – our theory that she's actually Tabby making sense in this context – didn't want it to get out. The second that we weren't absolutely sure it was her. Can you shed any light?'

'I don't want to talk about it on the show, it's not relevant.'

'Well, with respect, Rick, of course it's relevant. If Tabby had a history of lying, of deceit, the listeners deserve to know. They deserve the full picture.'

'Tabby had a lot of demons, let's just say she let a few of them loose on me. But she did the right thing, in the end. She dropped the allegation.'

I nod enthusiastically, rewarding Rick for confirming that story with a metaphorical pat on the head.

'We went through a lot together,' he continues, buoyed by the praise. 'A miscarriage, a suicide attempt, and, going through those extreme events, they brought us closer together. As you know, we ended up getting married pretty young and moving in together, starting a new life here in London.'

'How quickly did things start to go wrong? There was infidelity in the marriage, I believe?'

'The trauma of what we went through brought us closer, that was for sure. We were each other's support systems. I couldn't talk to anybody else about what I'd been through with Tabby, except Tabby. But, though it was what drew us to one another, ultimately it also pushed us away.' He chews the inside of his cheek, biting back his emotions. 'As we got older and our scars healed, just looking at her was a reminder of our painful past. And not just for me, for her as well. We both craved the peace we felt when we weren't together. We could start again, be whoever we wanted. It wasn't her fault, it wasn't mine. It just was.'

'So, what do you think pushed Tabby over the edge? Why would she commit this horrendous injustice against you if your relationship was ending amicably?'

I wet my lips and recant the theory Rick's so desperate to subscribe to. 'Do you think it was as simple as rejection? Suddenly, you could move on but she was stuck… She was so angry with her friend Annabella, for having the qualifications she didn't and the looks she coveted, that she flew into an impulsive and jealous rage and killed her best friend. Then she went through a raft of cosmetic procedures using her connections in the industry to create a look as similar to her old friend as possible, living as her for five years. She even hired a private detective in the interim, after "Tabby" went missing, to check that what she was up to wouldn't come to light. Then she waited for the case to die down, for your life to just about begin returning to normal… And that's when she struck. She was eager to get involved with this show. She stalked you, you know, for weeks, gathering information. She broke into your home to find 'evidence' that you were up to no good. She even started a dating you. Did you have any idea, any at all, that Annabella wasn't who she said she was? That Annabella was actually your wife Tabitha Rice?'

I watch him shift in his seat.

'It's funny,' Rick says. 'I know now, obviously, about Annabella and the podcast and I can't say I wasn't hurt that she was using me to feed information back to you. That one will sting for a while.'

I rearrange my skirt and sit in a different position.

'But you have to understand, I knew Annabella when Tabby was alive. And I was *married* to Tabby.'

His eyes change, he's about to pounce.

'No amount of plastic surgery would be capable of convincing me that Tabby had become Annabella.'

I stammer, caught off-guard, Rick's admission punching through me. This isn't what he said he was here to say. *Is he playing me?*

'How do you explain the procedure that Annabella butchered? She's a qualified nurse, she wouldn't make a mistake like this,' I retort.

'She's been under a lot of pressure. She makes mistakes when things aren't right, when things aren't perfect.'

'Or the break-in? That was her, you know, in your home.'

'She had her reasons. I know she was desperate to find out what happened to her friend. But, what I think's particularly interesting is the thread that holds her actions together.' He pauses.

'You.'

There's a brief hiatus as I reach for the power supply.

'The puppet master pulling the strings behind the scenes – always everyone else getting their hands dirty. Never you –'

At that moment I pull the plug on the broadcast and cut Rick's microphone.

'What are you doing?' I shout. 'You can't say things like that, I've given you the benefit of the doubt here, let you into my home and this is how you want this to go?'

I stand up, jabbing an angry finger at his face, mouth frothing.

'I know it was you, Kay,' he says slowly. 'There's a car in the garden, it has a Polish number plate and, if a forensics team got their hands on it, I'm sure they'd find Tabby's DNA in the passenger seat.'

I take a step back, my leg contacting the chair. It scrapes the floor as it moves, the only sound now, between us.

'How do you...' I half-ask, the horror that this all might be about to unravel paralysing me.

'Annabella sent me this picture.'

Rick shows me the car everyone's been looking for, the one with the Polish number plates, obscured by the tall grass in the garden. How had she found it? She must have crawled in there, searching, sniffing, smelling it out.

'Then she sent me this address.' He takes a step towards me. 'And I haven't heard from her since.' His eyes narrow. 'Where is she?'

If he was a step closer, I wouldn't have the advantage, but I do and my black hair billows as I sink to the cupboard below the sink and rattle with a catch that holds Tomasz' old shotgun. Rick doesn't understand at first, making no move to stop me. As I pull it out from its position already loaded, his face colours, pumping red back into his cheeks.

'Stop,' he demands, which almost makes me laugh.

Standing in front of him, I prop the weapon up to my chest, I can't give him a chance to make me change my mind. My heart thuds against the barrel and my finger clasps the trigger, slippery with my sweat. Rick moves quickly, then ripping his jacket and jumper and shirt from his torso.

'What are you doing?' I growl at him, distracted, unable
take a clean shot.

'I'm wearing a wire, Kay, the police, they've seen the
cture, they're here, they've heard everything.'

Inside the four walls of my kitchen, I smell gunpowder.
y shotgun, an ancient barrel of a thing, floats its residue
a gust of air that blows from the outside in. The back
por has been forced open and I hear Rick shout. I picture
onfires, flames licking up wooden kindling, a puppet
opped on top, the character burning, consumed by fire in
way that's not normal. That's how they'll see me now. Not
someone fighting for justice, as a mother fighting for her
aughter, but as a killer. As someone to be burned for
r crimes. Tomasz could have stopped this, could have
lped, but he left, his character somewhat failing him when
ush came to shove. Uncomfortable with 'what the podcast
d turned me into', apparently. Perhaps it's true what they
y about a mother's love: it burns far brighter.

'This is for you, my darling girl,' I whisper, the wind
cking up again as my front door crashes off its hinges, an
my of boots on their way towards me. I close my eyes and
cus, let Orla do the aiming, my knees rattling as I pull the
gger and fire once more.

In the moment, I picture being with her again, my
aughter, flashing through the memories we would have
ared over the years: leaving school, choosing a university,
e right course, setting her on her career path, helping her
ove into her own home, meeting partners, imagining the
ildren she'll never have. Misshapen tears spout from
neath my eyelids and clump my lashes as I think about
hat Tabitha Rice took from me. I hear the sirens, next, and

I know that it is over. I've known it for a while. It was over when Annabella found the car. Or perhaps it had been over since the moment I picked Tabitha Rice up from the side of the road and told her I only wanted to help. I've been running on fumes ever since. Perhaps Tomasz was right to escape.

I slop into the ground, feel the pull of Earth's gravity as it keeps me there, holding me in place until the officers arrive and drag me from it.

Annabella

Now

First, the police found Rick. He'd been shot and was bleeding heavily when they picked him up and loaded him into the back of an ambulance. Then they found Kay, part of her skull blown from her head in a last-ditch suicide attempt. She was still breathing when they found her.

They searched the house, next. They found Kay's investigation room. They kept it intact and officer after officer went to the house to look at it – to marvel at the exceptional detail that had gone into planning such an intricate deceit. It was better than anything they'd seen at the station, and one of the policewomen joked that they would have used a woman like Kay on the force. Shortly afterwards, they found me. I was sedated and bruised but otherwise unharmed, saved by Rick answering my text, saved by Rick doing the right thing.

I sit inside the police station, rubbing my hands round

one another in frustrated loops, waiting for the officer I'v
grown to know so well over the last few months arriv
Each time someone new comes in through the automat
doors, a new gust of Baltic air crawling into the space, I s
up meerkat-like to look out for him.

Twenty minutes later, Gerry barges through the door an
tells me this:

'We've got her. Bang to rights. DNA. Blood. Gunsh
residue. Her defence team had been running us in loop
trying to pin Tabitha's murder all on the husband, tryir
to get the gunshots written off as self-defence against Rick

'How is Rick?' I ask, eager for an update. I'd heard h
shoulder had been completely obliterated, that he'd had t
have it rebuilt with plates and wires in the weeks after h
was shot.

'Discharged.' Gerry tells me, a glint in his eyes.

I pick up on his silent meaning but choose to ignore i
Rick's better. That's all that matters.

'Seen this?' Gerry asks, throwing a paper in my directio
Mandy Evans tells all, the headline screeches from th
paper's red top. I roll my eyes and throw it back in h
direction. 'Inevitable. Next she'll be a reality star.'

Gerry smiles strongly at me and sits down.

'Not on the Christmas card list, then?'

'Not exactly.'

We stare at each other, talking as friends, and Gerry pick
at a spot on his arm.

'They'll want you to talk about Kay in court, you know
How are you feeling about that?'

I'd been relatively coy with Gerry about Kay. She kille
Tabby, she tried to kill me, she tried to kill Rick but, even s

I'm fearful of getting involved. Everything I seem to touch when it comes to Tabby ends up going wrong. If I spoke out about Kay… what if I got it wrong again? What if she got off because of me?

'You still treading lightly?'

I think of Rick, of the way I've let him down.

Gerry sighs and tells me straight. 'You should go and see him, Annabella.'

True Crime Criminal

A report by the London Times

The woman behind the world's most-downloaded true-crime podcast was charged this week with the murder of her podcast victim: Tabitha Rice.

Kay Robero, described as a 'hoarder' by a close neighbour, released this year's most successful true-crime podcast that delved into the particulars of Tabitha's missing persons inquiry. But the show was nothing more than an orchestrated investigation constructed, behind the scenes, by the show's host.

Kay, in the off-beat and eccentric style for which she'd become known, led listeners through twists and turns that, listening back, were far closer to fiction than fact.

But it worked. Kay was in talks with a major film production company to bring her podcasts to the screen in a series of televised episodes. That was, at least, until Annabella, close friend of victim Tabitha Rice, discovered the truth. Hours earlier, Kay's podcast had pointed the finger at Annabella – had accused her of masquerading as her deceased friend. But, behind the scenes, a ferocious struggle was taking place. In an explosive final episode,

Rick Priestley outed Kay live on air. The broadcast was cut short and, shortly afterwards, Kay shot Rick, then turned the gun on herself. Her condition is officially described as 'stable' but reports from inside the hospital suggest she is severely brain damaged and unlikely to lead a normal life again.

Annabella

One Year Later

The gold-gilded patterns on the side of the bridge glow under the nearby streetlight, my mind preoccupied with how many people had been wronged. Orla, Rick, Mandy, Tabby, Kay, Me. All of us, really, to varying degrees.

I don't know if I'll ever be completely fixed – I was already a little broken to begin with – but I'm on the road to recovery. I've accepted help, I talk to a counsellor every week. I've been trying my best to make new friends, new connections.

Kay Robero has been convicted for the kidnap and murder of Tabitha Rice and, though that's a good thing, I'm surprised I don't feel happier. I think I understand, now, what people mean when they talk about closure.

I stop to look out across the river, staring in the distance at Tower Bridge, the sparkling lights of the city all around me and think about how long it has been since I last saw Rick Priestley. I chew on the side of my nail as I mull it over, then make the decision.

I catch the train across town and alight at Queen's Road ation in Battersea, pavements lining the way, curtained indows either side.

Rick hasn't moved to a new house – he probably can't ll – and looks exactly as I remember. He walks around the ey-silver kitchen in a loose sweater and jeans, poking his nd into the refrigerator, tilting his face towards his phone, s broad shoulders and wide smile laughing at something the screen. The same dangerously handsome man I'd met many years ago.

I freeze, for a moment, in the darkening sky, trapped in e memories of him. Of us.

had been exhausting. Hiding it. I'd be wildly anxious, lame with guilt whenever we were together, but Rick had en impatient, desperate to end things with Tabby, to get r partnership out in the open and deal with the fall out it happened.

Rick and I grew into each other's lives just as Tabby d I intertwined and, rather than sever the relationship, wrapped Tabby closer, hurting her behind her back made sier by being such a steady and reliable friend to her face. *eflecting*. Would we have been such good friends, such se friends, if it hadn't been for Rick? I'm not sure. Tabby ould take me to CBT classes, confused by my anxiety, and e'd sit, holding my hand, as I discussed the crushing guilt elt every day when I woke up, made bearable only by a ries of strange rituals I found comfort in.

There was the night of the *Perspextacular*, not long after ck and I first realised there was something between us, my

feet strapped in a pair of plastic sandals as I limped Tabby
back to their house. She was out of it, her heart fluttering
in her chest, the faint whiff of vomit on her breath. I cleaned
her face with warm water and tucked her into bed. I headed
downstairs. And there was Rick. Waiting in the kitchen
for me to come down. I really liked him. I'd known it for
a while. He was bright and successful, kind and cheerful.
There was a light spray of freckles across the bridge of
his nose, a fittingly sunny accessory to the warmth I felt
in his company. His hair was dark chocolate, his teeth
spotless ivory. So, I drew closer that night, under this light
and stayed there.

I became a fixture in their lives, I would cook dinner
with them, sleep over, make breakfast in the morning, play
house. Tabby would ask me questions about my love life
and I'd tell her there was someone, but I wasn't ready to
introduce him. Rick would press his foot against mine under
the table, warning me. When Tabby was at home, Rick
would sometimes come to my place. I was comfortable with
him being there, even when Rick disordered my carefully
ordered apartment, it was OK, because it was Rick. While
we grew, he and Tabby shrank, increasingly cold toward
one another. She was letting it affect her, coming in late to
work, obsessing over his messages, hurt by the betrayal she
suspected, the person causing her suffering listening to her
talk all about it. One day, hanging by a thread with Caroline
at work, I saved her. If she lost her job, then lost Rick, then
me, she'd have nothing. The guilt crept closer, wrapped its
cold fingers round my throat.

One night, I woke with Rick in my bed, awake beside
me. 'It would be so much easier if she just, I don't know.

st disappeared.' He'd laughed, he'd been joking, but it
d stuck with me, the throwaway line with which I later
me to build his guilt on top of. Because that's exactly
hat happened. Now I know it was by coincidence and not
sign, of course, but Tabby disappeared, just a few days
er Rick had wished for it. Consumed by fear – at first
lidn't want to believe he was to blame – I went to his
ace to find out what he knew, if he thought there was
y danger, any at all, that our affair would be exposed.
e guided me into the lounge, sat me down on the sofa,
apped his hands around my sweaty palms, pushed the
ir from my face. He opened his dull blue eyes and said,
want you to move in with me.'

It had been three days.

I made my excuses. I cried so hard my eyes dried up. Rick
d murdered Tabby to make way for our relationship, it
s obvious. I couldn't live, I couldn't cope. I pulled my
othes from my head that day, poured a cap of toilet bleach
o the bathtub and ran the hot tap. 'Clean body, clean
oughts,' my mother's voice trilled as I stuck my foot into
e steaming water. It stung as I made contact, the smell so
t, so thick, it made me cough. Part of me wanted to drink
to clean myself from the inside out.

I dropped down into it, naked, pushed slimy red limbs to
e edges of the tub, jagged bones sticking out of my chest,
nt and back. I hadn't eaten properly since she vanished.
ouldn't bear to. I would try tomorrow, I thought. I pulled
legs to my chin. 'My friend,' I whimpered. 'It's all my
lt.' My tears turned the bathwater salty. I vowed to do
re, to catch him. Though I let her down in life, I would
everything I could not to let her down in death.

★

It took years to pull myself from the darkest of places.
shut Rick out completely. I hired Chad to find out wha
he knew about Rick and, more than that, I hired him t
find out if there was anything about Rick and me to l
found. I sent Chad fishing, I told him there'd been anothe
woman when Tabby went missing. But he never found he
Me. Even though I was right there.

When Kay got in contact, she told me Rick had move
on with Mandy. I couldn't understand it. *He'd killed fo
me... and yet he was happy with someone else?* It didn
make sense. I grew angrier, red skin under my work unifor
as I watched from afar, still punishing myself for what I'
done. When Kay pushed me to see Rick, our reunion wa
complicated. We didn't speak about what had come befor
It was an unwritten rule between us, our tryst had been
secret we weren't sure the other would even admit. But beir
with him again, even duplicitously, unlocked something i
me. He won me back with his honesty. He told me thing
about Tabby I didn't know, hadn't thought to question. H
proved to me that he wasn't the monster I'd invented t
hide my own guilt. Because that was it, really, that was th
crux of why I was hell-bent on proving Rick's guilt: becaus
it would prove mine, too. I tortured Rick because I wante
to torture myself. How could Tabby have gone missing
few days after her husband begged for her to disappear s
he could be with me? She couldn't. I deserved to die, th
same as Tabby, for what I'd pushed Rick to do. The sto
was quite different, in the end, and I am grateful, for m
sanity, that I have seen it to its conclusion.

Now all that's left is the rest of my life. My future. Do I want to spend it hiding? Or do I want to change the narrative, flip the page, live the life I've wanted to live ever since I met him? Pepping myself up, I walk directly towards the black brick of his house. I stride across the street in a confident cadence, my face a little pinched with the nerves. Then, when the front door stands tall before me, I grab the brass handle in my grip and knock twice, with force enough to show I mean it, that I'm here, that I'm not an invisible woman skulking in the shadows.

Rick appears in the gap, the door opening, his face in muted surprise.

'Annabella,' he says. 'You're back.'

Author's Note

Do Her No Harm – a play on the Hippocratic oath declaration Primum non nocere, 'first, do no harm' – was inspired by the current state of the non-surgical cosmetics industry in Britain. In the UK, it is legal for procedures like Botox and dermal fillers to be injected by anyone, regardless of their training or experience.

With the proliferation of Instagram, and the perfect pouts and filtered faces that go with it, an increasing number of people are suffering serious consequences of being injected by untrained and unprofessional individuals. Save Face, a national register of accredited practitioners, received 934 complaints from patients in 2017-2018 regarding unregistered practitioners. Of these, the vast majority, 616, related to dermal fillers.

A BBC documentary, The Botox Bust, took this one step further and found beauticians across the country happy to give Botox to an undercover reporter without a valid prescription, and a struck-off doctor supplying Botox on the basis of telephone conversations. The BBC's One Show found that 17 out of 23 providers visited were happy to offer lip fillers to a 15-year-old.

In the process of researching for this book, I was stunne to find out that Botulinum toxin – Botox – is the mo poisonous biological substance known to humankind – couple of teaspoons would be enough to kill everyone in th UK – and yet it is so routinely used in an industry that is n currently well regulated.

If you are thinking of having non-surgical cosmet surgery, check the Save Face register first.

Acknowledgements

Thanks first to Hannah Smith at Aria, my brilliant editor, whose careful refinements and cracking plot-twists are second to none. Thanks also to Vicky, Rhea, Nikky and the wider Head of Zeus family who do such a fantastic job. most thanks to Kate Nash, my agent, who is always so helpful and gives great advice.

Shout out to my amazing family, especially my mum and sister who are such super beta-readers! Gratitude also to my uncle James for taking the time to look at some of my earlier work and offering such valuable comments. And to nna, I love that you read every book! Thank you to my friends who continue to be so supportive and wonderful; Georgie, Sophie, Fiona, Abby, Emily, Charlotte, Kirsty, Zoe, Eli, Kim – to name a few.

To Paula and Brendan who are always unbelievably kind and helpful in lending their time.

To Colin, too, for being ready to help in a heartbeat.

Finally, most thanks of all must go to you, the reader, thank you so much for choosing to read my book right to the end. Here's to you!

About the Author

NAOMI JOY is a pen name of a young PR professional who was formerly an account director at prestigious PR firm in London. Writing from experience, she draws the reader in to the darker side of the uptown and glamorous, presenting realism that is life or death, unreliable and thrilling to page-turn.

Hello from Aria

We hope you enjoyed this book! If you did let us know, we'd love to hear from you.

We are Aria, a dynamic digital-first fiction imprint from award-winning independent publishers Head of Zeus. At heart, we're committed to publishing fantastic commercial fiction – from romance and sagas to crime, thrillers and historical fiction. Visit us online and discover a community of like-minded fiction fans!

We're also on the look out for tomorrow's superstar authors. So, if you're a budding writer looking for a publisher, we'd love to hear from you. You can submit your book online at ariafiction.com/ we-want-read-your-book

You can find us at:
Email: aria@headofzeus.com
Website: www.ariafiction.com
Submissions: www.ariafiction.com/ we-want-read-your-book

f @ariafiction
🐦 @Aria_Fiction
📷 @ariafiction

Printed in Great Britain
by Amazon